They said no more.

After the music had stopped he bent over her hand—and kissed it. Georgie pulled it away, as though the kiss had stung her, and for a moment he thought that she was about to leave him there, stranded.

'No,' he said, and recovered the retreating hand. She stared at him, eyes huge in a pale face. 'Come, Mrs Georgie,' he said, still gentle. 'Admit it—we were both in the wrong.'

Her indomitable spirit surfaced again. 'What did it cost you to tell that lie, Fitz?' she demanded, still letting him hold her hand. 'You can't believe that you were in the wrong.'

Paula Marshall, married with three children, has had a varied life. She began her career in a large library and ended it as a senior academic in charge of History at a polytechnic. She has travelled widely, has been a swimming coach, and has appeared on *University Challenge* and *Mastermind.* She has always wanted to write, and likes her novels to be full of adventure and humour.

Recent titles by the same author:

THE WOLFE'S MATE
THE DEVIL AND DRUSILLA
THE WAYWARD HEART
REBECCA'S ROGUE

MISS JESMOND'S HEIR

Paula Marshall

*First published in Great Britain 1999
Harlequin Mills & Boon Limited,
Eton House, 18-24 Paradise Road, Richmond, Surrey TW9 1SR*

© Paula Marshall 1999

ISBN 0 263 81722 9

*Set in Times Roman 10½ on 12 pt.
04-9907-83463 C1*

*Printed and bound in Great Britain
by Caledonian International Book Manufacturing Ltd, Glasgow*

Chapter One

'Georgie, dear, have you heard the news? Louisa Manners came this morning whilst you were out and told me that the caretaker at Jesmond House had received word from the heir that he intends to take up residence there almost immediately. It seems that he is not aware of how derelict the place has become over the last few years. All in all, though, I don't think that it would be wise for you to take the children to play in the grounds. Miss Jesmond was happy for you to do so, but perhaps the new owner might not be so accommodating. Best wait and see.'

Georgie—more properly Georgina—was busy stringing a guitar. She looked across at her widowed sister-in-law who was only a few years older than she was, but was a semi-invalid who spent her life on the sofa.

'Who is the new owner?' she asked. 'Have you any notion when he is due to arrive?'

'No to both questions.' Caro Pomfret sighed. 'Louisa asked me if I knew who the heir might be, but all I could say was that I had no knowledge of any of Miss Jesmond's relatives—indeed, from what little she said of them, I thought that she had none. For that matter, I don't even know that it's a he. I thought that she might have said

something to you—she was as friendly with you as anyone…which isn't saying much.'

She looked disapprovingly at Georgie. 'You said that
you were taking the twins for a walk when you had finished
repairing poor John's guitar—do you really intend to show
yourself in public in those unsuitable clothes?'

Georgie, her self-imposed task nearly over, smiled at her
sister-in-law before looking down at herself. She was wearing jacket, shirt, breeches and boots, suitable for riding in,
which had belonged to her half-brother John when he was
a boy. Her russet-coloured hair was cut short after a fashion
which had died out some years ago—but then Georgie and
fashion had little to do with one another. She preferred to
wear whatever was most suitable for the task in hand.

Her sister-in-law often sighed regretfully over the un-
deniable fact that Georgie did not use her best features—a
pair of fine green eyes and a *piquante*, almost turned-up,
nose—to more effect on the local gentlemen who had come
courting as soon as they decently could after her husband's
death.

'I shall not be in public, Caro,' Georgie said, after playing a few testing chords on the guitar. 'I thought of taking
Gus and Annie to play at the far end of the Park where no
one at all will see us, except the birds and the squirrels.
The children like it there.'

'I know they do. But you are forgetting two things. First
of all, that part of the Park adjoins Miss Jesmond's land,
and secondly, you can never be quite sure that no one will
come across you. Suppose it were some gentleman? What
would he think of Miss Pomfret of Pomfret Hall, near Netherton, exhibiting herself in public dressed like a stable boy!'

'Hardly a stable boy,' returned Georgie, smiling. 'When
John wore these when he was a lad, no one ever thought
he was other than John Pomfret of Pomfret Hall. And be-

sides, you forget, I am a widow and no longer Miss Pomfret, but respectable Mrs Charles Herron of Church Norwood who chooses to live with you for the time being for our mutual convenience.'

This was not strictly true; the convenience was all on Caro Pomfret's side. The Pomfrets had been as poor as church-mice and, when John had died after a hunting accident, Caro and his twin children had been left with little to live on. Georgie, on the other hand, had been left a comfortable sum of money by her mother, her father's second wife. Her husband's death had left her with even more, and a fine house to boot, which was at present let to an Indian nabob and his wife who needed a temporary home while they looked for one of their own.

Georgie's decision to return to her old home to help Caro—who had taken to her bed after her husband's sudden death and had left it only to live an idle and helpless life—had been for her nephew and niece's sake rather than her sister-in-law's. For a variety of reasons, she had no wish to marry again, even though she was only twenty-five.

'All the same, no gentleman would think you respectable in those clothes,' moaned Caro, as though Georgie had not spoken—a bad habit of Caro's.

'I have no interest in gentlemen, respectable or otherwise, so that is no matter,' Georgie declared, beginning to sing one of Mr Tom Moore's songs in a low contralto, satisfied that she had made the guitar playable again.

She rose. 'Forgive me, Caro. Nurse will have the children ready by now and I have no wish to keep them waiting.'

'And you will remember what I told you about not going on Miss Jesmond's land. We really ought not to annoy our new neighbour by trespassing upon it.'

'I always remember everything you say,' returned Georgie untruthfully. 'Try to rest, my dear, and then we can have a game of cards this evening. Gus and Annie would like that.'

'If my poor head doesn't persist in troubling me,' wailed Caro, watching Georgie walk out of the room carrying the guitar, and thinking that it was fortunate that Georgie was something of a flat-chested beanpole who could certainly be mistaken for a boy in her brother's old clothes. Which I never could, Caro congratulated herself complacently, since my nicely rounded figure has always been the subject of admiration.

Besides, I mustn't be too unkind, for it is a most convenient thing for me that she takes the children off my hands when she visits so that I don't have the trouble of caring for them. I'm not in the least surprised that she ended up by marrying an elderly scholar—for his money, presumably. Considering the way she dresses and carries on, no one else would have wanted her! One wonders why Charles Herron did, such a hoyden as she has always been.

With which ungracious thoughts—considering all that she owed to her sister-in-law, both in love and money—she drifted off to sleep.

Georgie, meanwhile, went her own sweet way, across the small park where no one was allowed to play cricket on the carefully tended grass. Gus and Annie ran happily behind her. They were making for the far end of Jesmond House's land where there was a large stretch of flat green turf where she and the children could play cricket to their heart's content, far from the disapproving glare of Caro and her gardeners.

'You're sure of this, Jess? You know what you are doing? This is not a mere whim wham, I hope—the result of a more brilliant spring than usual.'

The new owner of Jesmond House was standing before the glass doors of the drawing room, looking out over ruined gardens and the desolate park beyond which a small folly stood, crumbling into ruin. He could almost hear his former employer's sardonic voice echoing in his ear after he had walked into his office to tell him that he had inherited his great-aunt's estate and wished to be relieved of his duties in order to start a new life far from the City of London and the to-and-fro of the business world there.

'No, not a whim wham,' Jess Fitzroy had said, shaking his head. 'And it's not because I am tired of working for you—after all I owe you a debt of gratitude which I can never repay.'

Ben Wolfe made a dismissive motion with his hand. 'Nothing to that,' he said curtly. 'You repaid me long ago. I only want to be sure that you have carefully weighed up what you are proposing to do. You know, of course, that if at any time you grow bored with country living and would wish to return, I shall always be ready to welcome you back—if only because I might have some difficulty in finding a lieutenant whom I can trust as completely as I trust you.'

Jess said simply, 'I shall miss working with you', and took the hand Ben held out in friendship. The two men could not have been more unalike. Both of them were tall and well built, but Ben was a great, grey-eyed, black-haired bear of a man, who looked more like a coalheaver or a pugilist than a wealthy man with an old name. Jess, on the other hand, was fair, blue-eyed and classically handsome, with the build and poise of an athlete.

Susanna, Ben's wife, had once likened Ben to a broadsword and Jess to a rapier, so far as physique went, that was. In business and in life, however, both were equally devious—Jess, because Ben, slightly older, had trained him to be that way, Ben being devious by nature.

'You will be easy financially, I hope,' Ben said, eyebrows raised a little, 'If not...?'

It was an offer of help, Jess knew. He said, carelessly, 'Oh, my great-aunt has left me a competence, and I am not strapped for cash myself.'

This, he knew, was evasion rather than direct lying. Ben was not to know—indeed, Jess had concealed it from him—that he had made himself wealthy by following his employer's example. Like Ben, he had made a financial killing in 1815 by buying rather than selling stocks because, old soldiers both, they believed that Waterloo would be a victory, not a defeat. The first news which had come from the Continent had wrongly reported that Napoleon had won.

Since then he had invested wisely and, although he would never be as inordinately wealthy as Ben Wolfe, he was rich in the way most people counted riches. It was not only Ben Wolfe from whom he wished to conceal his true financial position, but the people amongst whom he proposed to live. When a very young man, he had learned by bitter experience the wisdom of playing his cards close to his chest. Only Ben Wolfe's friendship and advice had saved him from ruin.

Now Jess felt that he no longer needed Ben's protection, that he could fend for himself, without needing someone powerful and daring to stand behind him, ready to rescue him if he failed. He was also beginning to believe that only if he left his familiar surroundings to strike out on his own would he ever find a wife as worthy of loving as Ben's Susanna was.

He would have liked to marry Susanna, but she had only

ever had eyes for Ben. Leaving London would mean leaving her shadow behind as well as Ben's.

He had had no notion of what he might find when he reached journey's end in the south Nottinghamshire countryside. He remembered Jesmond House from his days there as a small boy, when his great-aunt had always made him welcome. Days which he had almost forgotten, until the letter had arrived from her lawyers telling him that he had inherited the house which he had not seen since he had left for India as a very young man. And not only had she left him the house, but also her small fortune. His first reaction had been that he would sell the house, sight unseen.

Jess smiled wryly, wondering at the sudden impulse which had, instead, brought him back to this near ruin, which he could only just recognise as the well-run splendid mansion of his youth. He remembered it being a spotlessly tidy place with a warm kitchen where he was always welcome. Mrs Hammond, the cook, had fed him surreptitiously because his great-aunt had the appetite of a bird and thought that lively young Jess needed no more to eat than she did. She had baked the most appetising Sally Lunns and fed them to him on the sly in her kitchen.

Well, he would need to use some of his money, and all his aunt's, to restore the house to its former glory, and fill it with the servants who would keep up its splendour. It was perhaps appropriate that at this point in his musings, Twells, his aunt's aged butler-cum-footman, should walk deferentially in and murmur, 'The mistress always used to ask for the tea board at this hour of the afternoon, sir. Would you care to follow her custom?'

He was about to say 'No' when he had a sudden brief memory of a much-younger great-aunt sitting at the small table beside the hearth serving tea to him on many of the

long, golden, summer afternoons of his childhood, a
younger Twells hovering beside her. That, together with the
understanding that the old man found his presence bewil-
dering and disturbing—although one of his first acts on
arriving had been to tell his aunt's remaining few servants
that he had no intention of dismissing any of them—had
him changing his mind.

'Very thoughtful of you, Twells. Yes, indeed, and afterwards I'll take a walk into the paddock beyond the Park.
The servants used to play cricket there in their time off, I
believe.'

The old man's face filled with pleasure. 'Fancy you remembering that, sir! You were naught but a young shaver
when you last visited—and I was a deal spryer then than I
am now. I'll see that the tea board comes along instanter.'

He was as good as his word and departed, muttering,
'Mrs Hammond will be that pleased.'

Once he had gone Jess half regretted his hasty decision
to take a walk. He was still dressed for the town with fashionable trousers strapped inside light shoes, and a tight,
elaborate cravat which he had tied himself. He sometimes
wondered—frivolously—whether his valet Mason's deser-
tion of him, in order to take over his father's inn in Devon,
had been the real reason for his own sudden abandonment
of London and his old life. In the country he would be able
to dress more carelessly than in town where a man was
judged by his clothing and deportment.

He drank his tea and ate the Sally Lunns which arrived
with it. Astonishingly, Twells—or, more likely, Mrs. Hammond—had remembered his childhood love of them. Altogether it was an odd thing for Jess Fitzroy to be doing in
the middle of a mild May afternoon.

Back in London he would either have been at his desk
or engaged on some delicate—or indelicate—errand for

Ben Wolfe. Now the day was his, but he scarcely knew what to do with it. He walked slowly through the glass doors, crossed the terrace, and strolled down a slight incline, passing by the neglected flower-beds which once had been so trim. Finally he came to a wooden gate, badly in need of rehanging, which he remembered led towards the paddock. On opening it he heard voices: high voices, children's voices, and a cry of 'Well caught' came ringing through the mild summer air.

Jess grinned to himself. He had trespassers; village children, probably, who were using the paddock because no one else did. There used to be an elderly donkey grazing there, he remembered, who had most likely brayed and galloped off into the Shades long ago to eat grass in heaven instead of in Jesmond Park. There was a small stand of trees to pass through before he finally reached the spot where the trespassers were enjoying themselves.

For all the happy noise they were making, there were only three of them. A boy and a girl who looked to be about ten years old and, by their casual dress, were a tenant farmer's children, and a russet-haired youth, similarly attired, who was bowling at the girl. They were playing single-wicket with a crude cricket bat. They were so intent on their game that they did not see him, until the girl, skying a ball, was caught by the boy.

Jess clapped his hands together and exclaimed, 'Well bowled! May I have a go now?'

All three of them turned to look at him. The youth said in a clear, pleasant voice, 'You must be the new owner of Jesmond House. We really ought to apologise for playing here—but it's the only convenient piece of turf near to home. I suppose you'll want us to leave.'

He was a handsome enough lad with a cheeky face, who held himself well for all his rough dress. The boy said reproachfully, 'Oh, come on, Georgie, he said that he wanted a go. Give him your bat, Annie—unless you wish to bowl, sir.'

Another educated rustic. Jess said, stretching out a hand, 'I was never much use as a bowler, but with the bat—that was different.'

Annie handed him the bat, saying confidentially, 'Don't judge Georgie's bowling by what I was receiving—that's all,' she added, for Gus was putting his hand over his mouth to indicate that she was not to say too much.

So Georgie was a bit of a demon bowler, was he? And here he stood, scarcely dressed for a real game in his tight trousers and his fashionable cravat, which held his head stiff and high as it was intended to. On the other hand, Georgie was slight—although sometimes slight men were the most cunning and successful bowlers of all.

On yet another impulse—he was having a lot of them these days—Jess ripped off his cravat, tossed it aside and undid the top button of his shirt before taking guard.

The lad's run up was short and the trundling ball was artfully pitched, spinning away from him; nevertheless, he hit it hard and high, but not too much so, because of the youth of the players. Gus gave a squeal of excitement, Annie put an awed finger in her mouth to watch the ball's flight while Georgie ran towards where it was falling—only to miss it by inches when it hit the ground and ran into the scrub which bordered the paddock. The lad ran after it, his coat flying open to reveal his loose shirt which had fallen out of his breeches.

It also revealed something else which brought up Jess a little short, although he had half-suspected it. Georgie was plainly no lad, but a girl dressed in her brother's clothes, and when she scrambled enthusiastically into the bushes to kneel down to rescue the ball from where it was hiding, it was quite plain that Miss Georgie was a veritable tomboy—a romp, no less.

A judgement which was borne out when she threw the ball, overarm, straight and accurately at Gus, shouting, 'Catch, Gus—and now it's your turn to bowl.'

Gus caught it, moaning reproachfully, 'Oh, I say, Georgie, he's a regular Corinthian, I shan't stand a chance against him.'

Jess raised his bat in salute—amused that Gus should describe him with a word used of fashionable idlers who never did a hand's turn. His camouflage—something which he had sometimes adopted in London when on one of Ben Wolfe's missions—was obviously working well.

He was rewarded with a belligerent glare and a slow trundler from Gus which he treated with more respect than it deserved as he did the second and third he received. But he let fly at Gus's fourth, only to be caught by the rampant lass, Georgie—or more accurately, perhaps, Georgina.

She smiled triumphantly at him before Gus exclaimed, 'Oh, that was a gift, that was. He meant you to catch it, Georgie. He really knows how to play.'

Georgie's triumph disappeared immediately. She said reproachfully to Jess as she held the ball high, 'Was it, sir? Did you intend to be caught out?'

Before he could answer, she continued, her tone quite changed. 'Oh, it's very wrong of me to question you so rudely. You are most plainly the owner of this land, Miss Jesmond's heir, for who else would be strolling in her grounds dressed like a refugee from Piccadilly? And we are equally plainly trespassers. You have every right to offer me a dolly drop and, now I think of it, you were almost certainly being kind to Gus to let him take your wicket. Allow me to apologise to you at once.'

Jess, who had handed his bat to Annie, smiled at Miss Georgie's impulsive speech.

'Not at all,' he said, and walked towards her so that they stood face to face before he bowed elaborately to complete his portrayal of a Piccadilly lounger.

'Allow me to apologise for doing it too brown. I should have known that Master Gus was fly enough to grasp when he was being patronised. I wonder if you would agree to let Gus and Annie play at single-wicket alone for a few moments while I have a quiet word with you.'

Georgie looked at him closely for the first time. At a distance he had been an impressive figure of a man, tall and broad-shouldered, quite unlike her late husband who had been a stooped scholar. Near to he was, as she was later to tell an interested Caro, quite impossibly handsome—no man in the neighbourhood of Netherton could hold a candle to him. Golden-haired, blue-eyed, straight-nosed, with a long amused mouth, and—she noted a trifle dazedly—with trim ears, set close to his head, he was, indeed, the very model of a Prince in a fairy tale.

His voice was pleasant, too. It was also, she thought, the voice of a man who was accustomed to be obeyed. She wondered what he had to say to her privately as she told Gus and Annie to continue their game without them for a few moments.

Jess regarded her levelly. Close to, no one could mistake her for a boy, even though she had buttoned her coat so that her clinging shirt no longer revealed the lines of the small breasts which had given her sex away to him. He considered carefully what he was about to say: principally, that it was dangerous for her to parade around the countryside dressed like a lad. Her father should have more sense than to allow it. Particularly someone as young as she appeared to be.

He was not yet to know that he had quite mistaken Georgina's age, which he had guessed, wrongly, to be under twenty. Later, he was to think that it was her lack of artifice, her frank manner, and the lack also of any kind of fashionable face-paint which had combined to deceive him.

'I am, as you have guessed, the new owner of Jesmond House. My name is Jesmond Fitzroy. Miss Jesmond was my great-aunt and this is my first inspection of my property. Now, whilst I am not angry that you and your brother and sister have trespassed on my land, I am a trifle worried that your mother and father should allow so young a woman to go abroad dressed like a boy.

'It is, I would submit, highly dangerous for you to put yourself at the mercy of any rogue who wanders the countryside, of whom there are many these days, and I consider it to be one of my first duties, seeing that I am the owner of Jesmond House, to so inform them—if you will be so good as to tell me your name.'

The play of feeling on Georgie's mobile face was revealing. She was smiling at him when he began to speak, but by the end of his well-meant—but unfortunate—words of advice her face turned black as thunder. She thinned her lips and said nothing, but she was thinking a lot.

Jess waited for her to reply but, seeing that she apparently had no such intention, he continued, a little less agreeably, 'Your name please, Miss Georgina. If you would be so good.'

Georgie said, keeping her voice low, but plainly furious, 'Has anyone ever told you how pompous you are, Mr Fitzroy—or do they expect it of you? In which case, everyone has ceased to remark upon it. Gus and Annie are not my brother and sister, and we shall certainly leave your land to you in future. I shall be careful not to sully it again either

in skirts or breeches, so you may take your sermons elsewhere.'

Later, she was to regret the violence with which she had
answered him, but he had touched a nerve by reproving her
for wearing breeches. She had endured quite enough of that
from Caro! Her anger was the greater precisely because for
the first time she was beginning to think that Caro, foolish
though she usually was, had some right on her side.

But, faced with this attractive stranger who was speaking
to her as though she were a naughty child, her temper ran
away with her. 'For your information,' she continued, her
voice as cutting as she could make it, 'my mother and father are both dead, and I am perfectly capable of looking
after myself.'

She turned away from him before he could answer her,
calling peremptorily, 'Gus, Annie, please pull up the stump
at once, and bring the bat and ball to me. We are leaving
immediately.'

Jess said in his usual mild way, 'One moment, if you
please.'

'No moments at all,' she flung at him, incontinent, something which back at Pomfret Hall she was to recall with
growing shame, 'for we shall be gone in a moment.'

'No,' Jess said, stung at last into abandoning his normal
equable manner. 'You will tell me your name and where I
may find you. Someone near to you may be pervious to
sense and try to control you.'

'Oh, indeed,' she returned fiercely, thinking of Caro and
her whining. 'There certainly is someone, and you may find
her—and the three of us—at Pomfret Hall. I bid you good
day. I trust that you are sufficient of a gentleman not to try
to detain me.'

He stepped back. She had breached his resolve always

to conduct himself with quiet dignity, a resolve which dated back to his earliest days with Ben Wolfe.

'Oh, indeed,' he informed her through gritted teeth. 'I have not the slightest wish to detain such a termagant in breeches. I bid you good day—and may the future invest you with a little more common sense.'

All the way back to the Hall, Georgie blushed with shame every time she thought of her recent encounter with Jesmond House's new owner. What on earth could have possessed her to make her behave so badly, so completely outside the bounds of a young gentlewoman's normal conduct?

She could find no useful answer to her own self-questioning, for what she did not wish to admit was that at first sight she had been bowled over by Miss Jesmond's heir, only to have him treat her like a foolish child who needed advising and reprimanding! Her pride and her vanity were alike hurt. The second did not matter, but the first did.

And the worst thing of all was that, although he had been right to warn her, it was his refusal to see her as anything but a silly chit which hurt the most.

Chapter Two

'You're quiet tonight, Georgina. Is anything wrong?'

Caro, after a great deal of complaining, had played cards with Gus, Annie and Georgie before an early supper. After it she had retired to her favourite position on the sofa in order to read, but *The Forest Lovers* did not interest her, even though it was by her favourite author, who had written *Sophia*.

Georgina was repairing Annie's doll's dress, which had been torn by Caro's pug Cassius in an unusual fit of temper. He was usually as sleepy as his mistress.

She said nothing in reply until Caro came out with, 'Really, Georgina, you might be civil enough to answer a reasonable question.'

'Forgive me, I'm somewhat *distraite* tonight,' Georgie said with a sigh after removing some pins from her mouth. She had been wondering a little wildly how best to answer her sister-in-law since she really ought to have informed her earlier of her meeting with Jesmond Fitzroy. In the normal course of events, she would have done so immediately on returning home.

Gus and Annie, who had heard nothing of her final encounter with him, had babbled to their mother about meeting a strange man in the paddock, but Caro had been too full of her own affairs at the time to take much notice of them.

Something of Georgie's disquiet must have affected Caro; she said anxiously, 'I do hope you're not sickening for a chill. It would be most inconvenient, for I should not like to catch it. Dr Meadows has often said that in my delicate state I ought to avoid having anything to do with anyone affected by any form of ill health.'

'No, I'm not sickening for anything—at least, I don't think I am. It's just that this afternoon we met Miss Jesmond's heir when we were playing cricket in her paddock, and I must confess that I think that you were right to advise us not to take advantage of him by trespassing on his grounds.'

Caro sat up sharply, her face a picture. 'And you said nothing of this until now! Really, Georgina, it's most inconsiderate of you. So little happens in Netherton, and when it does you invariably keep it to yourself.'

'Don't do it too brown, Caro,' retorted Georgie, a little stung. 'It's not three hours since I met him, and until now we've not had an opportunity for a private conversation.'

Since she had no answer to make to that Caro said, somewhat stiffly, 'I take it that he was the gentleman who came to the paddock this afternoon about whom Gus and Annie were prattling.'

'Indeed. His name is Jesmond Fitzroy. He is Miss Jesmond's great-nephew.' It was all Georgie could bring herself to say of him. It was not enough for Caro.

'But what is he like? How old is he? He *is* a gentleman, I take it?'

Georgie thought of the perfectly turned-out Mr Jesmond Fitzroy in his exquisite town clothes.

'Very much a gentleman.'

Georgie's reply was short, but it gave her away a little. Perhaps it was its very brevity that was betraying.

Caro said sharply, 'And that is all? Surely you could tell his age. Was he old or young?'

'In his thirties.' Georgie was still brief. 'He is extremely handsome. Very fair. Tall.'

'Did he say anything about a wife?' There was an unwonted eagerness in Caro's voice which surprised Georgie a little.

'Our conversation was not a long one, and I did not quiz him about his personal particulars. He was on his own. He did say that we might continue to play cricket in the paddock but, bearing in mind your reservations about that, I am not sure that we ought to accept his invitation.'

'Nonsense. Of course we must accept such a kindness. A handsome young man—possibly without a wife—will be a great addition to Netherton. I wonder what he is worth. We must be sure to invite him to supper when he is settled in. You must call on him formally.'

And then, a trifle anxiously, 'Did he notice your breeches? I told you not to wear them.'

Georgie said dryly, 'He could scarcely not notice them. And, *if* I do pay him a formal call, I shall be sure to wear skirts.'

'*If?* Why if? *Of course* you will oblige me by calling on him. You have nothing better to do! I grow intolerably bored these days and you would please me greatly by arranging matters so that I may enjoy a little entertainment. I would prefer that we extended the hand of friendship to him before Mrs Bowlby does. She is always to the fore these days. One would not think that I was Mrs John Pomfret of Pomfret Hall!'

Georgie nobly refrained from pointing out that if Caro were to exert herself a little and not perpetually live on her sofa it would be more difficult for Mrs Bowlby to claim to be the *grande dame* of Netherton, and that it was she, Georgie, who did most of the work which provided Caro with some sort of social life. That she did so willingly was for the sake of Gus and Annie, who would otherwise have been neglected, and in memory of a brother who had been unfailingly kind to her.

'Very well,' she said, squirming inwardly at the thought of calling on Mr Jesmond Fitzroy, with or without skirts. 'On the other hand, if you wish to rival Mrs Bowlby, why do you not make the effort and call on him yourself? After all, he does live virtually next door.'

Caro gave a long-suffering sigh. 'You know quite well why I go out so little, Georgie. The effort is too much for me. Dr Meadows says it is essential that I take things easily and that does not include running round Netherton extending supper invitations to all and sundry. And you know that you like being busy.'

But not with Mr Jesmond Fitzroy, was Georgie's dismal response. Oh, dear, who would have thought that Caro would take such an interest in a new neighbour? And then something else struck her: what a slowcoach I must be! John has been dead these three years, she is scarce thirty, and there are few men in this part of Nottinghamshire whom Caro would think fit to marry Mrs John Pomfret.

Hence retiring to the sofa.

But the arrival of a handsome man, who is only a little older than she is, and who must be presumed to have some sort of fortune, is obviously considered by her to be quite a different proposition from the local squires and the odd unmarried poor parson who frequent these parts!

For some odd reason, this new thought distressed Georgie a little. Odd, because her memories of Mr Jesmond Fitzroy were bitter ones. After all, she told herself firmly, he and Caro would make a good pair, united in disapproving soundly of me if in nothing else!

Caro was still talking—it was time Georgie paid some attention to her. 'So that's settled,' she was saying. 'You will pay him a courtesy visit tomorrow morning before the rest of Netherton stands in line at his doorstep to try to monopolise him. Poor John was the Squire here before he died, even if Banker Bowlby does seem to think he has inherited a position which Gus will fill when he comes of age.'

She sank back against the cushions. 'You may also invite Mr Fitzroy—and his wife, if he has one—to supper tomorrow evening. It is possible that he has had a long and hard journey and might not wish to visit anyone tonight.'

The last thing Georgie wished to do was to have another lengthy tête-à-tête with her recent tormentor. While not directly contradicting Caro—which would only have resulted in starting a lengthy and complaining argument—she privately decided to send one of the footmen around in the morning with a note asking him to supper on Friday evening, two days hence, which would give him time to find his bearings.

On second thoughts, she decided that, by the look of him, Mr Jesmond Fitzroy would never need time to find his bearings. By his looks and manner he appeared eminently capable of landing on his feet at whatever spot he chose to arrive—whether it be Netherton or elsewhere.

Netherton, being somewhat more than a village, had decided to call itself a town, albeit a small one. It had numerous good shops, two posting inns, a bank, and, although it could not claim to be a genuine spa, possessed a set of impressive Assembly Rooms where one might drink pure, and supposedly health-giving, water brought from a nearby spring which had been dedicated to Saint Anne. Balls were held there and, on two afternoons a week, tea and cakes were served in the Grand Hall to the sound of a string quartet.

The sum of which caused its inhabitants to remark with great satisfaction, 'We may not call ourselves a spa, but we have all the advantages of one without the disadvantages of large numbers of idle—and sometimes disreputable— visitors.'

Besides Pomfret Hall and Jesmond House, there were also a large number of respectable country houses around the town whose gentry owners were responsible for a lively social life. One of Netherton's wits had recently remarked that 'in imitation of the north of Nottinghamshire, nick-named the Dukeries by virtue of the large number of Dukes' mansions there, this southern part of the county ought to be nicknamed the Gentries!'

Because of the lack of visitors from the outside world, the news that Miss Jesmond's heir had finally arrived at Jesmond House was the cause of a good deal of excitement among the ladies of the town. The gentlemen, whilst shar-ing their interest, were much less noisy than their wives and sisters in expressing it.

Mrs Bowlby, Banker Bowlby's wife, was holding court in her drawing room surrounded by cronies and toadies on the afternoon after Georgie's encounter with Jess, and she could scarcely contain her enthusiasm on learning of his arrival.

'You are sure, Letitia,' she announced, addressing the poor gentlewoman who was her cousin, dependent and vic-tim, 'that he really has taken up quarters here? I would not like to make a fool of myself by visiting an empty house in order to be patronised by that awful butler. One might imagine that, if the heir truly has taken up residence here, one of his first acts will be to dismiss him and engage someone more suitable.'

'Oh, I am quite sure that he *is* the gentleman now in residence,' Miss Letitia Markham reassured her demanding mistress. 'The cook there told our cook that he arrived here two days ago, but has not advertised his presence to the generality. He wished to inspect the house and grounds in private, he said. Far from sacking the butler, he immediately rehired the few servants left to look after the house—so I'm afraid you will have to put up with him, Maria.'

One of poor Miss Letitia's few comforts in life was to administer small pinpricks to annoy her irascible employer, whose only concession to her poverty-stricken cousin was to allow her to use her Christian name. Fortunately for Letitia, Mrs Bowlby was never quite sure whether the pinpricks were accidental or intended.

'The more fool he, then!' she exclaimed. 'He had a fine opportunity for a clean sweep. Have you any notion who he is? Of what family or fortune? Or how old he might be? Has he a wife, for example?'

Miss Letitia smiled and nodded. 'Oh, yes. He is Mr Jesmond Fitzroy, Miss Jesmond's great-nephew who used to stay with her, I am reliably informed, many years ago when he was only a lad. He is not married. Of his own family or fortune, I have no information—or rather, our cook had none.'

'Hmm, Fitzroy,' murmured old Miss Walton of Walton Court. 'An odd name. I seem to remember a boy of that name visiting Miss Jesmond some twenty-odd summers back.'

'It means King's son,' declared Mrs Bowlby, nodding authoritatively. 'Probably goes back to the Middle Ages.'

'Oh, how romantic,' gushed Mrs Firth, whose own family only went back to Elizabethan times, although Letitia often privately thought that that meant nothing since all families went back to Adam and Eve. This was an opinion so seditious that she never voiced it aloud.

Instead, she added slyly, 'I understand that Mrs Pomfret sent Mr Fitzroy an invitation to supper which—according to what his cook said to ours—he gratefully accepted.'

'Did he, indeed! One would never have suspected that she might be so forward—she being such an invalid these days. What does puzzle me,' added Mrs. Bowlby, 'is how it is that the servants always know these things before we do. You must have spent a great deal of time gossiping in the kitchen with cook today, Letitia, to have learnt all that.'

This last came out as a piece of overt criticism.

Miss Letitia was in no way daunted. 'Yes, wasn't it fortunate that I did? Otherwise we should all still be in the dark about our new neighbour!'

'Has Mrs Pomfret invited anyone other than Mr Fitzroy to supper?' asked Miss Walton, looking around her. 'I have heard nothing—has anyone else?'

No one confessed to having been invited. Mrs Bowlby, giving a ladylike sniff, said, 'You may be sure that she will monopolise him if she can. I will not be at all surprised if he is her only guest.'

Mrs Bowlby plainly felt that her desire to be the first lady of Netherton—spurred on by Caro Pomfret's retirement from public life—was under threat if Caro decided to leave her sofa and return to it.

She was just about to say something even more cutting than usual about the Pomfrets when the butler opened the door and announced 'Mrs Charles Herron,' and Georgie walked in, looking charming in a leaf-green walking dress which showed off her russet hair and green eyes to advantage.

So much so that, looking at her ladylike self in her mirror, she had felt so composed and *comme il faut* that she had a sudden wish to call on Mr Jesmond Fitzroy and dazzle him in her character of Professor Charles Herron's wife, to demonstrate how mistaken he had been to dismiss her as a hoyden in breeches.

She had, on the other hand, not the slightest desire to visit Mrs Bowlby, whom she disliked intensely, but, having defied Caro's wishes over meeting Mr Fitzroy again and inviting him to supper, felt that she was compelled to oblige her over Mrs Bowlby.

'Try to find out,' Caro had said eagerly, before she set out, 'whether there is any useful gossip about our new neighbour to be gleaned. Mrs Bowlby's cook is Miss Jesmond's cook's sister, you know.'

Georgie didn't know, and was sadly amused by the vacuous tittle-tattle which formed the staple of provincial life. Her marriage to a gentleman-scholar who had been a pillar of academia at Oxford University had introduced her to a far different society. It had necessitated making herself over into a demure and outwardly conventional wife, but she had considered that a fair exchange for her entry into the world of ideas in which he had reigned supreme.

Her return to Netherton had shown her its emptiness— but she could not say that to Caro, nor that her reversion to her previous lively ways was a silent rebellion against Netherton's dullness. Nevertheless, to please Caro, she smiled at Mrs Bowlby, pretending that the greatest desire of her life was to sit in her drawing room, to drink weak tea and to engage in prattle about all those neighbours who were not present.

Mrs Bowlby was not slow to attack. 'I understand that Mrs Pomfret has already asked our new neighbour to supper. May I ask if you have met him, Mrs Herron?'

After a night's rest and a private determination that she

was making a cake of herself over Mr Jesmond Fitzroy, for whose opinion she did not give a damn—to use a phrase which her brother John had been fond of—Georgie found it easy to answer the Gorgon, the name with which she had privately dubbed Mrs Bowlby.

'Oh, indeed. By pure chance, I assure you. I was walking with the children in the paddock between the Hall and Jesmond House when we came upon him.'

She paused, surveying the expectant faces around her who were finding her narrative much more exciting than the tale of what one cook had said to another.

'And what did you make of him?' burst from Miss Walton, who had the reputation of being both downright and forthright and tried to live up to it.

'I thought that he appeared most gentlemanly and agreeable. He was dressed in the London fashion,' said Georgie with a smile, as though she and Jess had been exchanging civilised pleasantries on the previous afternoon instead of engaging in a slanging match.

'We hear that he is young—in his thirties,' stated Mrs Bowlby. 'Did he mention anything about having a wife or a family?'

'Oh, our conversation was brief and we never touched upon personal matters. Neither of us thought it the time or the place. We shall shortly know everything about him, shall we not? Until then we must possess ourselves in patience.'

The smile she offered the assembled company this time was that of Mrs Charles Herron of Church Norwood at her most cool and commanding and brooked of no contradiction. It killed further conversation about Jess Fitzroy dead, and the ladies were reduced to gossiping about the next Assembly Ball, due to take place in a fortnight. Since Mrs Bowlby's husband was the chairman of the committee which ran the Rooms, her opinion on whether the Ball was to be a formal, or an informal one, was deferred to.

'Oh, informal, please,' Georgie begged. 'Formal ones are so stiff, I think, and the younger girls would like something a little freer. Do try to persuade Mr Bowlby to incline in that direction, please.'

'I rather think not,' Mrs Bowlby enunciated firmly. 'There is too much freedom among the young these days. It is never too early to learn to conform!'

'But only think how we longed for a little freedom when we were young,' Georgie pleaded—but in vain.

After she had left them Mrs Bowlby remarked, 'Mrs Herron is a deal too sure of herself for so young a woman. I note that she is not affecting the tomboy today.'

Mrs Firth leaned forward to say confidentially, 'Jepson, my maid, told me yesterday that she runs round the grounds at Pomfret Hall wearing—of all things—breeches!'

Hands were raised in shock. Miss Walton pronounced the last word on the subject. 'One has to hope that Mr Fitzroy has not seen her in such a get-up. What kind of impression would that give him of the way we conduct ourselves in Netherton!'

A judgement which was received with universal acclamation.

Jess Fitzroy was introducing himself to Netherton on the morning of the day on which he was invited to supper at Pomfret Hall—a visit which intrigued him since it would mean meeting the young termagant on her own ground.

He drove into Netherton in his gig. He had decided not to bring his flash curricle into the country immediately, since it might give away the extent of his wealth. To be regarded as comfortable, he had decided, was his aim: an impression he certainly gave when he reached the inn yard of the White Lion and handed the reins over to a willing ostler.

'Which is the way to the bank?' he asked, adjusting his hat to the right angle, neither too jaunty nor too serious. He was not dressed in his London fine, but something discreet, more suited to a small country town. His boots were not dull, but neither had they been glossed with champagne.

'To your left, sir, when you leave the yard. On the main street. You can't miss it.'

His reward was an unostentatious tip.

Jess found the main street to be busy. He was the subject of a few curious stares, as he had been when he drove in.

The ostler had been right. The bank was unmissable. He pushed open a big oak door with a brass plate in the centre proclaiming itself to be Bowlby's. Inside it was like every country bank he had ever visited—quite different from Coutts, where he had his account in town.

A small man dressed in decent black advanced towards the stranger. 'Pray, what may I do for you, sir?'

Jess said briefly. 'I am Jesmond Fitzroy of Jesmond House, Miss Jesmond's heir. I wrote to Mr Bowlby from London, explaining that I wished to do business with him and possibly open an account here. I would like to speak to him, if you please.' He looked towards the door which plainly opened into the bank's parlour.

'One moment, Mr Fitzroy. I will discover whether he is free to see you.'

Jess sat down in the chair indicated and gazed at the bad oil paintings of bygone Bowlbys on the walls. He reflected amusedly that it had been easier for him to see Mr Coutts in his London office than Mr Bowlby in his country one— but then Mr Coutts knew exactly who he was and all that Mr Bowlby knew was that he was Miss Jesmond's nephew.

The door opened and Mr Bowlby emerged, followed by his clerk. He extended a welcoming hand.

'Always honoured to meet the late Miss Jesmond's nephew,' he boomed, his fat face one smile. 'Pray step this way, sir,' and he flourished a hand towards the parlour where he offered Jess a seat in an armchair facing his large and imposing desk.

'Now, sir, what may I do for you?'

Jess looked round the comfortable room before saying, 'First of all, I should like to take charge of the deeds of Jesmond House, which I believed are lodged with you. Was there any particular reason why they were not given to the keeping of her solicitor, Mr Crane?'

'None, sir, none. But I had been a friend of Miss Jesmond's for many years and when she indicated that she wished me to retain them for safekeeping after she had paid off her mortgage, I did not argue with her. I shall have them delivered to you at Jesmond House tomorrow. What else may I do for you, sir?'

'I would like to open a small working account with you, so that I have a source of income here in Netherton. Nothing large, you understand. My main account will remain at Coutts.'

Mr Bowlby rubbed his fat hands together and said in the manner of a wise man instructing a foolish one, 'Will not that present some difficulties for you, sir, if you intend to remain in Netherton? Would it not be wiser to have your main account here, rather than at a distance? Our reputation is an excellent one.'

For some reason Jess found that he did not like Mr Bowlby. He could not have said exactly why, but years of working with Ben Wolfe had first honed his intuition and then had led him to trust it. Nothing of this showed. He poured his charm—noted among the circles in which he moved in London—over the man before him.

'Since I have not yet made up my mind whether I intend to make Netherton my permanent home, I think it wise to retain my present financial arrangements. You are happy to have a small account on your books, I trust.'

He did not add that transferring his full account to Bowlby's Bank would have enlightened the man before him of the true extent of his wealth—something which he preferred to remain a secret. His trust Mr Bowlby would have to earn, since Jess Fitzroy had long since learned that nothing was ever to be taken for granted in the world of business and finance. Only time would tell how far he could trust Mr Bowlby.

'Certainly, certainly, no account too small, sir. I was but trying to assist you. Finance is a tricky business and gentlemen frequently find themselves adrift in it.'

Not surprising if their metaphors are as mixed as yours, was Jess's inward comment while Mr Bowlby roared on, 'And is there nothing further we can do for you?'

'Yes, indeed,' said Jess sweetly. 'You may inform me of the way to Mr Crane's office where I also have business.'

'With pleasure, sir,' and he walked Jess to the bank's front door before pointing out Mr Crane's front door as cheerfully as the ostler had done.

But Jess did not leave him a tip.

Instead, he bowed his thanks and walked the few yards down the street to Mr Crane's office, where something of a surprise waited for him.

The surprise was not Mr Crane, who was an elderly gentleman whose manner was as quiet and pleasant as Mr Bowlby's had been noisy and officious. His office was quiet, too. No oil paintings, Jess noticed, just a small water-colour showing a country view with sheep in the fore-ground and a river in the distance.

Instead, the surprise consisted of Mr Crane's information as to the extent of his inheritance.

'I fear that I misled you, sir. When I came to investigate Miss Jesmond's financial position more fully I found that, in fact, her estate was less than half of what I had originally indicated to you in my earlier letters. It seemed that she invested unwisely, sold off good stock and bought bad. I spoke to Mr Bowlby about the matter and he confirmed that she had refused his advice and depended on that of a friend who claimed that he had been an expert in the City. At one point, she did so badly that she was compelled to borrow from the bank, lodging her house deeds as secu-rity—although I understand that she later paid off the loan. In order to do so, she sold him a large part of what had been Jesmond land for many years.'

'But Mr Bowlby retained the deeds,' Jess said slowly, 'even after she had repaid the loan. He has promised to forward them to me tomorrow.'

'Oh, you must understand that she trusted Mr Bowlby, who had been so kind to her, and allowed them to remain with him. Of course, until she was compelled to take out the mortgage, they were in my charge. I saw no need to bring pressure on her to lodge them with me again. They were safe where they were.'

'Oh, that explains it,' said Jess—who thought that it didn't.

'I repeat that I am sorry that I unintentionally deceived you over your inheritance. I did not realise that matters had gone so ill with her. I hope that you have not yet made any unbreakable decisions based on its apparent original size.'

'Not at all,' said Jess, who had regarded his aunt's money as a bonus. He had been more interested in the house in which the bank no longer had any interest. He was surprised that Mr Bowlby had said nothing of these matters when he had indicated his misgivings over the bank's holding the house deeds. Or was he surprised? He wondered what advantage Mr Bowlby thought that he was gaining by holding on to them. Nor had Bowlby informed him that it was he who had bought his aunt's lands so that she might pay off the mortgage: that transaction had never been mentioned.

He also thought that Mr Bowlby had supposed him to be a gentleman who knew little of matters financial and therefore might be fobbed off with an incomplete story—which raised, in Jess's mind, further suspicions as to his motives.

Mr Crane was still speaking. 'There are some documents for you to sign, Mr Fitzroy, which will, in effect, transfer all her inheritance to you. It will then be your decision whether I continue to act for you as I did for her.'

'For the moment,' returned Jess coolly. 'Until I have made up my mind what I intend to do, you may continue as my solicitor here—for my business in Netherton only. It is only fair to inform you that I have a solicitor in London who will continue to act for me there. Your interests will not conflict with his. My London affairs have nothing to do with Miss Jesmond's estate.'

Mr Crane nodded. 'I understand. If they do, then I must ask to be relieved of my responsibilities to you."

Jess rose, bowed and sat down again.

'Now,' he said, 'let us get down to business. You will be good enough to tell me all the details of the late Miss Jesmond's estate which are in your possession and not those of Banker Bowlby.'

Mr Crane looked up sharply. Mr Jesmond Fitzroy had spoken coolly to him throughout in a most offhand manner, but he was not sure that his first impression of him as a charmingly lightweight young man was necessarily the true one.

And what had he meant by his last remark about Banker Bowlby?

He did not enquire and Jess said nothing further to make Mr Crane ponder on the true nature of his visitor. He listened quietly to the old solicitor's exposition of Miss Jesmond's admittedly muddled affairs, offering no opinions of his own before leaving with mutual expressions of goodwill.

He strolled along the street, familiarising himself with its layout before returning to the inn to collect his gig. After he had driven out of the White Lion's stable-yard, he found himself behind a chaise which followed the road which led to Jesmond House until it turned off into the drive to Pomfret Hall some half-mile before Jess reached his own gates. He noted idly that Mrs Pomfret had visitors and wondered whether he would meet them at supper.

His main preoccupation was with his morning's work and in particular with Banker Bowlby and with what Mr Crane had—and had not—told him…

'Garth! What brings you here? And why did you not inform us that you were coming to visit us? Georgie, pray ring for the housekeeper—she must prepare a room for my brother immediately.'

Sir Garth Manning made no attempt to answer his sister's questions. He was too busy smiling at Georgie, who was, for once, dressed demurely in Quaker's grey with a high white linen collar trimmed with lace, as were the cuffs of her long sleeves.

'Oh, don't fuss, Caro. I never stand on ceremony, you know that. I always do things on impulse. Much the best way—one never knows what or who one may encounter next. And, to prove my point today, I have found your sister-in-law. I had no notion that she was staying with you—which proves my claim about the unexpected being best. You look charming, dear sister—I may call you dear sister, may I not?'

Georgina, who had never cared overmuch for Sir Garth, would have liked to retort to him with 'No, you may not,' but her regrets over her recent encounter with Jesmond Fitzroy had made her a little wary about being needlessly rude to gentlemen.

She simply gave him an enigmatic smile which he took for agreement. 'Sister it shall be then. I cannot be constantly calling you Mrs Herron, most clumsy.'

'But accurate,' Georgie could not help retorting.

'True, true—but how boring the truth often is, you must agree?'

Georgie could scarcely contradict him. Nothing could be more boring than the truth which Jesmond Fitzroy had served up to her the other day. It seemed that thinking of him had almost brought him to life for Caro exclaimed to her brother, who had sat down beside her and was fanning her gently, 'Oh, Garth, it is most apropos that you have come. We shall now have not one, but two, handsome and unattached men with whom to entertain Netherton!'

'Two,' remarked Sir Garth archly. 'Pray, who is the other? I am not sure whether or not I am pleased to learn that I have a rival.'

It took Georgie all her powers of restraint not to inform him that he and Mr Fitzroy would make a good pair so far as being obnoxious was concerned. Caro, on the other hand, was only too happy to inform her brother of the new owner of Jesmond House.

'Plenty of tin, has he?' enquired Sir Garth negligently.

'So one supposes,' she said, 'but I have not yet met him.
He is to sup with us this evening and then you may pass
judgement on him. At least he has Miss Jesmond's inheritance, which cannot be small.'

Sir Garth raised dark eyebrows. He was dark altogether,
glossy-haired, with a saturnine hawk-like face, rather like,
Georgie thought fancifully, a villain in one of Mrs Rad-
cliffe's Gothic romances.

'Perhaps,' he returned enigmatically. 'The old lady was
light in the attic towards the end, was she not? Sold all that
land to pay for bad investments. If you want to hook him
for yourself, Caro, be sure that you find out exactly how
deep his purse is. Another unfortunate marriage—begging
your pardon, dear sister Georgie—would be one too many.'

Caro simpered, 'Oh, seeing that we have not yet met, are
you not being a little forward, brother, in handing him to
me for a husband?'

'My habit, Caro dear, is always to further your interests,'
he assured her. 'It's a cruel world we live in. One needs to
know one's way about it. All that glisters is not gold.'

Georgie thought that Sir Garth knew whereof he spoke.
She wondered cynically if he had arrived in Netherton to
lie low at his sister's expense—or to recoup himself, perhaps. She did not believe that Netherton was at all the sort
of place which he would choose to frequent—unless ne-
cessity drove him there.

'It's your good luck that I am here to inspect him, my
dear. I look forward to the evening.'

So, apparently, did Caro. She arrived in the drawing
room where Georgie was looking at an album of the Beau-
ties of Britain while waiting for Mr Fitzroy to arrive. She
received the full benefit of Caro's elaborate toilette.

For once her sister-in-law did not immediately make for

the sofa, but instead pirouetted in the centre of the room, waving her fan and looking coyly over the top of it.

'How do I look, Georgie? Will I do?'

Georgie, inspecting her, had to confess that her sister-in-law had seldom looked more enchanting. Her golden hair, her blue eyes and her pink and white prettiness were undiminished although she was nearing thirty.

She was wearing an evening dress of the palest blue trimmed with transparent gauze and decorated with small sprays of silk forget-me-nots. Her fair curls were held in place by a small hoop of the same silken flowers mounted on a ribbon of slightly deeper blue. Her slippers were frail things of white kid.

All in all it seemed that three years of sitting on the sofa doing nothing and letting others worry on her behalf had enhanced rather than marred her good looks. If she had become slightly plumper as a consequence of her lengthy idleness, her figure was so charmingly rounded that most gentlemen, Georgie conceded glumly, would have nothing but admiration for it.

And all this hard work over the past few hours was for Mr Jesmond Fitzroy—as Sir Garth immediately remarked when he entered to find Caro in her glory and Georgie, as usual, feeling eclipsed by it.

Her own green outfit with its cream silk trimmings seemed drab and ordinary, but Sir Garth bowed over her hand as though she were beauty's self and complimented her on her appearance with, 'When last I met you, many years ago now, you were only the humble little sister, but time has worked its magic on you to transform you.'

How in the world did one answer anything quite so fulsome? Georgie put down her book and offered him a meek thank-you, and was saved from further extravagant nonsense by the announcement of Mr Jesmond Fitzroy's arrival.

Any hope that she had possessed that her memory had played her false by enhancing his good looks and his perfect self-command flew away when he entered. If anything, she had under-rated his good lucks and the ease with which he wore his good, but unspectacular, clothes.

She heard Caro draw a sharp breath when he bowed over her hand. Sir Garth, more sophisticated in the ways of the great world, raised his quizzing glass to inspect the visitor more closely, drawling, 'I thought that we might have come across one another before in town although your name is not familiar, but I see that I was wrong.'

Jess surveyed him coolly. So this was Mrs Pomfret's brother, the owner of the carriage which he had seen earlier that day. He was a regular London beau with all the hallmarks of one who moved in good society and had been born into it.

'Oh, I live on the fringes of the *ton*, as many do, I believe.'

He offered Sir Garth no explanation of who and what he had been, and what he had just said to him was no more, and no less, than the truth.

Caro said suddenly, 'I believe, Mr Fitzroy, that you have already met my sister-in-law, Mrs Charles Herron, when she was looking after my two children, so no introductions are needed, although to make everything *comme il faut*, I will offer you a formal one.'

She took Georgie, who had been standing half-hidden behind the brother and sister, by the hand to bring her forward—and Jess found himself facing the hoyden in breeches whom he had rebuked the previous afternoon. Only she wasn't wearing breeches, but a plainish green frock with few trimmings. Her riotously short russet-coloured hair was held back and half hidden by a black bandeau, and the low collar of her dress and its artful cut left one in no doubt that here was a young woman in her early twenties and not the young girl whom he had thought her. Only her green eyes were the same—but even more defiant and mutinous than they had been the previous afternoon!

Caro Pomfret was explaining to him that Mrs Herron was a widow and was living with her so that they might keep one another company instead of being lonely apart.

'She's so good with my lively two, and keeps them in order, which I never could,' she sighed, as though Georgie was a rather helpful nursemaid.

It would have been difficult to know which of the pair of them, Jess or Georgie, was the more embarrassed in view of the unfortunate nature of their previous meeting, although nothing that they said or did gave Caro or Sir Garth any hint of their mutual feelings.

I ought to apologise, they both separately thought, but how does one do that without making matters worse?

Jess's other thought was that, unlike her sister-in-law, Mrs Caroline Pomfret was exactly the sort of unexceptional lady whom a wise man might make his wife. She would always, he was sure, say and do the right thing—indeed, was busy saying and doing them even while they sat and talked about Netherton and the late Miss Jesmond.

'I was so fond of the dear old lady,' sighed Caro untruthfully. She and Miss Jesmond had disliked one another cordially. It had been Georgie who, until her marriage, had provided Jess's aunt with congenial company. After she had been widowed and had returned to Netherton she had lightened the old lady's last days with her bright presence until death had claimed Miss Jesmond.

Caro was now giving Jess her version of her friendship

with Miss Jesmond—which was an accurate account of Georgie's transferred to herself.

'So,' she ended, smiling sweetly, 'you may imagine how pleased I am to meet at last the nephew of whom she was so fond.'

Great-nephew, thought Georgie a trifle sourly.

'And Georgie knew her a little, too,' Caro sighed. 'Although none of us was aware that you were her heir.'

'And nor was I,' returned Jess, who was enjoying more than a little the attention and admiration of a pretty woman. 'It is many years since I last visited my aunt, but I believe that I am the only member of her family left—which accounts for the inheritance, I suppose.'

Sir Garth said, 'I am never sure whether having relatives is a good thing or not, but one is supposed to commiserate with those who have none—so I shall do so.'

Jess bowed his thanks. 'It leaves one feeling lonely,' he admitted. 'However, I can well understand that there are occasions when relatives can be a liability—although I am sure that that term could never be applied to your sister or your sister-in-law.'

'True,' replied Sir Garth, 'and I was spared an unkind father so I am lucky.'

'And I also,' sighed Caro. 'Until I lost my husband,' she added hastily.

Georgie refused to join this mutual congratulation society. She was more than a little surprised by the resentment aroused in her by Jess's admiration of Caro. It was not that he was being obvious about it. Indeed, most people would not have been aware of his interest in her, but Georgie was finding that she could read him.

It was her late husband who had tutored her in the art of understanding the unspoken thoughts of men and women, and she was beginning to regret that anger had led her to misread Jess when she had first met him. It was not that she was interested in him—no, not at all, she told herself firmly—but in a small society like Netherton's she was bound to meet him frequently and it would not do to be at open odds with him, for that might cause unpleasant gossip.

So she said a few moments later, just before the butler came to announce that dinner was served, 'Have you found the opportunity to visit Netherton yet, Mr Fitzroy?'

'Indeed. I drove there this morning. I needed to find a bank and Miss Jesmond's solicitor. Not all my business could be concluded by correspondence before I visited Jesmond House. I was pleasantly surprised by how attractive the little town is—and how busy. I had no notion that there were Assembly Rooms, for example. There were none, I believe, when I visited my aunt over twenty years ago.'

Georgie replied, pleased that they were about to have a civilised conversation at last, 'They were built about fifteen years ago. My late father and Mr Bowlby headed a committee which thought that Netherton needed to have a more varied social life. They were also responsible for improving the streets and creating the public park and the small Arboretum which lies at the end of the main street. My father was a keen gardener; so, too, was your great-aunt when she was a young woman and they frequently made presents of flowers and plants to both the park and the garden.'

Jess privately noted that Georgie had been careful to refer to Miss Jesmond as his great-aunt rather than his aunt and had also informed him—or rather, reminded him—of her love of the outdoor world. He had already decided to restore the gardens around Jesmond House in celebration of her memory.

He told Georgie so.

Her face lit up. 'Oh, how pleased she would have been if she had known that! I think she rather feared that once she was gone the gardens might never recover their old glory.'

Caro was privately yawning at this discussion of matters in which she had no interest. So far as she was concerned, flowers and plants were things which the servants collected from the gardeners and placed in bowls and vases around the house for her to admire if she chose to—which wasn't often.

She was pleased that the butler arrived to announce that supper was ready immediately after she had seconded Georgie's remark by exclaiming, 'What a sweet thought. It does you credit, does it not, Garth?'

Sir Garth, whose lack of interest in things botanic was even greater than his sister's, drawled, 'Yes, indeed, great credit, I'm sure. I like a tidy garden.' A remark which would have killed that line of conversation even if the butler had not summoned them to the supper table.

'I thought,' Caro said, after they were all seated, 'that you would prefer a small private supper party with only a few present rather than a formal dinner where you might be overwhelmed by all those wishing to meet you. You must be aware that the whole of Netherton is excited by your arrival—we meet so few strangers.'

Georgie thought drily that she had rarely met anyone less likely to be overwhelmed than Mr Jesmond Fitzroy, whose reply to Caro was a model of tact and charm.

'Very good of you, madam. Most thoughtful of you. A slow introduction to all the curious would certainly be easier than encountering them *en masse*.'

Now Mr Jesmond Fitzroy was not being quite truthful in coming out with a remark made primarily to please his hostess. He had long been aware that in war, business and life, early reconnoitring of one's surroundings and their inhabitants was highly desirable—particularly when those surroundings were new. He would have been perfectly happy had Mrs Caroline Pomfret invited most of Netherton society to meet him, but no one would have guessed it from his manner.

Except for Georgie.

Her instincts were beginning to inform her that their guest was a far more devious person than his bland exterior might suggest. Consequently the eye she turned on him after that little speech was a trifle satiric—and, being devious and alert, Jess immediately read her expression correctly.

So, Mrs Charles Herron was not only a hoyden, she was also a minx! And a cunning one—unlike her artless sister-in-law. Unfortunately for him, his first encounter with Georgie not only had him continually misreading her, it was helping him to misread Caro too. Because she was so obviously Georgie's opposite, so delightfully conventional in her manner, he was crediting her with virtues which she did not possess.

His instincts were on surer ground with the ineffable Sir Garth, who entertained them over supper with tales of high life. He was, it seemed, a personal friend of all of those in the first stare of London society, throwing nicknames around with abandon. Lord Palmerston was 'Cupid', Lord Granville was 'Beamer', Lady Jersey was 'Silence', and so on…and so on…

Yes, the man was a fraud of some kind, Jess was sure.

If that were so, then what was he doing here in this quiet backwater where some small Assembly Rooms and a miniature park were among the few excitements of the little town?

Jess made a mental note that Sir Garth Manning would bear watching.

And all the time that he was exchanging small talk with

Manning and his sister, about the gossip surrounding King
George IV's determination to rid himself of his wife, Queen
Caroline, who, when she was Princess of Wales, had been
the bane of his life, the Herron minx remained unwontedly
quiet. And who, pray, had the late Mr Charles Herron been,
who had chosen to marry a redheaded termagant?

Which was being unfair, he knew, for Georgie's hair was
not truly red, and for a termagant she was being uncommonly backward in the assertion department!

Halfway through the meal the butler came in and spoke
a quiet word to Caro Pomfret, who looked sweetly up and
waved an airy hand at Georgie. The butler promptly went
over to her and further whispering ensued, at the end of
which Georgie rose from the table and addressed the company apologetically.

'Pray excuse me. It seems that Annie has had a bad
dream and is asking for me.'

Jess rose and bowed. Belatedly, a second later, Sir Garth
followed suit. 'No excuse is necessary,' Jess offered with
a smile. 'Bad dreams take precedence over supper.'

'Unless they are caused by supper,' guffawed Sir Garth
when Georgie had left the room.

'You see,' said Caro, all sweetness and light, 'Georgie
is so very good with them. A pity she never had any children of her own. My health, you understand, does not allow
me to run around after them too much. Georgie, now, is as
strong as a horse.'

For the first time where Caro was concerned Jess's critical faculties began to work. Mrs Pomfret appeared to be
the picture of health—but perhaps the picture was not entirely truthful.

Sir Garth, aware that his sister had sounded a false note,
and had said something which might put off a prospective
suitor, particularly one who had inherited Jesmond House,

drawled languidly, 'But you are recovering a little from the shock of your poor husband's death, are you not, Caro dear? Your health was feared for then, but I gather that you are doing much more than you were.'

He turned to Jess, smiling his crocodile smile. 'Dear Georgie has been a real tower of strength—so strong and commanding—everyone takes heed of her. Such a boon while Caro has not been up to snuff.'

Well, the strong and commanding bit was true enough, thought Jess, remembering Georgie's reaction to his well-meant advice. It was plain that she lacked poor Caro's sensibilities.

Georgie did not return until supper was over and the rest of the party was seated again in the drawing room, waiting for the tea board to appear. She had had enough of watching Caro charm Jess and had decided that seated on poor Annie's bed, reading her a fairy story, and occasionally comforting her, was a better way to spend the evening than in mouthing sweet nothings to persons she did not like.

Unfortunately, in the middle of the second story Annie fell into a happy sleep, leaving Georgie with no choice than to return to the drawing room where she sat, mumchance, watching Caro and Jess try to charm one another.

She soon realised, though, that Jess was not engaged in mouthing sweet nothings. His apparently idle remarks were intended to winkle information out of both Caro and Sir Garth without appearing to do so.

Caro was discoursing animatedly about Banker Bowlby and his pretensions. 'Had it not been for the untimely deaths of both my father-in-law and then my husband,' she was declaiming pathetically, 'Mr Bowlby would not be such a prominent person in Netherton. He quite sees himself as the Squire—which, of course, he is not. Even buying up Miss Jesmond's unwanted land does not entitle him to be considered other than a business man who claims to belong to the gentry.'

'The trouble is,' said Sir Garth, 'we have no notion of who old Bowlby—this man's father—was. He came to Netherton with a bit of money and, it must be admitted, a great deal of drive, and ended up taking over the bank from old Gardiner who had no heir but wished to retire. He claims that his grandfather was Bowlby of Bowlby village near Worksop, but has never shown any evidence to prove it.'

After that there was further gossip about the Wiltons and the Firths. It would be impolite to yawn, though Georgie had heard most of this before and wondered what Jesmond Fitzroy made of it.

Jesmond Fitzroy! What an absurdly pompous name. Fitz! That's what she would call him. It suited him better than his proper one. The thought made Georgie giggle inwardly. Her face flushed and her eyes shone. Yes, given the opportunity she would call him Fitz.

Jess, all ears, being enlightened as well as entertained by Netherton gossip, looked across at her sitting quietly in her chair and recognised the message of the shining eyes, so at contrast with the unsmiling and silent mouth. He decided that he would like to know more about her, about her dead husband and how she came to be here, running Caro Pomfret's errands and looking after her children.

The unwelcome thought struck him that she might be the reason for Garth Manning's presence. Why unwelcome? It was nothing to him if Manning might be after Mrs Herron's small fortune. He was sure that it was small. Although, if Manning were desperate, small might be enough.

Why did he think Manning desperate? Jess didn't know. What he did know was that Manning was a poor thing to be a gentle and pretty woman's brother and her hoyden of a sister-in-law's suitor.

Meanwhile he stayed talking until the proper time to leave, bending first over Mrs Herron's hand, and then—a little longer over Caro Pomfret's, watched by a benevolent Sir Garth Manning. He was suddenly sure that Manning would approve his suit if he decided that Caro was the wife for whom he had been looking.

Back at Jesmond House Twells was waiting up for him, a slightly agitated expression on his old face.

'You have a visitor, sir.'

'What, at this hour?'

'He arrived shortly after you left and said that he was sure that you would wish to see him. He was so insistent that I put him in the library. I didn't think that the drawing room was suitable.'

Jess was intrigued. Who, in the name of wonder, could his visitor be? He tossed his top coat and hat on to the medieval bench which stood in the hall and strode towards the library. Twells said agitatedly, 'Shall I announce you, sir?'

He sounded so tired and old that Jess turned to look at him. 'Certainly not,' he said. 'You are ready for bed and I need no trumpeter to go before me. And, Twells—' as the old man moved away '—you are not to wait up for me again. Surely there is a young footman about the house— Henry Craig, for example—who doesn't need his rest so much and who could be trusted to open the door for me.'

'I am butler here, sir.' Twells's tone was both dignified and rebuking.

'I know that, but you could consider that you are training up a useful deputy—one who can stand in for you at any time. I shall not value you the less, you know—merely commend your good common-sense in agreeing with me. Now, go to bed. I can see myself there later.'

He walked into the library, wondering whom he might find. A man was seated in a chair, reading a book by the light of a candle. He rose when Jess entered.

'Kite!' exclaimed Jess. 'What the devil are you doing here?'

'A good demon to invoke,' said Kite smoothly. He was a tall, slender man with a clever face, decently dressed, a cross between a clerk and a gentleman. His voice and accent were good, although Jess knew that he could speak London cant when he wished. 'You might like to look at my letter, sir.'

He handed it over to Jess who broke the seals and began to read it. It was from Ben Wolfe.

'Dear Jess,' it said, 'I am sending you James Kite to be your lieutenant because I am tired of seeing his damned dismal face around the counting house since you left us. It was either him or Tozzy who had to go, seeing that they were both being glum together—I believe they thought that I had dismissed you, and I wasn't prepared to tell them that you went of your own free will.

'I chose him for you rather than Tozzy because I thought that he is smooth enough to fit into your new life as Lord of the Manor of Netherton. Pray don't turn him away. He can do for you what you did for me—he made it plain that it was you he wished to serve, not me, so I have lost two good men at once. My only consolation is that he will keep you, as well as himself, out of trouble. Knowing him, you will take my meaning.

'Susanna joins me in sending you our best wishes for your future.

'Your humble servant, Ben Wolfe.'

Jess looked at Kite. 'You are aware of what is in this?' he asked, waving the letter.

'Not the exact words, no, but the gist of it.'

'And it is what you wish?'

'Yes—as Mr Wolfe understands.'

'Mr Wolfe understands a damned sight too much,' said Jess. '*You* must understand that being my lieutenant, my man of all work, will be very different here in the country from what it was in London.'

'You need a man at your back anywhere in the world, begging your pardon, sir. Here as elsewhere.'

'And will you, on occasion, be my valet—should I ask you? I don't want a regular one.'

'Anything you ask, sir.'

'But I have already discovered that I may need your special skills as well—although practising them may not be as dangerous as in London.'

'Only time will tell.'

He should have remembered how brief and sardonic Kite was. A cross between himself and Ben Wolfe.

'Your official position will be as my secretary. Tomorrow I shall be seeing the man who was my great-aunt's agent until she lost her reason, and you will be present, taking notes—and listening. You were good at listening.'

'My forte, sir.'

Jess rang for the footman, Henry Craig, who he hoped was now standing in for Twells. 'I shall have a room assigned to you—it won't be comfortable. The whole damned place is derelict. You can help me to restore it.'

'With pleasure, sir.'

Jess watched him follow young Henry, who was to be Twells's new deputy. Craig was carrying the bags which Kite had brought with him. He did not know whether to laugh or to curse—or to congratulate himself.

On the whole, he decided on the latter—but God help Netherton with Kite loose in it.

And Sir Garth Manning and Mr Bowlby in particular, both of whom Kite could track for him.

Chapter Three

Jess had underestimated the size of the social life in Netherton and the ingenuity of its inhabitants in organising it.

The following morning Kite, who had already taken up his secretarial duties, handed him a letter from the Bowlbys which had arrived by special messenger.

It invited him to a fête to be held in the grounds of the Bowlbys' mansion, Nethercotes, on the afternoon of the immediate Saturday. It also welcomed him to Netherton and hoped that Mr Fitzroy would enjoy his stay in the town.

'Shall I answer it for you? I take it that you wish to accept.'

'You take it correctly. I shall be seeing Parsons, the former land agent here, at two of the clock this afternoon in the library. You will, of course, be present. This morning I intend to ride around the countryside, familiarising myself with the lie of the land.'

'You have a map of the district, sir?'

'Yes,' said Jess, holding up a tattered scrap of paper. 'It purports to show the boundaries of the local estates, including those of the land my aunt used to own. I'll see you at lunch. In the meantime, you might go up to the attics and see if you can find anything useful there. And by useful

I mean not only bibelots, pictures and furniture, but also papers and documents, however old.'

'Understood, sir.'

Kite ghosted out of the room. Jess had forgotten how unobtrusive he was—and how immediately obliging. The letter would go straightway to the Bowlbys and the attics would be searched.

It was a glorious morning for a ride and his horse—named Tearaway because he was nothing of the kind—like Jess, was, for once, eager to enjoy a little exercise. He turned down the main street, openly watched by the villagers—he could not yet think of Netherton as a town.

Occasionally stopping to read the map, he quartered the countryside after the same fashion he had employed long ago in India, only the scenery being different. He had just begun to ride down a green lane at the back of his little property when he saw young Gus running along the bank of a shallow river, one of the tributaries of the Trent, waving his arms and shouting.

Jess grinned. He'd bet a mountain of tin that the young hoyden was at her tricks again! What could it be this time? He ought to find out in case she were in real trouble. He dismounted, tied Tearaway to a fence post, and pushed through the low hedge which bordered the field where he had caught sight of Gus.

By now Gus had seen Jess and was running towards him.

'What luck to find you here, sir,' he gasped breathlessly. 'I thought I'd have to run to your home farm to find help.'

He began to tug at Jess's coat. 'It's Georgie,' he said. 'She went into the river after one of the village children who had strayed from home, fallen in and was like to drown. She saved the child, but she's wet through and has hurt her ankle. She said not to fuss, she could manage, but

I disobeyed her because I thought she needed help. This way, sir, this way.'

He had been pulling Jess along while he told his story.

So, he had been right. Georgie Herron was in trouble again. No, that was quite wrong. She had not been in trouble when he had found her playing cricket on his land. The trouble had come after that when he had tried to advise her.

He wondered how badly she had been hurt. He doubted whether Gus was the most reliable of witnesses, although he seemed to have plenty of common-sense.

How like mad Mrs Georgie to hurl herself into a river— even a shallow one—after a drowning child! He couldn't imagine the ladylike Caro doing any such thing. But then Caro would never have been roaming the countryside with two small children, either.

He found Georgie sitting on the river bank not far from where he had first seen Gus. She had stripped off her boy's jacket in order to go into the river and was soaked through, her wet shirt clinging revealingly to her. She was cradling on her knee the soaked and crying child whom she had rescued and was trying to comfort her.

She had walked a few yards from the spot where she had rescued the little girl from the river, but the weight of the child, combined with the pain in her damaged ankle, had compelled her to sit down for a moment. She felt her heart sink when Gus and Jess rounded the turn of the river and came into view.

Of all the dreadful luck! What a fright she must look, like a drowned rat with her hair in strings about her face, for the child had sunk on to the river bed and she had had to bend down in order to lift her out. Of course, the poor little thing had had no more sense than to clutch at her so that she had lost her balance, landing in the water and wrenching her ankle at the same time.

Fitz was bound to ring a peal over her again and be full of sound advice on the proper behaviour of a young lady. She tried to stand up to greet him, but holding the squirming child made such an act difficult as well as painful.

Nevertheless, she managed to lever herself upright just before Jess reached her. He confirmed her worst fears by immediately barking an order at her in a sergeant-major's voice. 'Whatever do you think that you're doing? Sit down at once!'

'Oh, Fitz,' said Georgie sorrowfully, 'I might have guessed that you would begin to bully me the moment you saw me.'

'Of course I shall bully you,' said Jess, scarcely hearing the 'Fitz', but relieved to see that she still had enough spirit left to spark at him. 'You need to be bullied if you insist on running around the countryside doing dangerous things!'

'Goodness me,' she exclaimed, seething. 'I suppose I ought to have left the poor little thing to drown and fainted with shock at the sad sight instead.'

'I would never have expected that of you,' announced Jess firmly. 'And before you try to walk, allow me to have a look at both the ankle and the child. You could let Gus hold it while I do so.'

He looked around him. 'And where's Annie? Have you lost her as well as half-drowning yourself?'

'It! It! She's a girl, Fitz—or were you so busy reprimanding me that you failed to notice that she wasn't wearing breeches? And Annie isn't with us—she didn't feel up to a long walk.'

'Fortunately for her, she appears to be unlike you in every way,' said Jess severely, 'seeing that she was obeying the normal conventions which govern the behaviour of females and didn't want to go gallivanting around the countryside. Take off your wet sock at once so that I may inspect your damaged ankle. And, by the way, who gave you leave to call me Fitz?'

'The same person who gave you leave to shout orders at me every time we meet. The deity, if you like. He's supposed to arrange our life, I believe, although where females are concerned he's made a poor fist of it!'

Jess, bending over her ankle, gave a crack of laughter at this spirited sally. Gus, now cradling the wet and crying girl child, saw nothing to laugh at, particularly since Georgie had begun to shiver with cold.

He said, rebuking Jess a little, 'It was jolly brave of Georgie to rescue her. You mustn't be cross with her.'

'No, it wasn't brave and I don't think that he's really cross. And I was stupid to allow myself to lose my footing in the water,' announced Georgie, who was finding that there was something strangely intimate and pleasant in having Fitz examine her bare foot and ankle. That stroking motion, now, as he tried to assess the damage, was quite delightful and soothing. She was sorry when he stopped.

'No real harm done,' he pronounced at last. 'A light sprain only. But I don't think that you ought to walk on it. I left my horse tethered on the byway. If you will allow me to carry you there, he may take you the rest of the way home. Gus can lead Tearaway and I'll carry the child. Have you any notion of who she belongs to?'

'None. The first time I saw her was when she was falling into the river. And you don't need to carry me. I'm quite capable of walking.'

'Contrary infant that you are,' Jess told her pleasantly, 'you cannot really wish to make a light sprain worse. You will miss the Bowlbys' fête and the Assembly Room dance if you do.'

'Infant! Fitz, I'll have you know I'm an old married

woman, or widow rather. A little respect from you would not come amiss.'

But Georgie was laughing while she spoke, her green eyes shining and dancing and Fitz—dammit, he was already beginning to think that was his name—held her lightly against his heart. She was really no weight at all despite the one boot she was still wearing and her sodden breeches. Now that he was holding her, he could feel her shivering.

He sat her down for a moment and pulled off his coat. 'Wrap that around you,' he told her. 'Unwise for you to get too cold.'

'No need,' declared Georgie, staring at his magnificent shirt which covered an equally magnificent torso. 'I'm so wet that I shall ruin it. Though it's kind of you to offer it, Fitz.'

'All the more reason for you to wear it,' he told her briskly. 'And come to think of it, no one has ever called me Fitz before. Odd that, for one would normally expect it to be my nickname.'

'Oh, everyone was too frightened of you to give you a nickname at all, I suppose. Have you always behaved as though you were the Lord of All?'

'Now that,' he told her severely, joining in with her light-hearted game, 'is really unkind. I've a good mind to drop you and leave you to the wolves.'

'There aren't any wolves round here,' said Gus glumly, 'and if you did any such thing I'd tell on you to the village constable.'

'He doesn't mean it, Gus,' Georgie reassured him. 'He's only teasing me. He'd never do any such thing.'

'Really?' said Jess, raising his perfect eyebrows. 'Care to twit me again and find out?'

They had reached Tearaway; before Georgie could answer, Jess had lifted her on to him.

'Your breeches do have some practical use,' he told her. 'You can ride astride. We're not far from Pomfret Hall if my map is correct. Once there, you must take a warm bath, put on some dry clothes and lie down for a little.'

'Orders, orders, always orders, Fitz. What were you in your previous incarnation? An Army officer?'

Something in his expression gave him away.

Georgie said exultantly, 'Caught. I knew it! You were.'

'You are,' he told her, but his voice was kind, 'the most knowing minx I have ever had the misfortune to meet.'

He had a sudden memory of an occasion on which Ben Wolfe had said something similar to his future wife Susanna. The thought made him smile. Georgie saw the smile. It transformed a face whose expression was usually a trifle severe.

'What sort of a soldier, Fitz?' she asked him.

'The usual,' he said drily, 'but that was long ago and not worth the telling.'

'Long ago,' exclaimed Gus, delighted to meet a real live soldier. They had been thin on the ground since Waterloo. 'You must have been quite a babe then.'

'Indeed, Master Gus. Older than you, though. And green, very green.'

'Green, Fitz?' called Georgie from her perch. 'I can't believe that!'

'Believe it, Mrs Georgie, believe it. I may call you that, may I not?'

'If you will allow me to call you Fitz—though we must behave ourselves in public. There I propose to be good. You shall be Mr Fitzroy with just the slightest stress on the first syllable. You're not green now, though. By no means.

Was that the Army? Papa always said that being in the Army made a man.'

Jess decided to tell the truth. 'Partly the Army and partly a friend I made in it. And that is enough of me. Since you have questioned me so thoroughly, I believe that gives me the right to question you. Have you always been so downright, Mrs Georgie?'

Silence. She was not answering him. He shifted the child on his arm. Fortunately for his comfort, fright and tiredness had finally sent her to sleep. He wondered why Georgie had suddenly become shy, for she was looking away from him and by the set of her body for the first time since he had met her, her ready wit had deserted her.

'The truth, Fitz,' Georgie said at last. 'You want the truth? The answer is no. And it wasn't the Army which changed me.'

She had not known how to reply. The question had brought the past rushing back and Georgie hated the past and had no wish to live in it again.

Unknowingly it was something she shared with the man walking alongside her. Suddenly she felt desperately tired and very cold. The exhilaration which had consumed her from the moment Jess had walked into view had disappeared. She shivered, a long shiver. Even his coat could not warm her.

Jess felt the shiver. He turned to Gus and said, 'Can I trust you, young shaver? We are not far from your home. Do you think that you could carry the child there on your own if I mount Tearaway and gallop your aunt there before she expires with cold and shock? We are on what passes for a main road here and you should not meet with any danger. I'll have them send a footman in your direction when I reach Pomfret Hall.'

'No need,' said Georgie quietly. 'I am not about to faint, but I do feel so dreadfully cold.'

'The warm bath, remember,' Jess said, 'The sooner you reach it, the better. I shall ride in front of you. Loose the reins and allow me to mount.'

She did not argue with him, which told him that she was in need of his assistance. Nor did he twit her again, but concentrated on encouraging Tearaway to increase his speed so that they might reach Pomfret Hall the more speedily.

'How like you, Georgie,' wailed Caro gently, 'to throw yourself into the river after a chance-met child. I don't say that it's not worthy of you, only that it's foolish. Could you not have sent Gus for help instead?'

'By which time the child would have been drowned dead for sure,' said Georgie sturdily, some of her old fire returning now that she was back home and about to enjoy the warm bath which Jess had demanded and Caro had ordered. 'You didn't really expect me to sit on the bank and watch her dying struggles?'

Jess watched, amused, when Caro threw him a helpless look, saying, 'I never know what to expect from you, Georgie, so I suppose I shouldn't be surprised at this morning's adventure. Do either of you have any notion of whose child it is?'

'It,' began Georgie belligerently, 'she's not an it,' only for Jess to put a gentle hand on her arm and say soothingly,

'Time to go upstairs, I think. That must be your maid approaching.'

It was. Georgie's maid, Madge Honey, was in her fifties and had been her old nurse. She arrived in time to hear Georgie fire at Jess, 'Orders again, Fitz!' and to say reprovingly to her, 'Now, now, Miss Georgie. None of that.

You're soaking wet through and there's a nice warm bath being prepared for you. I've put some dry clothes out and readied the bed so that you can have a good lie-down. Come along, do!'

Georgie was led away, clutching her head melodramatically and exclaiming, 'It's a conspiracy, it really is. Has Mr Fitzroy been coaching you, Madge, that you should echo what he has been telling me every few yards on the way home?'

'Has he, now, my pet? Then he's a right sensible gentleman, isn't he? And you'd do best to heed him.'

Jess tried not to laugh. Caro smiled wearily at him and said, 'Madge is the only person who can control her these days. When I think what she used to be like…' She shook her head. 'I'll have the butler fetch you one of John's old coats before you catch your death of cold, and you'll oblige me by taking tea—I've already ordered the tea board.'

Jess began to demur, but Caro looked so charmingly welcoming that he gave way, and obediently put on one of her late husband's jackets which fitted him quite well, although it was not of a colour he liked.

Caro began to chatter about every subject under the sun until he said, 'I would be grateful if you would enquire whether Gus has brought the half-drowned mite home.'

'Oh, that!' said Caro, waving an airy hand. 'The butler informed me when I ordered the tea board that Gus had arrived home safely and that the housekeeper was arranging dry clothing for it. And now we have the bother of discovering whose it is.'

This last came out with a great sigh.

Fortunately for Jess—he could think of no reply which would not sound critical of his hostess—Sir Garth came in, saying, 'Heard m'sister-in-law had been in the wars and that you had rescued her, Fitzroy. What's she been up to now?' and he gave a knowing laugh.

Jess, to his great surprise, found himself defending Georgie. 'Nothing discreditable,' he said coolly. 'Quite the contrary. She went into the river to rescue a drowning child. Most enterprising of her. Fortunately I happened to be nearby to see that she reached home again without dying of cold. She has damaged her ankle, but not too seriously, I believe. Mrs Pomfret has sent for the doctor.'

Sir Garth smiled, ignoring the hidden rebuke. 'Noble of her, I'm sure. Shouldn't expect anything else of her. She'll make some fortunate man a useful wife.'

By his expression he obviously considered himself to be that man, which, Jess decided, would be a pity. She deserved something better than this conceited jackanapes. He decided to take his leave. He could not stomach too much of Sir Garth's company.

That gentleman, once Jess had gone, sank into an armchair, remarking to his sister, 'Which of you does he fancy? You or Georgie? He looked down his nose at me when he thought that I was criticising her.'

'Georgie!' exclaimed Caro with a scandalised laugh. 'He doesn't fancy Georgie. They are quite at odds with one another, I believe. Thinks her a hoyden by the way he spoke when he brought her home.'

'Does he, now?' Sir Garth was thoughtful. 'Some men have a penchant for hoydens, though.'

'Not Mr Fitzroy. You must have observed that he is very *comme il faut*.'

'Secretive devil, too,' said Sir Garth, ignoring this last comment. 'Wonder where he comes from. Would bear looking into.'

A verdict similar to the one which Jess had already passed on him!

* * *

Parsons, late Miss Jesmond's land agent, arrived in the afternoon and was shown into the library, that repository of battered books.

Kite had earlier placed a box of grimy documents which he had salvaged from the attics on one of the tables for Jess to inspect. Before that he had had a distracted visitor: a young farm labourer, Jack Wild, one of Jess's tenants, whose little daughter had disappeared that morning from the garden at the back of his cottage and had not been seen since.

'I need a search made, sir,' he had said hoarsely. 'I thought you might be able to help me, seeing that you are my master now.'

Jess had the pleasure of telling him that his daughter was safe at Pomfret Hall after falling in the river and that she had been rescued by the bravery of Mrs Herron. 'Go to the stables,' he ended, 'and ask one of the grooms to drive you over in the gig, collect her and take you both home.'

'That I will, sir, and thank you and thank Miss Georgie, too—begging your pardon, but we all called her that before she married—it seems odd to think of her as Mrs Herron.'

'One question for you before go on your way. You work at my home farm, do you not?'

'Aye, that I do,' agreed Wild eagerly. 'Worked for old Miss Jesmond all my life. Don't have much to do since Mr Parsons left. Miss Jesmond paid my wages—belike you'll do the same.'

'I am hoping to re-employ Mr Parsons—if he is not already committed elsewhere.'

'Doing piece-work for Banker Bowlby, he is. Would probably like his old job back.'

He left, still thanking Jess profusely. Jess thought that he ought to thank him for revealing that Banker Bowlby seemed to have a finger in every pie.

Parsons turned out to be a large square man with a weathered face, dressed in country clothing.

'You wished to see me, Mr Fitzroy?'

'Indeed. You were my aunt's land agent, I believe. When did she dispense with your services—and why?'

Parsons had not known what to expect of Miss Jesmond's heir. He looked a right soft gentleman and no mistake with his pretty face and his pretty clothes, sitting there in the ruins of a once-fine library.

On the other hand, his first words had been direct and to the point.

'After she sold most of her land she no longer needed an agent, nor, she said, could she afford to pay one, so she told me that my services were no longer needed.'

It was a straight answer to a straight question. Jess, leaning back a little in his chair said, almost as though he were not interested, 'Why did she sell her land? Do you know?'

'She said that she had made foolish investments and Banker Bowlby was helping her to pay back what she owed by taking the land off her hands as quickly as possible.'

Parsons's face when he came out with this was expressionless, passing no verdict on what he was saying.

'Have you any notion of how much he paid her?'

'None, sir. She seemed happy with it, but…' He paused and fell silent.

'But?' prompted Jess, eyebrows raised.

'But, begging your pardon, sir, she was weak in the head by this time, and I am not sure that she quite understood what was what.'

'You were present?'

'When Banker Bowlby visited her here. Yes.'

'Was no sum mentioned then? Or any account given of her debts?'

'None. I understood that these matters had been raised

in a meeting at the bank and this meeting was for her to sign the documents which he had prepared for her. The butler and I were simply there as witnesses.'

'You did not read the documents, then?'

'No, sir. I asked—but Mr Bowlby and Miss Jesmond both assured me that they had gone over them together and that they were both satisfied with their contents.'

'But you said that Miss Jesmond was weak in the head.'

'Aye, sir, but when I tried again Miss Jesmond grew petulant and sent me away. She said that I was trying to ruin her. One of the footmen signed the documents instead. Soon after that she dismissed me. I think Banker Bowlby recommended her to do so—although he took me on to do piece-work for him, saying he was sorry for me.'

'And did you believe him?'

'No, sir, but I needed the work, so I said nothing. I have a family to keep.'

'And would you work for me, in your old capacity?'

'But you have little land, sir, and so have little use for an agent.'

Jess smiled coldly. 'You must allow me to be the best judge of that.'

Parsons stared across at Kite, busy taking notes.

'Begging your pardon, sir, but what is that man doing?'

'Mr Kite is keeping a record of our meeting in case my memory fails me. He will now write down that I have offered you your post back at slightly more than Miss Jesmond paid you. He will also note down your answer—which is?'

'That I accept, sir, except that I am a little troubled about what my duties might be.'

Jess said over his shoulder, 'You have that, Kite?'

'So noted, sir.'

'Good, and you, Parsons, have no need to be troubled.

You will start work tomorrow, and we shall then have a brief discussion about your future. Is there anything further you wish to know?'

Parsons stared at Jess now, fascinated. 'No, sir, but you will forgive me for saying that this is a regular rum do.'

Was that a smile on Mr Kite's impassive face? Parsons wasn't sure. If he had feared that his answer might ruffle Mr Jesmond Fitzroy, he was quite mistaken.

'You are not the first person to make such a remark to me, Mr Parsons, and I doubt that you will be the last. You will report to me in this room at eight of the clock on Monday morning. I am sure that I need not say that I expect punctuality at all times. Good day, Mr Parsons. The butler will show you to the door.'

A rum do, said Parsons to himself as he left Jesmond House, and a regular rum gent. Is he the clever one or does that man of his, Kite, do his thinking for him? But I've my old post back so I shan't complain.

'Well, Kite, are you thinking what I'm thinking?' asked Jess when the door had closed behind Parsons.

'That Banker Bowlby will bear investigating? Certainly.'

'And soon.' Jess was a trifle abstracted. 'I had not thought that the country would prove so lively.'

'Begging your pardon, sir, but in my experience liveliness may be found anywhere. Best to be ready for it.'

'So noted,' replied Jess, in a slight mockery of a clerk's formal answer. 'I shall remember your advice when I next meet Banker Bowlby at his fête on Saturday. For the present I shall not ask you to make a formal investigation of him—I need a little more information first. I shall go through the papers you have discovered—there might be something interesting to be found in them.'

'I fear that there are a sight more in the attic.'

Jess sighed. 'I thought that I had done with investigating

dubious ventures, Kite, but I ought to have known that I was wrong. Bring them down slowly. Who knows, the answers to some questions which I am beginning to ask myself may be found there.'

'So noted, sir.'

From Kite's tone it was impossible to discern whether he was mocking himself or Jess.

Jess decided to let sleeping birds lie!

Chapter Four

The Bowlbys' fête had been in full swing for some time and still Fitz had not appeared. There was an unexpectedly large number of people present, Georgie conceded, but even so Fitz was such a distinctive figure that she could not have missed seeing him if he were present.

And why in the world, she told herself crossly, should I worry whether His High Mightiness is present or not? Later in the day on which she had gone into the river, the little girl's father had arrived at the Hall, sent on by Fitz with a short note in his own fair hand saying that Mr Wild was one of his farm workers and had been informed that his daughter owed her life to Mrs Herron's courage.

Wild's gratitude to her when she entered the entrance hall where he was waiting for her, the child's hand in his, was so great that it was embarrassing.

'I only did what anyone ought to,' she told him.

'That's as may be, but there's many a fine lady who'd have stood by and let her drown. I shan't forget what you did, Miss Georgie.'

Nor would Georgie forget Fitz's kindness in the manner in which he had sent Wild to the Hall in his gig. Yes, that was it. She was in such a lather to see him because she wished to thank him—and for no other reason.

And there he was, cool and confident, not a dandy, but wearing his ordinary clothes after such a fashion that he might as well be one. He was talking to Caro—of course. The Bowlbys had put a *chaise-longue* out for her and she was reclining on it with her usual airy grace, fluttering her eyelashes and her fan at the handsome man bending over her.

Georgie acknowledged desperately that she would never be able to lie on a sofa and make charming small talk. It was quite beyond her. She had never done such a thing, and now it was too late to learn.

She made her way slowly towards them, using her fan for the day was hot—unlike the one on which she had jumped into the river.

Caro saw her first. 'Oh, there you are, Georgie. I thought that you might have gone home. This kind of affair always bores her, Mr Fitzroy. Is not that true, my dear?'

'Not today,' returned Georgie as coolly as she could. 'I am fast learning the social graces, Caro, and if you would lend me your *chaise-longue* I could practise a few more.'

Her sister-in-law gave a charming screech. Jess's face lost a little of its usual impassivity on hearing this two-edged comment.

'Might you not find a *chaise-longue* a little constricting, Mrs Herron?' he asked her.

'Caro doesn't appear to find it so, so why should I?'

'Dear Georgie—' the words flowed from Caro's mouth like cream from a jug '—you know as well as I do how different we are. For one thing, you are as strong as a horse…while I—' and she sighed dramatically '—am quite otherwise.'

She might have known that her sister-in-law would

wrongfoot her, so she ought to have held her tongue. As strong as a horse, indeed! This was the second time that Caro had so described her to Fitz. How off-putting! It suggested a red-faced and brawny female and she was far from being that. Salvation came from an unexpected quarter.

'Strong, I agree, but a horse, never,' said Jess. 'I am exercised as to precisely which animal Mrs Herron resembles the most.' He put his head on one side before offering, 'A gazelle, perhaps?'

Georgie could not help herself, 'Oh, Fitz,' she exclaimed, 'you always do and say the unexpected! A gazelle! I am indeed honoured!'

She was aware that she was conversing in exclamation marks, egged on by the petulant expression on Caro's face. Fortunately for all of them—particularly herself, she afterwards thought—Banker Bowlby came up and said, 'So pleased that you have honoured our little party with your presence, Mr Fitzroy. I have already welcomed the ladies. I understand that no introductions are needed since you have already met and supped with Mrs Pomfret and Mrs Herron.'

'And I am delighted to be here,' returned Jess truthfully. He had had a strong desire to see Banker Bowlby on his home ground and, at the same time, to become acquainted with as much of Netherton society as possible. 'You must introduce my hostess to me: I was on my way to her when I had the good fortune to meet Mrs Pomfret—and Mrs Herron, of course.'

So I am an afterthought, raged Georgie silently, always to be second to the ineffable Caro! She could not know that Jess was laying false trails for the Banker. He had no wish to be seen as a charming philanderer laying waste among the ladies. Unknowingly using the word Georgie had privately employed to describe Caro, he wanted the Banker—

and Netherton society generally—to view him as an ineffable and uncommitted idler until he had solved to his own satisfaction a number of puzzles which that society—and his dead great-aunt—presented to him.

Mrs Bowlby had early retreated into the house, a large one on the outskirts of Netherton which had once belonged to the Bank's previous owner. It was furnished in expensive rather than good taste. Poor oil paintings of Banker Bowlby's supposed ancestors hung on its walls.

She had taken up a vantage point by the open door where she could watch 'the goings-on'—her favourite words to describe any social occasion. Surrounded by her sycophants, she was fanning herself. Her face was unlovely, fat and red like her husband's, and her dress sense was non-existent, but power, Jess well knew, does not need beauty to support it and, by virtue of her husband's position and his wealth, Mrs Bowlby was a power in Netherton.

She had just handed her fan to Letitia, announcing that she was too heated to fan herself, so Letitia could earn her pay by keeping her cool, when Jess was presented to her. Like everyone who met him she was immediately struck by his good looks and his air of idle and unconscious ease.

'Ah, we meet at last, Mr Fitzroy,' she said, giving him her large hand to kiss—which he duly did. 'I knew your aunt, of course, but not so well as I might have hoped, since she was very much an invalid in her last years.'

'So I understand,' he replied. 'It was unfortunate that I lost touch with her after I left Netherton many years ago. No one was more surprised than I was when she left me her fortune. It came at a time when life in the country suddenly held renewed attractions for me.'

'You could not have come to a better place than Netherton,' she assured him. 'We are all one big happy family here—thanks, of course, to my husband.'

Jess gave her an indolent smile. 'So I understand. I am indeed fortunate to have arrived at such a rural paradise.'

It took him all his strength to keep a straight face while he came out with this outrageous lie. He already suspected her husband of being a swindler. He had also discovered from Parsons confirmation of what he had seen for himself: that, due largely to mismanagement by the local gentry and farmers, the labourers on their lands were living in the direst poverty so that Mrs Bowlby and her kind could sit in state. The system of poor relief which an earlier government had instituted actually encouraged them to keep wages low.

He had already instructed Parsons to put in hand certain reforms on the running of the land remaining to him, and to set in motion plans to improve immediately the tumbledown cottages of his workers. At the same time he and Kite arranged to set about restoring Jesmond House more slowly. He must not give the impression of being over-rich—even though he was. Later, when he had established himself, he would try to buy back some of the lost Jesmond lands.

Mrs Bowlby took his answer at face value. She simpered at him after sharply instructing Letitia to fan her with a little more vigour.

'I always suffer in the heat,' she informed Jess. 'Something which I can never get poor Letitia to understand. The other side of my face needs cooling,' she snapped at her unfortunate dependant. 'I should have thought that you would know that by now without me having constantly to remind you.'

Without pausing for breath she continued trying to charm Jess. 'I do hope that you intend to grace the ball at the Assembly rooms tonight. Everyone who is anybody will be there.'

Jess was truthful this time. 'You may be sure that I have every intention of being present. It is not, I dare say, an occasion to be missed.'

'No, indeed, and we must instruct the Master of Ceremonies to introduce you to as many pretty and eligible young women as possible. Mrs Pomfret and Mrs Herron are not the only charming young ladies who live around Netherton, you know. My own daughters, for example, Cecilia and Frances, would be delighted to meet you. Have you been introduced yet?'

Jess gave a sad sigh. 'Alas, no.'

'Then I shall arrange matters at once. Letitia! Pray find Sissy and Fanny, and inform them that I wish them to come here in order to meet Mr Fitzroy. Don't gape at me, but be on your way immediately. That is an odd name of yours, Mr Fitzroy—pray, what is its origin?'

This set Jess lying again. 'Now, madam, you have me there. My father died when I was but a boy, before I showed curiosity about such matters, and thought mine a name like many others so I never asked where it came from. It probably, I understand, dates back to the Middle Ages.'

'How delightful! I should have so liked to live then. People really knew their place—none of this horrid rioting, hayrick-and machine-burning which we have to endure today—although,' she hastened to add lest her vision of Netherton as Arcadia be destroyed, 'I am pleased to say we have little of that here.'

'So I understand,' Jess returned, happy to have her attention diverted from his name. He would have liked to move on to other pastures, but was compelled to wait in order to meet Sissy and Fanny.

He was unaware that Georgie Herron was standing behind him during his tête-à-tête with Mrs Bowlby and had

been listening to it with mounting amusement. She had followed him and Mr Bowlby into the house, leaving Caro to
act as siren to the unattached gentlemen of Netherton in
whom Georgie had no interest. No, her interest, she now
knew, was fixed on Fitz, and what the nature of that interest
was she did not enquire of herself.

She could hardly bear to wait to see what sort of effect
the Bowlby twins would have on him. If he thought that
she was a hoyden, what in the world would he make of
them? Of course, they didn't wear breeches, but...

Her wait was soon over. Miss Letitia was arriving with
a sulky pair in tow. They had been playing hide and seek
with the elder sons of the neighbouring squires—none of
them more than twenty—and did not wish to lose their fun
in order to meet Mr Fitzroy who was supposed to be more
than thirty.

They knew better than to disobey their mother, though.

Jess found himself confronted with two large and flushed
young girls, dressed in the worst of fashion and quite obviously in the sulks at being summarily pressed to meet
him.

'Cecilia, Frances, my two dear twins. I would like you
to meet Mr Jesmond Fitzroy, the great-nephew of that dear
old lady, Miss Jesmond, who has come to live in Netherton.
Make your best curtsies to him, dear girls, and then I would
like you to show him around the house and grounds.'

'Must we?' were the words which could almost be seen
to be hovering on Miss Cecilia's lips, while Jess made them
his most elaborate bow, secretly horrified at being condemned to the company of such a pair of raw chits who
would, he was sure, possess neither conversation nor manners.

Georgie, on the other hand, was highly delighted at the
sight of Fitz pretending to be honoured by Mrs Bowlby's

tactless offering. Let him learn what real hoydens were like, who a few moments ago had been screaming their pleasure around the Bowlbys' gardens.

On the other hand, they would be most likely to be so awestruck by Fitz's magnificence that they would descend into a sullen silence. Either way, she could scarcely hide her own pleasure at seeing him wrong-footed. She had moved so that he could see her after he straightened up from his courtier-like bow, and, as usual, she had misjudged him for, turning his head slightly, he favoured her with a complicit wink which none but she could see.

Now what was she to make of that?

Georgie watched him being led off by the twins, who dutifully pointed out the supposed likenesses of Grandfather Bowlby and his wife, Charlotte, hanging opposite to the hearth above a breakfront bureau filled with new china.

'Papa says,' remarked Fanny, 'that it was a set made for Catherine the Great of Russia which he got for a song—by accident. She died before it could be delivered and her successor refused to buy it.'

And no wonder, thought Jess, staring at the gaudy objects on display. Although the bit about buying it for a song was most likely the only true statement Fanny had made. The dinner service was undoubtedly well-covered in gilt, but he thought it unlikely that Catherine the Great had ever ordered anything so tasteless.

He was shown so much over-ornate furniture and so many bad oil paintings of dubious ancestors and equally dubious Greek myths that he began to feel quite dizzy and found himself wishing that Georgie had come with him so that he would have had the pleasure of sharing the cultural joke with her.

For some reason he thought that she would agree with his verdict on the Bowlbys' home—which was odd. Why was that? And why did he constantly think of her when he had not the slightest wish to do so?

The interminable—and grudging—tour ended at last. Cecilia announced with satisfaction, 'That's that, Mr Fitzroy. Would you mind if Fanny and I returned to the gardens? We find it stuffy in here, don't we, Fan?'

'Not at all,' returned Jess. 'I'm finding it stuffy, too.'

'Don't tell Mama we asked, though,' put in Fanny.

'By no means, most tactless.'

'Oh, splendid.'

He watched them race down the stairs towards freedom, thus destroying their mother's hopes that one of them would appeal to Miss Jesmond's heir whom their father thought might have money.

'That,' he had told his wife the night before, 'could be checked if he offered for either of them. He's a close-mouthed man.'

'A bit simple, perhaps,' Mrs Bowlby had suggested. This was before she had met Jess.

'I don't think so. Idle, rather—can't put himself about. Not a bad thing,' he added. Silently he also added to himself, Because, being idle, he's not likely to ask unfortunate and pointed questions or follow them up if he does.

After all, had he not already fobbed him off most successfully over Miss Jesmond's land and money? To have him marry one of the twins would successfully end any further possibility of him being awkward over his father-in-law's business dealings.

Back in the garden himself, walking through another room to arrive there, thus avoiding Mrs Bowlby's court, Jess met Bowlby himself, who led him to a long table laden with food and drink and urged him to indulge himself. Jess obliged him by accepting a large bumper of wine—which he later secretly poured into some bushes.

Only to have Banker Bowlby exclaim jovially when he espied his empty glass, 'I told you the drink was good. Do have another!'

Jess obliged him again—and the second glass, equally discreetly, followed the first. He had a strong suspicion that Bowlby wished to get him drunk, and he had an equally strong desire not to oblige him in that.

He walked back into view again—he had retreated into a herb garden hidden by a privet hedge in order to dispose of his wine—and immediately met Georgie, who was now on her own.

She had an expression on her face so curious that he said almost without thinking, 'What is it, Mrs Georgie? Does something ail you?'

'Not at all,' she answered, her expression turning into a grin. 'But I have a feeling something ails you, Fitz. Don't you like your wine that you upend it into the bushes?'

'You have been spying on me,' he said slowly and didn't know whether to laugh or to cry. He only knew that he had never been caught out before. Mrs Georgie would bear watching herself. She was a more complex character than he had originally thought her.

'I didn't mean to,' she confessed. 'I wanted to talk to you and followed you, being discreet myself. I had seen Banker Bowlby bully you into drinking, which I thought you didn't wish to do—and I was right, wasn't I?'

'Indeed you were—but what gave me away?'

'That I don't know,' she confessed. 'What I do know is that we ought to join the others. In a small town like Netherton unpleasant gossip is rife. It's the only entertainment there is. We ought not to go back together,' she added, when Jess offered her his arm.

'I bow to your superior understanding of village life,' was all Jess could find to say, and walked off in the opposite direction, not knowing whether he suddenly admired Georgie—or detested her even more. She had no business being so shrewd.

He was immediately caught up in a crowd of strangers to whom Banker Bowlby introduced him after pressing on him another unwanted glass of wine. He had just met the gushing Miss Walton when he saw Kite, dressed in his gloomiest black, walking towards him, stared at by Sir Garth for being a crow among peacocks.

Since he had arranged with Kite that he should arrive at about this time into the party he was not at all surprised by his presence, although when he reached him Jess said, brows raised, 'What is it, Kite? Did you really need to interrupt my pleasure?'

Kite said respectfully, 'If you will allow, Mr Fitzroy, I should like to speak to you privately.'

Jess turned to Banker Bowlby, who was hovering nearby, curiosity written all over him. 'You will forgive me, sir, if I ask if I may step aside for a moment? I cannot conceive what brings my secretary here.'

'Of course, of course!' Banker Bowlby was all joviality. 'By all means.'

Jess motioned Kite away from the curious crowd, and said once they were alone on the other side of a bed of flowers, 'Well done, Kite. Precisely as I asked. I hope nobody at the house was offensive to you when you asked to speak to me.'

'Not at all, sir. I was suitably humble, you see.'

They were speaking in such a highly confidential way that their watchers could only assume that they were discussing most urgent matters.

'And you won't be offended if I bad-mouth you to Bowlby and the others after you have gone, but I have a particular reason for asking you to do this.'

'I understand. And there *is* something I have to tell you.'

'Which is?'

'That I have found an interesting document among a batch of papers from the attic. I'm not sure of how important it is, but I shall leave that to you to decide.'

'Don't tell me about it here,' said Jess. 'Later.'

He raised his voice so that he could be heard by those nearby who possessed acute hearing. 'Really, Kite, fancy disturbing me here for something so minor as that. Use your own discretion, man. You don't need me to dot your i's and cross your t's. That's what I pay you for—to take the burden of work from my shoulders.'

He was reasonably sure that Banker Bowlby had overheard enough to confirm that Jess Fitzroy was an idler of the first water who could be safely dismissed as one unlikely to cause trouble or make difficulties if he decided to extend his swindling from the great-aunt to the great-nephew.

'What in the world was all that, Fitzroy?' asked Sir Garth, who had strolled up to speak to Bowlby and to find out 'what the crow wanted,' as he inelegantly put it.

'Only my man of business,' complained Jess, 'who wants me to attend to the business instead of him. He didn't need to disturb me when I'm enjoying myself. Whatever does he think I pay him for?'

'What, indeed?' Banker Bowlby smiled whilst some of the watchers tittered at the spectacle of an inane and idle gentleman annoyed by being disturbed at his pleasure.

Only Georgie, who had been an interested spectator of the whole episode, remembered the wink and the wine poured into the bushes and asked herself what the devil Fitz was really up to now!

Chapter Five

A Very Important Personage sat at his desk in Whitehall. A Less Important Personage stood before him, receiving orders.

'You do understand all that I have told you, I trust, and that you must act with the utmost discretion. You are to discover exactly what Mr Jesmond Fitzroy is up to at Netherton in Nottinghamshire and report back to me. The person who was originally keeping an eye on him was, unfortunately, struck down by an illness and, when he returned to his duties, failed to discover immediately that Mr Fitzroy had left London after parting company with the nabob, Mr Ben Wolfe—one of the Duke of Clarence's friends. You will, of course, be as discreet as possible whilst conducting these enquiries.

'We need to know whether there is anything more to Fitzroy's removal from his old haunts than a mere desire to enjoy country life. It seems that his parting from his old patron and employer was an amicable one.'

'Begging your pardon, m'lord, but it would be advantageous to me to know why it is so important that we need to keep Mr Fitzroy under constant surveillance.'

Lord Sidmouth sighed. 'This information is not to leave

this room, you understand. Mr Fitzroy is the last direct descendant of Frederick, Prince of Wales, the father of the late King George III. His line is illegitimate, although the Prince's mistress was a lady of a good family who subsequently took the Royal by-blow in and brought him up as a gentleman. The Prince settled a small sum of money on the son whom he never saw—and who was older than the late King, his legitimate half-brother. This man is the direct—and last—descendant of Frederick's son.

'Hence the name Fitzroy—often given to Royal bastards although, perhaps fortunately, Frederick never became king. You must be aware that such persons can cause great trouble for both king and government by making extravagant claims on them—hence an eye is always kept on their doings. Any change of habit or of life must be viewed as suspicious. Your task will be to inform me if his behaviour is such that it might cause us to worry about him.

'I stress that it is essential that he remains unaware of our interest. One point: he has a secretary named James Kite, whom I believe you already knew as a man of infinite cunning—another worrying fact.'

Yes, the lesser man knew of James Kite. He nodded and said slowly. 'You mentioned Nottinghamshire, I believe that there is a man visiting Netherton where you said Fitzroy has settled who owes me a favour. I shall call that favour in—although I shall also employ an ex-Runner who is versed in this kind of work.'

'Do as you think fit,' said m'lord. 'I wish to know no details of how you arrange matters. Just forward to me immediately any useful information relating to Fitzroy himself. He is aware of his relationship to the Royal family, although, so far, neither he nor any of his relatives has traded on it. It is essential—given the scandals about the present Queen when she was Princess of Wales—that we have no long-dead ones revived to cause excitement and delight the Radicals. The public dislike of the King, shared by all classes, has created a dangerous situation. I say again, royal by-blows have a nuisance value which must not be underestimated.

'On the other hand, the whole thing may be a mare's nest—it is for you to find out.'

He waved an airy hand which the Less Important Personage, Mr Courtney Beauchamp, took as dismissal. Bowing his way out, he reassured his lordship that the matter would be dealt with promptly and with the utmost secrecy.

'Kite!' Jess called. 'You may help me to tie my cravat— it's the one item of clothing I can't control.'

Unaware that he was arousing interest in Whitehall, Jess was dressing himself for the ball at Netherton's Assembly Rooms. He thought drily that two pieces of excitement in one day might be too much for the Nethertonians, especially since some of the gentlemen had already drunk heavily at Mr Bowlby's fête.

Kite, also unaware that high and mighty gentlemen in Whitehall were taking his name in vain, obeyed his master's voice and tied his cravat for him.

Jess stared at Kite's handiwork in the mirror. 'Are there no limits to your talents?' he enquired.

'I try to please,' returned Kite modestly. 'Will that be all?'

'For now, yes. But I would like you to start investigating Banker Bowlby as soon as possible. I want to know everything about him—particularly his financial standing—and how many estates he has bought up since he took the bank over after his father died. His father we can leave until later. You said that you had found an interesting document in the attic—I'll look at it tomorrow.'

'I have put it on your desk in the library, sir. It may be important, I doubt whether it is immediately urgent. As for Banker Bowlby, you shall have the information you require as soon as possible—although I shall doubtless need to visit London for a few days to make my search as complete as possible.'

'Do that, Kite. And now, am I sufficiently well-dressed not to offend, but not so much that I look ostentatious?'

Kite took this question seriously and walked around Jess, nodding his head. 'Perfect, sir,' he said at last. 'No offence and certainly no ostentation.'

'Good, then you may arrange for the chaise to be brought round. I won't destroy my perfection by driving the gig, thus ruining my carefully arranged hair.'

Neither man was aware that in arranging to investigate Banker Bowlby they had been echoing in little what the Important Personages in London were doing to them in large—although both of them would have been cynically amused if they had known!

Never known him trouble so much about his appearance before, Kite mused—although he's always been a natty dresser. Wonder if there's a woman in view—one he's serious about for a change. That would be a wonder, that would, and no mistake.

Kite was by no means as terse in his thoughts as he was in his speech.

Jess, meanwhile, was torn between two women, not concentrating on one. Common-sense told him to pursue Caro Pomfret, so charming and so proper, who would never embarrass a man, either in private or in public. On the other hand…

On the other hand, there was no doubt about it. Mrs Georgie Herron was the woman he lusted after. His annoyance when he had first seen her in her skimpy boy's clothing had been, he admitted, a device to cloak the undoubted fact that she had excited him after a fashion that he had thought had disappeared at the same time as his extreme youth: the period of his life when he had lusted after every pretty woman he saw.

The devil of it was that he didn't want to marry Georgie Herron, she was not the sort of woman he had ever admired, and he hated the notion that he could be led by his appetites to want someone who would be so unsuitable a wife for a man on the make.

Jess was honest with himself. His disgraceful origin, the sense that his branch of whatever family he might claim was a dishonourable one, had been with him ever since he had learned the truth from his great-aunt so many years ago. He needed to recreate himself. He had thought once of changing his name, but that smacked of deceit as well as cowardice. Fitzroy he was, and Fitzroy he would stay. He laughed a little at himself—for a man who practised deceit so assiduously in his business life, it seemed a trifle captious to balk at it when it came to changing an unwanted name.

His arrival at the Assembly Rooms ended that line of thought, but not before he had decided that Caro was the woman he would try to make his wife, but Mrs Georgie was the one to have fun with—provided that the fun became neither too dangerous nor too serious.

For once, he was not being entirely honest with himself for, on entering the Rooms, the first person he saw was Georgie, dancing with Sir Garth Manning—and the sight annoyed him more than it should have done.

The most annoying thing of all was that for the first time she was dressed to look purely feminine. She was wearing a plain white satin frock with a gauze overskirt decorated with lemon silk roses, another rose was pinned to her frock's low neckline and a chaplet of them circled her curly russet head. Her ear-drops were small topazes, and she carried a fan whose parchment was painted with roses to match those she wore. Add to that tiny white kid slippers with silver rosettes and Georgie looked good enough to eat—or to bed.

There, it was out, and the devil was in it and in him that he should be tempted so. If she sparked at him, could he resist her? It did not bear thinking of. Instead, he made his way to Caro who had been found—as usual—a *chaise-longue* on which she was gracefully reclining. If he married her, would she get off it long enough to entertain him in bed—or would the *chaise-longue* have to do?

Yes, decidedly the devil was in him to make him think such dreadful thoughts about a virtuous woman. Was Georgie virtuous? There were times when he thought not. She didn't look like it tonight, laughing up at Sir Garth. Caro was too idle to be other than virtuous—perhaps Georgie was too busy?

Caro was speaking. 'I am not alone, I hope, in finding it tiresome that after weeks of so little entertainment we have two events on the same day. I am quite exhausted—I do beg that no one asks me to dance.'

She rolled her eyes at Jess, who leaned forward to say gallantly, 'I had hoped that you would take the floor with me, Mrs Pomfret, but since you wish to…'

Caro interrupted him immediately. The current dance was over and Georgie was being led back to her by Sir Garth. To refuse Jess now would make it certain that he would ask her sister-in-law for the next one.

'I think,' she said, casting her eyes down modestly, 'that I might make an exception for you. This is your first dance at the Assembly Rooms and I should not like to see you fall back on the MC to find you a partner.'

She leaned forward to whisper confidentially, 'There are some quite unsuitable persons present. The Bowlby twins, for example. Such hoydens. You would not wish to take the floor with *them*. Yes, I will partner you, Mr Fitzroy.'

Georgie, hearing the end of this conversation, was sadly amused to see that Caro was making it quite plain to Fitz that she was making an enormous sacrifice by agreeing to dance with him.

Jess, who had also twigged (one of Kite's words) Caro's ploy, murmured, 'If it is going to be too much for you, pray do not put yourself about.'

'By no means,' Caro faltered prettily. 'The pleasure is all mine.'

She rose, making her rising something to see in its resigned charm.

She called me a horse again recently, thought Georgie, disgusted, but she must resemble one, too, if she can lie on the sofa all day and remain in perfect health.

Sir Garth whispered in her ear, 'Wise girl, m'sister. No way to hook Fitzroy by being too much of an invalid. It would be a good gambit if she slowly prised herself off the *chaise-longue* over the next few weeks—convince him that she's ready to start a family for him. And if you'd show me a little pity we could make it a double wedding.'

This naked opportunism set Georgie fretting inwardly. 'There's only one thing wrong with that last sentence,' she told Sir Garth sturdily. 'I have not the slightest wish to marry you—or anyone else for that matter. I had one reasonably happy marriage, I doubt that I should have the good fortune to achieve another.'

'Oh, most women refuse the first offer,' said Sir Garth carelessly, 'it makes them feel important.'

'I am not most women,' retorted Georgie, 'and I always mean what I say. Do not trouble yourself to ask me again:

the answer will remain the same. Your friend I will be, but your wife never.'

'No reason why the two cannot be the same.'

Sir Garth could not lightly give up the chance to marry a woman whose fortune, while not remarkable, would enable him to take his place at the gaming table and on the racecourse again. He thought that Georgie's refusal of him was due to female whim whams and had no notion that she actively disliked him.

'Not in this case.' Georgie was adamant. She had a shrewd idea of why Sir Garth was pursuing her so relentlessly and had no intention of being fleeced so that he could indulge himself while neglecting her. She was rightly cynical about the nature of the husband he would make.

She sat down on the *chaise-longue* and arranged herself prettily on it, smiling up at the baffled Sir Garth and several local squires who came to ask her for the next dance or whether she would drink tea or eat ices with them in the supper room next door. She refused them all equally prettily for she was determined to be laid out *à la* Caro when Fitz returned and flutter her eyelashes at him as remorselessly as her sister-in-law did.

That should show him that she could play the social game as well as any other female!

When he returned, however, Caro on his arm, he merely raised those splendid eyebrows of his and murmured, 'Are you ill, Mrs Herron? A megrim, perhaps. Your eyes seem affected. Shall I call your carriage?'

Georgie gritted her teeth in rage. Damn him, he undoubtedly knew what she was about and was having the impudence to roast her. But she would not let him overset her. She cast down her supposedly afflicted eyes and said shyly, 'I was carrying out a small…experiment…I believe the word is. I was testing the notion that gentlemen behave with more gallantry to a lady reclining on a sofa than to one sitting on a chair.'

Jess's mouth twitched. 'Indeed? And have you reached any conclusions? Or would it be tactless to enquire?'

Caro, seething at having lost her usual favoured position, continued to cling to his arm as though, without it, she would fall down.

'More tactless not to,' riposted Georgie, still charmingly demure. 'Judging by the last ten minutes, I find being disposed on a *chaise-longue* seems to work wonders in the popularity stakes. I am thinking of having another installed at Pomfret Hall—opposite to Caro's, of course.'

Caro could contain herself no longer. She dragged her arm from Jess's and burst out with, 'Really, Georgie, you do talk the most utter nonsense! May I remind you that the *chaise-longue* was brought out specifically for my use, and not for that of any chance passer-by.'

'I'm scarcely a chance passer-by, Caro, and, seeing that you were prancing on the floor with Fitz and didn't need it, I thought that I would take a little rest, too. If you are feeling faint, I shall be perfectly happy to relinquish it to you.'

She put her head on one side and announced naughtily as she rose, 'It's true—you *do* need the *chaise-longue*. You don't look at all the thing. Would you like Mr Fitzroy or me to fetch you some smelling salts while you have a nice little lie-down? I don't recommend dancing again.'

She was barely on her feet before Jess seized her by the arm, saying loudly, 'I believe that you are engaged to me for the next dance, Mrs Georgie. Allow me to lead you on to the floor, the music is about to begin,' and virtually dragged her away from the enraged Caro and the amused spectators.

Once across the room he turned on her, and now he was

speaking through gritted teeth. 'What the deuce do you mean by baiting poor Caro so? Just because you are not as delicate as she is, is not an excuse for you to behave like a hoyden in the Assembly Rooms as well as in Miss Jesmond's park. Prancing with Fitz, indeed.'

Georgie tried to pull away from him. She knew that she had gone too far, but who was he to be her moral arbiter? And Caro delicate! That was a joke—she was about as delicate as a crocodile. Were all men so blind that they could not twig that the *chaise-longue* pantomime was really an act put on to attract them? It had truly worked wonders for her during her ten minutes sojourn on it, had it not?

'Which word enraged you the more?' she asked haughtily. 'Prancing or Fitz? I apologise for calling you that in public, but not for anything else. And, by the by, the music is beginning. Do you intend to continue to reprimand me before all Netherton?'

How could he explain to her that his anger was so great because seeing her reclining there, her eyes sparkling with mischief, had appealed to the unregenerate side of him so much that he would have liked to fall on her on the instant. For very shame he felt compelled to deny her attraction for him by denying her.

'No,' he returned, telling his treacherous body to behave itself. 'I simply wished to take you away before you said something you might regret. Asking you to dance seemed a happy solution.'

'For whom? You, me or Caro?' The music had begun and she shot this at him as they processed hand in hand down the floor, other fascinated couples following them.

'For all of us, Mrs Georgie—but particularly for you.' This last came out in a gentle voice, despite his resolution to be firm with both himself and her, and nearly overset

Georgie. Her eyes filled with tears. His anger she could cope with, but his kindness—that was something else.

Her head drooped and she nearly lost her way in the patterns of the dance. 'Oh, Fitz,' she whispered humbly, when they came together again, 'don't be kind. I can't bear it.'

This was such a *cri de coeur* that it was Jess's turn to be overset. He saw the green eyes sparkling with tears, the recent joy with which she faced him and life quite gone— and he had dispersed it.

Insight suddenly struck. Could it be that she had played second fiddle to Caro all her life? That her determination never to be put down came from the fact that she had been put down so often in the past?

His face softened. In the light of what he thought that he might have discovered, his selfish desire fled. He wanted, instead, to comfort her, but that would have to wait for the end of the dance. He wanted her to spark at him again, anything to remove her forlorn expression which seemed to reproach him.

They said no more. After the music had stopped he bent over her hand—and kissed it. Georgie pulled it away, as though the kiss had stung her, and for a moment he thought that she was about to leave him there, stranded.

'No,' he said, and recovered the retreating hand. She stared at him, eyes huge in a pale face. 'Come, Mrs Georgie,' he said, still gentle. 'Let me take you to the supper room. Not to drink lemonade, no, something stronger than that, while we make peace with one another. Admit it—we were both in the wrong.'

Her indomitable spirit surfaced again. 'What did it cost you to tell that lie, Fitz?' she demanded, still letting him hold her hand. 'You can't believe that you were in the wrong.'

'I should not have behaved like an angry papa,' he told her, walking her along to the supper room. 'And since angry papas don't feed their erring offspring with Madeira, my doing that for you will cancel out our joint misbehaviour.'

Georgie nodded, breathless. The overpowering feeling which being with him was beginning to create in her was quite unlike anything which she had felt for her late husband. She looked up at him, at his grave face, impassive again.

From across the room Sir Garth watched them. He turned to his sister who was back on the *chaise-longue* again.

'I'd advise you to get off that,' he said abruptly. 'It's not the way to catch a husband and, if you do want Fitzroy for yourself, you'd best follow my advice. Otherwise....' He paused meaningfully.

'Otherwise, what?' asked Caro petulantly.

'Otherwise you'll lose him.'

'To whom, pray?' remarked Caro, laughing.

'To Georgie. She has her eye on him.'

'Don't joke, Garth. It doesn't become you.'

'And if I said that he has his eye on her?'

Caro sat up at last.

'He hasn't. I swear he hasn't. You saw how he behaved just now when he dragged her on the dance floor to make her behave properly.'

'Aye, and I saw his face change for a moment when he walked her off to the supper room. He rarely shows his feelings—or hadn't you noticed? Don't make the mistake of thinking that you can see her off as easily as you did when she was a shy young girl. Many men like a spirited filly. I know I do. Fun to break them in, you see.'

Caro moved restlessly. 'I still think that you're talking

nonsense. They've been at odds ever since they first met,
I do believe.'

'None so blind,' remarked Sir Garth morosely. 'Best
think over carefully what I've been telling you. Don't let
him wriggle off your hook.'

His sister made a distasteful moue. 'Must you be so
coarse?'

'Face it, Caro, the truth is often coarse. Georgie knows
that, that's why she roasted you just now. You're overdoing
the lying on the *chaise-longue*. She was doing you a favour
by pointing it out—though that wasn't her intention.'

Something which Georgie was also thinking when Jess
handed her a glass of Madeira and a plate of Bosworth
Jumbles in the supper room.

'I shall grow fat,' she announced solemnly, 'if you insist
on me eating all these.'

'Not you,' Jess told her, 'you run around far too much
for that.'

He was relieved to see that she was slowly recovering
from his recent unkindness. He had once thought her so
hardened that criticism would flow off her like water off a
duck's back, but he knew now that he was wrong. He promised himself to go carefully with her in future: what he
could not promise himself was that he would be able to
resist the growing attraction which she held for him.

'Tell me,' she said abruptly, in an effort to change the
subject, 'is the man who came to see you at the Bowlbys'
garden party really your secretary?'

Jess replied as off-handedly as he could, 'Of course,' and
then, curious, 'Why do you ask?'

'Because—' she wriggled a little in an effort to give him
a sensible answer '—he looked dangerous to me—despite
his drab clothing.'

She was constantly surprising him by her acuity. 'You

have been reading too many Gothic novels, I do believe. Italianate desperadoes rarely run round the English countryside in real life. I would have thought poor Kite looked almost painfully innocent.'

This answer came out in his most teasing mode—which, naturally, set Georgie off again. She had become an expert at detecting false notes, in life as well as in music. She thought that she detected one here.

'True—perhaps that's why I suspect him. Those who look as though butter wouldn't melt in their mouths often turn out to be those who can make butter melt by merely looking at it.'

Georgie didn't add that this insight also applied to Fitz himself. His charming impassivity of expression, his determination—or so she thought—to be delightfully anonymous might be nothing but a form of trickery. She was, indeed, beginning to think that his whole mild manner cloaked something quite different.

Even his name was suspicious. Fitzroy, indeed! Hence her mockery of it. And Kite, who sported another interesting name, that of a bird of prey.

Jess's respect for her grew. He wanted to ask who and what her husband had been and how she had come to be so aware of the wicked complexities of the world.

Another task for Kite, perhaps. He didn't wish to ask her directly about her marriage, thus making her even more suspicious. Come to think of it, she was as shy as he was about mentioning her past.

He was about to turn their conversation into something time-wastingly banal in an effort to avoid giving himself away even more, for her questions and responses had made him aware that somehow she had sensed something false in the images which he and Kite were presenting to the world, when Banker Bowlby and his fat wife, accompanied by Sir Garth, came up to the little table at which they were sitting.

'So this is where you are hiding,' he cried. 'It's no way for you to introduce yourself to your fellows in Netherton, is it, Fitzroy? I believe that you have not yet had the honour of partnering my wife on the dance floor. She would be delighted to take a turn with you, wouldn't you, my dear?'

So saying, he fairly flung her into Jess's arms. Georgie choked into her glass of lemonade, which had succeeded Jess's recommended Madeira, at the spectacle of him being most ineffably pleasant to the entranced Mrs Bowlby while he led her towards the ballroom.

Let him try his clever tongue on her for a change! That she would take everything he said to her literally could only add to Georgie's private pleasure. Translating Fitz's remarks and his slight changes of expression was becoming a habit with her.

What did intrigue her was that he was not annoyed by Banker Bowlby's over-familiar manner in calling him plain Fitzroy, but was secretly amused by it. Did she amuse him? Now, *there* was a thought, and not, perhaps, a pleasant one. It all depended on the nature of the amusement, of course, and it might be best not to enquire further of herself as to that nature.

She certainly couldn't ask him.

Sir Garth, watching her, asked, a trifle sourly, 'What is amusing you so, Georgie?'

'Life,' she told him, in lieu of a better, more truthful, answer.

'I'm glad you find it amusing. Some of us are not in your fortunate situation.'

Georgie put down her empty glass of lemonade. 'I don't quite follow you, Garth. I was not aware that my position was in any way more fortunate than yours or Caro's.'

'It's scarcely the proper place to inform you,' he told her, 'but I think I ought to tell you straight-away that Caro's hold on Pomfret Hall is tenuous. Both her father-in-law and her late husband made unwise investments in the late wars—as so many did. And now the wars are over farming is in a bad way.

'Banker Bowlby, who is her chief trustee, is trying to save Gus's inheritance for her. So far he seems to be succeeding. To make herself really safe, though, she ought to marry someone like Jesmond Fitzroy who would bring her enough money to prevent the estate from being sold. After all, think what a tragedy it would be if Pomfret Hall and the lands around it passed out of the family's hands after six hundred years!'

'Can you not be of help, Garth?' Georgie had not the slightest notion that Caro's financial position was so dire. She had never spoken of it, nor given any hint that matters had reached such a pass. Her own fortune was so tied up that there could be no question of her advancing Caro other than a small sum which would plainly not solve her problem.

'Alas, my own position is not so remarkably secure that I can do other than offer her moral support. Now you, on the other hand, could assist her by promoting her marriage with Fitzroy. He undoubtedly needs a wife who is a lady and the joining of the remnants of Jesmond lands to those of the Pomfrets would be of benefit to both of them. After all, you cannot wish to marry him. You always seem to be at odds with him while Caro is most definitely at evens. He would make Gus a good father.'

'And Annie, too,' murmured Georgie under her breath. 'I suppose that you mean I ought to discourage him even more—thus leaving the field free for Caro. But, Garth, I think that I ought to inform you that Jesmond Fitzroy is a man who will make up his own mind, regardless of what others think, or how they might try to influence him.'

'But you could hold off, couldn't you, Georgie? You have me to fall back on, you know. What's more, you're safe and Caro isn't. None of the small squires who live around here could save Pomfret lands—or so she tells me—and she can't afford a London season, and besides, at her age without a fortune who of substance would offer for her?'

'Who, indeed?' murmured Georgie, feeling stifled—as Garth had intended. He was subtly and shrewdly playing on her pity for Caro's plight by suggesting that a marriage to Jesmond Fitzroy would be a useful way out of it and so Georgie ought to retreat and leave the field open for his sister.

Something else struck her. Garth must be aware that her own feelings for Fitz were rather different from those which the watching world might assume as they wrangled and sparred together. He was no fool—and perhaps he also thought that Fitz's feelings for her were such that he might turn his attention away from Caro.

Her mouth dry, she said as coolly as she could, 'I can scarcely answer for my own feelings, Garth, so I certainly can't answer for Caro's. If Jesmond Fitzroy—' it took her all her strength not to say Fitz '—shows genuine signs of wishing to offer for her then I shan't stand in her way. I can't say fairer than that.'

She picked up her fan, which lay on the table before her and rose to leave. 'More to the point, so far as you are concerned, inform yourself most strongly that I shall never agree to fall back on you. I haven't the slightest wish to fall back on anyone and, in the unlikely event of my having to undertake such a distasteful thing, you would be the last person I should choose.

'I am sorry for Caro and the twins and I wish that I could assist her in a more tangible fashion, but my own money is tied up in such a manner that I may not raise capital on it. I have contributed to the costs of running the house and even lent Caro small sums. More than that I cannot do. I would advise you to consult Banker Bowlby to try to discover whether there is any way in which he could offer help—a loan, perhaps.'

Sir Garth shook his head—he had no intention of treating Georgie's rejection of him as final—and blandly told her that Banker Bowlby had already made Caro a large loan of which little had as yet been repaid. 'He can do no more,' he ended.

'Nor I,' said Georgie sadly. She wanted to get away from him to think over what he had told her. The news had cast a dark shadow over what had, so far, been an entertaining evening. She bowed distractedly at him and made for the ballroom—to meet Fitz returning to the supper room, doubtless to rejoin her if she were still there.

For one brief and remarkable moment she found herself wishing that she could ask him his opinion of what Garth had just told her. Not of his wish for Caro to marry him to save her financially, but the fact that she was in such dire straits, and what his advice would be to someone in such a position.

Common-sense, or so she thought, saved her from doing any such thing. Why suppose that Fitz knew anything about finance and bankers and loans and estates ruined by extravagance and bad investments in the late wars? And she certainly couldn't tell him that Garth had warned her off trying to attract Fitz in order to gain her for himself!

'I have never, Mrs Georgie,' Jess told her when they met in the doorway to the ballroom, 'seen you with a furrowed brow before. I've known you angry, excited, charmed and talkative, yes, but worried, no. What can be troubling you in the middle of an Assembly Room Ball—and may I do anything to help?

'Unless, of course, it's a torn hem, or a ripped piece of lace that's worrying you. There I could not be useful.'

Georgie began to laugh. 'Oh, you are ridiculous.' She stood back in order to tease him, extending her foot a little above the ground. 'I really would like to see you try to mend a torn hem.'

'That's better,' he said, approvingly. 'We have only danced once, and I believe that convention permits me a second. Will you take the floor with me when the music starts again? The musicians are having a rest.'

'Of course, Fitz. You have only to ask.'

'And in the meantime let us sit and gossip and you may point out to me all the people to whom I have not yet spoken and to whom I ought to have done. I gather that provincial society is even more scrupulous about such matters than the *ton*.'

Georgie could not stop herself from asking a direct question of him. 'You have mixed with the *ton*, then?'

'A little. Enough to know what they are like. I have ridden in Hyde Park.'

'And seen Number 1, London, where the Duke of Wellington lives?'

'That, too,' he said. 'Have you been there?'

'Once, with my late husband, on our honeymoon. A friend took us into the Park in his four-horse curricle. We didn't see the Duke himself, but our host pointed out Mr Canning and Lord Palmerston. I was astonished to see that they looked quite ordinary.'

'No halos and no fangs,' suggested Jess, smiling.

'No, just middle-aged gentlemen taking the air—not demi-gods at all.'

He had the goodness to laugh at that, too, and then the music began and he led her on to the floor.

Caro, watching them, saw that Garth was right. There was something in the manner in which they looked at one another. One could scarcely call it lover-like, but there was something particular about it which set Caro furrowing her brow.

Garth was right about something else. She must engage Jesmond Fitzroy in a much livelier way. There he was, looking quite animated for once about something which Georgie had said to him.

Yes, she must leave the *chaise-longue* and try to pretend that she liked dancing, exercising, and doing all those tiresome things which she had spent her life avoiding if that was the way to hook him. Oh, dear, Garth's coarseness was having a bad effect on her.

Interest him, yes, that was the word, interest.

Otherwise—otherwise she would have to agree to Banker Bowlby's advice and sell the Hall and its lands, pay off the Pomfret debts and with what was left buy an annuity and a little villa in the main street of Netherton which would barely have a room large enough to accommodate her *chaise-longue*—misery indeed!

Chapter Six

Relative quiet fell on Netherton's social life. Two events in one day as Caro had complained and then, nothing—other, of course, than the occasional nuncheon, dinner or supper party, some large and some small. To most of which Jesmond Fitzroy was, of course, invited.

On the following Monday, however, he went back to his desk, not only to read the document which Kite had placed there, but also to send for that gentleman and inform him that he was to go at once to London where he was to enquire discreetly not only about Banker Bowlby, but also to try to find out as much as possible about the Charles Herron whom Miss Georgina Pomfret had married.

If Kite thought that the last query was an odd one, he didn't say so.

The document of which Kite had spoken turned out to be a commonplace book kept by his great-aunt in her old age and presumably before her mind began to fail. Only four pages were written on. The first two contained fragments of poems by Cowper and others which had probably interested her, all written in a fair neat hand.

The last two pages were quite different—the writing was agitated and at the end of the second page it descended into illegibility. Jess was of the opinion that they were written some years after the first two. The writer appeared to be arguing with herself.

'I have,' she had written, 'been debating with myself about whether I ought to tell Jesmond the truth. I know that his father never informed him of it, and in that I believe he failed in his duty to his son.

'And yet I understand his reluctance, for I share it. What can the truth profit him—or any of us, for that matter? I have thought of writing it into my will, but that would mean that Mr Bowlby would read it and that would be unwise, to say the least. It must remain a most secret matter to be known to the Jesmonds and the Fitzroys alone. To that end, if I were to write this down for Jesmond I would leave it where he might find it after my death.'

After that the handwriting became a scrawl but Jess could just make out a few of the words. 'So much time has passed, that perhaps the truth might safely be buried—and yet, I feel that he ought to know.'

Know what? he asked himself. What was it that was so important that his great-aunt had felt it necessary to begin to write it down? This was tantalising indeed. On the other hand, it might be nothing but an old person's vague fears about nothing in particular.

There was another page and a half of which little was decipherable—or, when deciphered, made no sense. Jess thought that this must almost certainly have been written after the old lady's descent into senility.

He thought for a little time before calling for Kite, who was already making preparations to leave.

'Where exactly did you find this?' he asked.

'Among a great pile of notebooks and accounts, which I think ought to be gone through by one of us—or both of us, there are so many. I took the liberty of reading it.'

'And what do you make of it?'

Kite hesitated. 'I understand that she lost her mind at the end of her life—so perhaps this business of truths and a secret matter was just the ravings of an old woman who no longer knew what the truth was. So far I have come across nothing resembling the writing down of which she spoke.'

Jess nodded. 'But,' he added, 'on the face of it, the first part was, by the excellence of the writing, written when she was still sane. It was something which troubled her greatly.'

Kite nodded. 'And now she is dead and can no longer tell us what it was, nor where she might have left an account of it—if she wrote one. However, among the piles of papers in the attic which still remain to be fetched downstairs, never mind looked at, there might be something which would throw light on what was troubling her.'

Jess nodded. He did not see fit to inform Kite of his own descent from Royalty, albeit on the wrong side of the blanket. It had never been a secret in the Jesmond and Fitzroy families, of whom he was the last surviving member, so it could not have been that of which his great-aunt had been writing. His father had told him the story when he had reached twenty-one and had advised him to forget it.

He had never valued his royal descent, rather the contrary: he wished, as his father had suggested, to forget it. The only persons he had ever told of his grandfather's birth were Susanna and Ben Wolfe. Nothing in Kite's face and manner betrayed that he thought that perhaps his employer was not telling him all he knew. He was there to carry out Jess's orders and only queried him as to their nature when he had good reason.

Jess handed him the little book. 'Keep it safe for me, Kite. It is one of my last links with her. I feel a little ashamed that I lost touch with her after I left for India— she must have been a lonely soul.'

For the first time since Jess had known him Kite showed a touch of common humanity.

'Do not distress yourself on that account, sir. The old butler tells me that she was a lively person with an active interest in all that passed in Netherton until extreme old age struck her down. She visited Buxton every summer, he said, to take the waters there and enjoy the company.'

'That doesn't absolve me,' said Jess gently, 'but it was kind of you to tell me.'

Kite remained impassive, merely saying, 'May I remind you that the artisans and labourers are arriving this morning and that you and Parsons are due to meet them and discuss the improvements to the house and grounds with them.'

'You may indeed remind me. I hired you to save me from having to remember too much myself.'

If Kite thought that a Banbury tale, knowing that Jess's memory was an exceptional one, that appeared to pass over his head, too. He silently gathered up his books and papers preparatory to starting off for London.

I wonder why my great-aunt never married, Jess asked himself after Kite had gone. She was a handsome woman in her youth, if her portrait in the Hall is anything to go by. She must have had some offers of marriage for her fortune was a good one before she lost it. Which brought him back to Banker Bowlby again and that he had been invited to dine with him on the coming Wednesday.

He wondered if the Pomfret Hall women would be there, too. The Banker had said something to him during the Assembly Rooms ball which seemed to indicate that he was involved in their financial affairs—which was perhaps not surprising seeing his importance in Netherton's life. Jess had already discovered from Parsons that two local farmers carried mortgages with him, and one, Unwin by name, was reported to be on the verge of bankruptcy.

He decided to visit Pomfret Hall that very afternoon and see whether, in apparently idle gossip, he could discover how many more fingers Bowlby had in Netherton's pies.

To Georgie's astonishment, Caro had risen early that Monday morning and had announced that she intended to take up riding again.

'I have spent far too much time on the sofa lately, and perhaps a little exercise might banish the cobwebs.'

'Very wise,' announced Sir Garth over his two-days-old copy of *The Times*. 'You frowst indoors far too much these days, Caro. Take a leaf out of Georgie's book.'

'Not if taking a leaf out of Georgie's book means I have to wear breeches.'

Sir Garth swiftly lowered his *Times*, exclaiming, 'That's a trifle eccentric, Georgie, is it not?'

'But more comfortable when riding than skirts and a side-saddle,' riposted Georgie. 'Do you propose to start this afternoon, Caro? If so, I can accompany you. It must be years since we have ridden together.'

'Tomorrow,' announced Caro, 'will be quite soon enough.'

Georgie privately wondered whether Caro's tomorrow would ever turn into today, but did not say so.

Sir Garth was about to pass a similar remark when Forshaw, the butler, entered.

'There is a person asking to see you, Sir Garth. He says that he has a message for you and that the matter is urgent. I have put him in the library.'

'Urgent!' Sir Garth's eyebrows rose. 'It must indeed be urgent if he needs to trouble me at breakfast! Did he say what the matter was?'

'No, sir. He said that it was for your ears only.'

Sir Garth threw down his napkin. 'Lead me to this urgent

fellow, and if the matter is not urgent I shall ring such a peal over him as he has never heard.'

He recognised the man immediately when he entered the library, and was careful to send Forshaw away before he asked sharply, 'Why have you followed me here? What is so urgent?'

The man grinned insolently at him. 'I have a message for you from your master and mine. Here it is.'

He handed Sir Garth a letter, which the latter put in his pocket, saying, sharp again, 'You may leave now, your errand is over.'

The grin grew. 'Not so. When you have read that you must come to London with me on the instant. I have a post-chaise waiting outside.'

It would be pointless to argue with him. He was plainly his master's voice. Sir Garth dragged the letter from his pocket and read it. It bade him return to London immediately in the company of the bearer, making what excuses he could for his sudden departure.

He crumpled it up in his fist. He would have liked to throw it in the insolent face of the lackey before him, but caution and self-preservation told him that it would not be wise to do so.

'I shall need time to pack,' he said, 'and to inform my valet.'

'No valet. You are to come alone.'

'But…'

'Those are my master's orders.'

There was no gainsaying him. Sir Garth swallowed and grunted, 'Very well. See that the kitchen feeds you.'

'Aye. I've already arranged that,' was all the answer he got.

And now to make his excuses to Caro and Georgie. Fortunately women were not very shrewd and would take his statement that business called him back to London as gospel.

Georgie, who was waiting for Annie and Gus to arrive so that she might take them for a promised game of cricket, said, 'It must be very urgent, Garth, to have you haring back to London so soon after you have reached here.'

Damn the woman! She was too sharp for her own good. It was probably not a good idea to try to make her his wife: the money she might bring him wasn't worth it.

He offered her a patronising smile. 'Ah, it's plain to see that you ladies have no notion of the busy life of a man of affairs. I shall return as soon as I can.'

I thought that all your affairs involved the bedroom, not the office, was Georgie's down-to-earth and private reaction to Garth's pomposity. Her antennae told her that there was something odd about his sudden departure and her learning later that his valet was not accompanying him did nothing to quell her suspicions.

She tried a delicate hint to Caro, who riposted with, 'Oh, you know that men have a public life of which we women have no notion. Perhaps he's going into politics. He did say once that Bobus Wright had talked of putting him up for a Parliamentary seat which the Wrights own.'

God help the House of Commons and the country if there are many such as Garth in it, was a further private comment of Georgie's which she could share with no one. It suddenly occurred to her, that if she only knew Fitz a little better, she could almost certainly share it with him! Thinking about Fitz was becoming a commonplace of her internal life and simply would not do. To think about her game of cricket with Gus and Annie instead would be more to the point.

The only drawback about that was that when they reached the field at the back of Jesmond House, Fitz was

already there with a group of labourers and workmen
headed by Parsons, who had been Miss Jesmond's agent.

'Does this mean we have lost our cricket pitch?' she
asked him cheerfully after they had greeted one another,
and she had congratulated Parsons on having his old post
back.

'It does if you were banking on playing here,' Jess told
her. 'But I see no reason why you shouldn't come and play
on my back lawn. I take it that Caro's flower-beds are still
sacred.'

'Always sacred...' Georgie smiled '...and I shall certainly take up your offer,' for Annie and Gus's faces had
fallen when they had seen Jess and the workmen preparing
the field.

'If you would care to wait for a moment I shall accompany you to the lawn and, if Master and Miss Pomfret will
agree, I shall join you in your game. Mr Parsons and I have
already given the workmen their orders. I face a summer
of having them about the house and grounds, for everything
has fallen into decay and ruin, both inside and out. I am
extending the Park into the field; when it is done you may
return to play on it—so long as you don't object to sharing
it with the sheep.'

'You are going to introduce sheep here?'

Jess nodded. 'Into the Park, certainly, and also on to the
fields beyond. They do well, I understand, in this part of
the world, and I intend to be something of a working farmer
myself. If old Coke of Norfolk, that rampant aristocrat,
could run his farms himself instead of letting them out and
still make a good profit, then I don't see why I shouldn't.
I shall be in the market for any land that's going in order
to extend my holdings.'

They were both aware that he was speaking to her as
commonsensically as though she were a man and that Geor-

gie did not object to him doing so. Gus said prosaically, 'I like sheep, sir, both to look at and to eat. Do you intend to have any cattle, sir?'

'A small dairy herd, perhaps.'

'Could I milk one of the cows, sir?' asked Annie. 'One of the little ones.'

'Whoa,' said Jess, laughing. 'I haven't even bought one cow yet, neither large nor small. But if I ever have a little one, I shall certainly invite you to milk it.'

Georgie could not help comparing him with Garth who acted as though neither Gus nor Annie existed. She could scarcely recall him having so much as spoken to them.

'Have you all been invited to Banker Bowlby's dinner party this Wednesday?' he asked her on the way to the back lawn.

'Yes, but Sir Garth will not be there. He was called back to London this morning and has already left. Urgent business, he said.'

Privately Jess thought that Sir Garth's absence was something of a blessing. Aloud he said, 'Mrs Pomfret will miss her brother, will she not? He has only just arrived.'

'Indeed. Although I am not sure how much he would have enjoyed dining at the Bowlbys. He is used to a somewhat more illustrious society than Netherton can offer.'

Was there a satiric note in Mrs Georgie's voice? Jess thought that there was.

'And you will enjoy dining there?' he asked her, keeping his voice strictly neutral.

Georgie decided to be frank. 'The food is good, but...' She hesitated. She ought not to gossip.

They were on the back lawn now, which gave her a good opportunity not to say any more as Jess helped Gus with the wicket and took off his coat with a murmured apology to Georgie.

'I trust that you will not object to my dishabille, but playing cricket in a tight jacket and cravat is not my notion of fun—something you might have gathered from the last time I played with Gus and Annie.'

He did not see Georgie wince at the memory of her first meeting with him, which was perhaps just as well, for the rest of the game passed off happily. There was only one commotion when Georgie, running between the impromptu wickets, caught her foot in her skirts and fell headlong.

She lay there for a moment, the small bat in her outstretched hand, until Fitz, who had been bowling, ran up to her.

'You are not hurt, I trust?' he asked, his face anxious. 'That was a nasty fall.'

'Not at all,' Georgie retorted, or rather panted, for the fall had winded her. 'You see what comes of not wearing breeches. I should never have fallen if I'd not been a perfect lady and kept my skirts on!'

She was not telling him the whole truth. Her knees hurt her and the ankle which she had strained a little when she had gone into the river was feeling decidedly ill-treated. It was, however, imperative that she put on a brave face in front of Fitz or he would never allow her to play cricket with them again.

He insisted on helping her to rise, 'But not until you have collected yourself,' he told her, 'and are quite sure that nothing is damaged. You do manage to land yourself in a series of pickles, Mrs Georgie,' he added a trifle severely. 'I am always having to rescue you.'

'That's because I'm not a perfect lady, but actually do things.' This came out when, with his help, she tried to stand up—only for her ankle to buckle slightly so that she fell against him.

He caught her immediately to him and for a moment they

stood breast to breast and heart to heart. The effect on both of them was immediate. Jess was instantly aroused and Georgie found herself afflicted by the most contrary sensations. Half of her wished him to continue holding her, and the other half was appalled that her unruly senses, starved for so long, were demanding any such thing.

It can't be just Fitz causing this, she told herself wildly. I'm sure that I should feel the same for any man who held me so intimately. But she knew that that was a lie. She could not have endured Garth to be holding her thus. Garth who smelled of cigars and drink while Fitz smelled of soap and clean linen—and, most potently, simply of Fitz, the strong man.

She pulled herself away—and it was over. So each of them silently vowed. But it was not over, and only the presence of Gus and Annie and possible curious faces at the windows of the house kept them apart. To recover himself Jess thought of icy water and snow and Georgie thought of anything at all, other than Fitz, that was.

'You are fit to continue? If not, you may wish to act as umpire—or even sit down and rest a little.'

Georgie smiled, a painful smile. 'Had you not been rescuing me, you would have been running me out. Allow me to field. I think that I could manage that.'

Goodness me, it's not the fall which is distressing me, it's what I have just learned about myself—and him. For Georgie knew quite well the nature of the effect which she had had on Fitz.

'I think that you could manage anything you wished—although whether that would be wise is not for me to say.'

'I might have expected sweet reason from you, Fitz,' she mocked him gently. 'Do you ever do anything daring, unexpected, or irrational?'

Yes, he wanted to say. I think that I have done something

irrational which might also be daring. I have fallen in love with you, of all impossible people! I wanted someone quiet and ladylike who will never answer me back, or, if she does, will easily be silenced by my superior sex and my superior position as her husband. What was your husband like, Mrs Georgie, that he failed to tame you?

'May we get on with the game?' asked Gus, his voice plaintive. 'If Georgie isn't hurt, why are you both standing there talking? And if Georgie is out, it's my turn to bat.'

Recalled to common-sense, both Jess and Georgie recovered themselves.

Georgie moved to mid-wicket and Jess picked up the ball again to bowl at Gus who, having brought his seniors back to their senses, proceeded to hit Jess's dolly drops all round Jesmond House's lawn. Georgie, distracted by what had passed, distinguished herself by dropping the ball twice, until a final lucky catch from her had Gus dismissed and Annie taking over.

Her short innings ended when Twells arrived, a pair of footmen following him carrying a pitcher of lemonade and glasses on one tray and Jess's favourite Sally Lunns, hot from the oven, on another. It was a measure of both Jess and Georgie's distraction that, although they both drank the lemonade, they refused the Sally Lunns.

'I do hope the Master isn't ailing that he can't eat my cooking,' said Cook anxiously when Twells returned to the kitchen. The old man favoured her with a smile. He had been watching the little game from the window and had seen the by-play between his master and Mrs Herron.

'Oh, he ain't ailing,' he said cryptically. 'There's more than ailing which keeps a man from eating. And a woman, too,' he added as an afterthought.

Cook sniffed. 'If you spoke plain English, Mr Twells, I might know what you were saying.'

Craig, standing by, gave a discreet smile and winked at Twells.

'The place needs a mistress,' he said.

'Aye, and so does he,' said Twells, grinning.

A conclusion which Jess was already reaching as the game ended. But Mrs Georgie was not of the stuff of mistresses, he was sure. She was far too straightforward to engage in intrigue. So where did that leave him if he didn't want her for a wife and she wouldn't consent to be anything less? Which also, he acknowledged ruefully, begged the question of whether she would accept an honourable proposal if he were foolish enough to make one.

Rational she might call him, but sometimes, he acknowledged, reason might not be enough. He would have liked to tell Mrs Georgie so, but thought that that might not be wise, either.

What might be wise, so far as he was concerned, was to ask her a question about something which she had begun to say earlier. He remained silent whilst they pulled up the pair of stumps and he resumed his coat and cravat whilst Georgie put on the light shawl which she had discarded.

Her face twitched when he turned to her, restored to respectability again—almost.

'Goodness,' she said, 'whatever have you done to your cravat? It's so limp and drooping that it looks as though you are about to surrender to the French. It wasn't much better when we met you in the field.'

'Since I have no valet at present, I'm reduced to tying my own.' He decided to be daring, unexpected and irrational by adding, 'I suppose you think that you could do better.'

'Indeed I could, Fitz. If you would allow me to try, that is.'

This was madness. He should not be encouraging her in

her wilfulness, but the devil must be in him this morning
for he found himself saying, 'If you wish,' pulling his cravat undone and handing it to her.

Georgie's eyes sparkled mischief. 'You will need to remove your jacket if I am to do it properly.'

'Oh, very well. But you had best be quick. Gus and Annie are growing impatient.'

'They must learn to wait. Now, bend down a little. You
are so tall and I am so short that since I haven't a stool to
stand on you must oblige me.'

A few minutes and some deft manoeuvring of her fingers
later, she had finished, her last act being to tie him a magnificent butterfly bow.

'It feels better,' he admitted grudgingly.

'Better! It's a masterpiece, no less. Look at your reflection in the first window we come to and see if I am not
right!'

So he did, then turned to her and said, 'Whatever else,
Mrs Georgie, you would make a splendid valet. Do you
have a name for your *chef d'oeuvre*?'

Georgie put her head on one side. 'Would Fitz's Surprise
do?'

'Eminently. Another *chef d'oeuvre*. I think that you
ought to have named it Mrs Herron's Surprise, though.'

'Oh, it's your cravat, not mine.'

They had reached the glass door on the terrace which
led to the faded drawing room. An elderly spaniel was lying
before it in the sun. Both Gus and Annie began to pet it.

'Yours?' asked Georgie.

'No, Kite's. He's away at the moment and Paris is beginning to feel lonely.'

'Paris, that's a noble name.'

'Kite acquired him in Paris,' he said, 'and being a literal
soul, that saved him the problem of finding a name. Speak-

ing of names reminds me of Banker Bowlby, who has an unusual one. You began to say something about him earlier, but stopped. Was an unusual fit of tact causing you to pause? Surely not?'

Georgie began to laugh. 'Tact, of course—something, I gather, that you don't credit me with. I must confess that I do not like him and wish that he was not managing Caro's affairs. It is no secret in Netherton that he is her chief trustee so I see no harm in telling you that.'

'No, indeed. And you have answered my question and in your own favour—by assuring me that when it is necessary you and tact are not enemies.'

'Although not exactly friends,' Georgie laughed. 'And now I must take Gus and Annie home before Caro begins to fret at our prolonged absence. She is probably fearful that we are being pursued by a bear which has come from nowhere like the gentleman in the play by Shakespeare.'

What a curious mixture she was! There were times when she surprised him by a sudden display of erudition. Something which she had said at the Assembly ball had led him to believe that she understood not only Latin, but possibly Greek. To be a learned hoyden was almost to be a contradiction. Jess admired learning because he had been blessed with so little of it and had read widely of recent years to make up for that deficiency.

'*A Winter's Tale?*' he ventured.

Georgie's eyes shone. 'You have read it? That puts you in a class by yourself. No other gentleman of my acquaintance would, I am sure, have picked up that allusion. Rationality has something to be said for it.'

Jess bowed. 'Do not misunderstand me. That was an accident. I have had no real education—other than that of life, but I do try to read a little, and that was something I came across. Quite by accident.'

He said no more. He had already said more than he meant to—or had said to anyone else. She had the trick of leading him on—probably because she provoked him. If he were not careful he would be telling her his secrets next. He must guard his tongue—and that other part of him which responded to her so readily!

Jess watched the three of them walk across the Park towards their home before he returned to the house to stare at his reflection in a Venetian mirror and admire her handiwork all over again.

Had she tied her husband's cravat for him? More than ever he wished to know about him, for in doing so he might solve the enigma which Mrs Georgie—or more properly, Mrs Charles—Herron presented.

Besides that, he had to admit that he owed her a debt of gratitude as well for her information about Bowlby: so, the spider had another fly in his web, Caro Pomfret by name. Was the Banker, as he was beginning to suspect, in the process of relieving her of her estate so that he might add it to that of Miss Jesmond's—and possibly of others of whom Jess knew nothing?

He began to look forward to his dinner with the Bowlbys. What else might he accidentally learn if he could persuade the egregious Banker that he was an idle fool?

Nothing could be easier, Jess thought, than to deceive Banker Bowlby after enjoying, by country standards, an excellent meal. Mrs Georgie had not been wrong about that. By now he knew most of the company and conversation at the dinner table had been free and easy, led by Mrs Bowlby who, he was beginning to learn, dominated every social occasion at which she appeared.

Except of course, after dinner, when Bowlby, his face redder than ever from the wine he had drunk, waved to his wife to lead the ladies into the drawing room and leave the men to the port which the butler had just placed upon the table.

Jess had only drunk lightly of the wine set before him. Not so the rest of the company. The chamber pot was dragged from its cupboard in the large oak sideboard ready for those who were not so abstemious as he was and were free to use it now that the ladies had gone.

Pipes were brought out, too, and the room soon reeked of tobacco smoke and alcohol fumes. Jess didn't smoke, and neither, he noticed, did old Crane, the solicitor, and one or two of the younger men. He also noticed that most of the men were stopping short of becoming helplessly drunk. Merry was the best adjective for them.

It was not long before Banker Bowlby, passing the port to Jess, who being compelled to drink rather more than he wished to in order not to look odd, said, 'Thought over what we were discussing when you visited me over Miss Jesmond's estate, have you?'

'Oh,' returned Jess, trying to look slightly fuddled and simple with it. 'What was that, then? I've forgotten.'

'About transferring your moneys and business from London to my place here at Netherton. Much handier for you, you know.'

Jess took a long swig from his glass of port before saying, 'Oh, I'm not sure whether I can. Kite looks after all my business affairs. Not sure he'll agree.'

Bowlby raised bushy eyebrows. 'He's your servant, ain't he? Save him from writing to and visiting London. Tell him what's what.'

'Can't do that,' announced Jess, slurring his words. 'Know nothing about business. Kite does. Trust him, always have. Might lose him if I tried to run him. Wouldn't do.'

He unloosed his cravat and lay back in his chair, the picture of an unknowing idler.

'I could look after your affairs for you,' offered Bowlby who, despite his reddened face, hadn't drunk as much as most of his guests.

Jess shook his head. 'Kite wouldn't like it.'

'Think it over, anyway. Lot to be said for it.'

His victim stared owlishly at him before putting a hand to his brow and groaning, 'Can't…m'head hurts.'

Bowlby narrowed his eyes and puffed smoke at the ceiling.

For a moment Jess thought that he might have overdone it.

'Shouldn't have troubled you when you were drinking,' he came out with at last. 'But, tomorrow morning, if you remember what I've just said, have a word with your man about it. He might be pleased at not having to drag himself all the way to London, but simply ride over to Main Street instead.'

He rose. 'Time we joined the ladies, I think. Don't want anyone on the floor, do we? Need an arm, Fitzroy?'

So he hadn't overdone it. Jess allowed that an arm wouldn't hurt and Georgie had the supreme pleasure—and surprise—of seeing him enter the drawing room on Banker Bowlby's arm and being tenderly lowered into an armchair. She needn't have been worried about being tactless after all. Fitz must have ignored her reservations about the Banker, for it was plain that he and Bowlby were getting on famously.

Worse than that, it was also plain that Fitz was a little merry—no, drunk was the proper word. Perhaps he had been tipping wine into the bushes the other day because he couldn't hold his drink, but somehow she didn't believe that was true. He must have been tippling pretty freely after the ladies had left the room to be so unsteady now.

She hoped that he hadn't walked or driven himself into Netherton but had come in the neat little chaise which she had seen delivered there recently and so could be driven safely home by his coachman.

Georgie had to confess that she was somewhat disappointed in him. She hadn't thought him a toper—but then, so many gentlemen were so she shouldn't have been surprised. Fortunately he behaved himself well, quite unlike some men on other occasions who had got above themselves and had needed to be gently removed and manoeuvred into their waiting carriages before they disgraced themselves. It was one of the expected trials of provincial society, was it not?

Jess had a pretty good notion of what she was thinking and found himself regretting it, but at the moment deceiving Banker Bowlby was more important to him than being in Mrs Georgie's good books. No one else seemed to notice his supposed condition. Caro, sitting for once on a chair, carried on over his nodding head a conversation with Mrs Bowlby about the rumour that the Hansons, who were not present, had bought a new carriage. It was to be hoped, she said, that they were not spending a touch above their means.

'After all,' she ended, 'his father was only Lord Bretton's land agent, even if he did inherit a little money from one of his mother's brothers and set himself up as a gentleman farmer.'

'Which?' asked Jess, a trifle vaguely as befitted a gentleman not totally in command of himself. 'Which was it became the gentleman farmer? The father or the son?'

'The father,' Mrs Bowlby roared at him. She obviously thought that being a little tipsy had affected his hearing.

'Gave up being a land agent when he inherited. Been above himself ever since.'

By which Jess rightly deduced that both Caro and Mrs Bowlby felt that Mr Hanson was not sufficiently respectful of their own superior station. The petty nature of much country life was something which did not surprise him. It was, after all, exactly like the major nastinesses of life in the *ton* writ small. Mrs Bowlby possessed neither the looks nor breeding of Lady Cowper or Lady Leominster, but her preoccupations were remarkably similar to theirs. Like them she dominated the society in which she lived.

Similarly it must be supposed that, if Banker Bowlby were a swindler, then his swindling would be on a much minor scale than if he were practising it in the City—but the people who were his prey would end up just as ruined as though he were a major shark.

Georgie, who was watching Fitz while Caro and Mrs Bowlby carried on dissecting the Hansons and their doings, was thinking hard. Nothing he had ever said or done when she had been with him had suggested that he would lapse into folly so easily as he seemed to have done at the Bowlbys. Quite the contrary. She also thought, by the way in which both Bowlbys spoke of him, that there was a certain amount of contempt for him in their manner. She was so busy watching Fitz that she didn't notice that he was also being closely and discreetly watched by someone else: Solicitor Crane…

What neither of them knew was that Jess, lying back in his large armchair, his eyes half-closed, was aware that both of them were watching him, and was amused by it. Georgie's interest he thought he understood. Solicitor Crane's, though, would bear thinking about. Was he being watched because Crane thought that he might need protecting or because he suspected something quite different? There was another thing which would bear investigating when the opportunity arose.

In the meantime he thought that he might appear to doze, so he closed his eyes, smiled vacantly, and offered the world the happy spectacle of a gentleman who had dined well but only half-wisely!

He thus did not see Solicitor Crane walk over to Banker Bowlby or hear him, nodding at Jess, ask in a low, dry voice, 'Tied hand and foot to his clerk, Kite, is he? Have you ever met him?'

'Who? Kite? No. No one's met him. Hasn't come into Netherton once. Almost as though the fellow doesn't exist.'

'Oh, he exists, no doubt of that. Parsons met him—says that he has the eye of a hawk and the manners of one. Queried all the papers Parsons handed to him regarding the improvements being made at Jesmond House and in the grounds. Made him justify and explain everything. Most impressed, Parsons was.'

'And what does Parsons make of Fitzroy?' asked Bowlby, walking Crane away from his other guests so that they might not be overheard.

'What everyone does—a charming idler. Not over-rich. He apparently droned on to him and Kite about being careful not to exceed the remit for the expenses. Thinks Kite is the brains behind Fitzroy.'

'Hmm.' Bowlby stared out of the window at the encroaching night. 'What did *you* make of him?'

Crane shrugged. 'He has never said enough to me for me to make anything of him.'

He looked across the room at the peacefully sleeping subject of their conversation. 'On the other hand, it always pays to be wary. Particularly when dealing with strangers.'

'Hmm,' snorted Bowlby again. 'Can't hold his drink, though, can he?'

'Apparently not,' said Crane drily. 'Let's join the others again. Shouldn't be doing business at a dinner party.'

Which, if Bowlby had cared to think about it, was an indirect criticism of him for questioning Jess while the port was circulating!

Chapter Seven

'Garth never told us how long he might stay in London,'
said Caro.

'He didn't have time to say anything before he left,' was
Georgie's answer.

Caro, Georgie and the children were taking a walk along
one of the lanes which lay between their property and that
of Jess's. This untoward show of energy on Caro's part was
a consequence of her resolution to take a little more exercise. She had been wailing gently and continually about her
feet aching ever since they had left the Hall.

Gus, who was holding his aunt's hand, asked, 'Do you
think we might meet Fitz, Georgie?'

'If you mean Mr Fitzroy,' said his mother sharply, 'then
say so. Really, Georgie, you are ruining the children's manners by encouraging them to speak so familiarly to a
grown-up.'

'Fitz doesn't mind. He told me so when we last played
cricket,' said Gus. 'He said no one had ever called him Fitz
before and he liked it.'

'I vow and declare he's as irresponsible as you are, Georgie. Perhaps it's not surprising, though. Mrs Bowlby tells

me that her husband thinks that he's a regular flibbertigibbet!'

'Really?' replied Georgie tartly. 'I'd have thought that the word applied to her more than to Fitz. He's anything but. I suppose that puts him out of the running as a suitable husband for you.'

'By no means—quite the contrary. Mrs Bowlby thinks that it would make him a most indulgent one.'

So Caro had been gossiping with that awful woman about the likelihood of her marrying Fitz. And she was reproaching the children for indecorum! She would do better to reproach herself! Georgie was surprised by the strength of her own reaction to the thought that Caro and Fitz might marry.

They left the lane to walk along the country road which led past the gates to Jesmond House.

'May we go in?' asked Gus. 'It would be nice to call on Fitz. He might propose a game of cricket—much better than just walking. What's the point in that?'

'Hear, hear,' echoed Annie.

Caro sighed. 'Certainly not. We have come along this road solely so that we might reach home again as soon as possible. My feet are hurting me and I need to sit down in a comfortable chair before I become unable to walk at all.'

'They wouldn't hurt if you took as much exercise as Georgie does,' returned callous and truthful Gus.

'Aunt Georgie, please. I insist on you obeying me, all of you, and that includes you, Georgie. And regardless of what *Mr Fitzroy* says, you will not call him Fitz. Is that understood?'

'Very well, Mama. But if he particularly asks that we do?'

Georgie, concealing a smile, said, 'I will explain to Mr

Fitzroy when I next see him that your mama wishes you to address him formally.'

She added a silent rider, but I shall go on calling him Fitz when I meet him for I am not Caro's child, thank God.

When they reached the entrance to Jesmond House, Caro demanded to sit and rest on the grassy bank opposite to the gates which gave an excellent view of it since the drive led straight to its front doors. From the outside it still looked as splendid as ever. Not overlarge, it had been built in the reign of William and Mary and its mellow brickwork had worn well over the years.

Caro had just decided that she was feeling sufficiently recovered to walk on when a post-chaise stopped to allow them to pass before it turned into the drive. A man was seated in it—the mysterious Mr Kite, no doubt. Gossip said that he had been visiting London on an errand for Fitz— to do with the improving of the House and grounds, was the explanation current in Netherton.

Or so Caro had informed Georgie. Doubtless another piece of gossip gleaned from Mrs Bowlby. And what made Caro so friendly with the woman these days? It was not so long since her name had been anathema at Pomfret Hall.

'And I can't walk any further,' moaned Caro after they had gone only a few more yards along the road back to the Hall. She sank on to the grass verge by the road and stripped off both her light shoes, saying, 'You must leave the children with me, Georgie, and run home with all speed. Tell John Coachman to come and collect us.'

'No,' said Gus rebelliously. 'I won't be left with you. I want to go with Georgie. I mean Aunt Georgie.'

'Mannerless child. She will run all the faster without you to hold her back.'

'It seems,' Georgie could not prevent herself from saying, 'that it does not matter if I behave like a hoyden so long as I am doing it in your service. Suppose I wish to behave like a perfect lady…'

Caro looked up, real agony written on her face. 'Do not be unkind, Georgie. It is not like you at all, not at all.'

'Very well.' Georgie relented. 'I didn't mean to provoke you. You're sure you couldn't walk slowly along while I make haste. No?' she added quickly as Caro made a face. 'I see you can't,' and she set off towards home at a rapid trot.

She had just covered about half a mile when she saw a gig being driven towards her. Fitz's gig, no less. She breathed a sigh of relief when he slowed down and stopped.

'Mrs Georgie! Whatever you are at? Are you proposing to take up fell running now?' he called down to her.

'Oh, do stop funning, Fitz,' she told him breathlessly. 'It's no joke. Caro decided to take a walk this afternoon with the children and me. Her feet gave out about half a mile back and she has sent me on to the Hall to ask John Coachman to come and collect her.'

'Has she, indeed? Beyond the next bend? Near my gates?'

Georgie nodded.

'No need to run any further, then,' he said. 'Can you climb into the gig while I hold the horse steady? Yes? And then I can drive you back to where you left them. Caro can change places with you, I can drive her to Jesmond House while you and the children walk there. It's far less of a distance for you to cover than if you continued to the Hall. One of my men can drive you all home later. I'm expecting Kite and the post-chaise back this afternoon. Hop in.'

She duly hopped in and thankfully sat down beside him.

'Do you often perform this kind of mad trick for your sister-in-law?' he asked her.

Georgie shook her head. 'Nothing quite so demanding as

this. What I don't understand is why she has suddenly adopted this odd fit of taking exercise. Yesterday it was riding with me—which lasted all of fifteen minutes—and I'm wondering what she'll wish to do next. Swim in the lake, perhaps... And she's not sat on the *chaise-longue* for the last week.'

'Don't you?' asked Fitz, smiling oddly. 'No, I don't suppose you do.'

What a strange mixture Mrs Georgie was, so knowing in some ways, so artless in others. It would be easy, he thought, to misjudge her.

They found Caro and the children where Georgie had left them, and the proposed change-over was soon made.

'I'll come back for you in the gig,' Jess promised Georgie. 'I shouldn't be too long.'

'May we have a game of cricket after you pick us up?' begged Gus, never one to let an opportunity slip.

Jess laughed and answered him before Caro had time to begin an expected reprimand.

'Not today, I'm afraid. We have to look after your mama first. Another day, perhaps.'

Both children pulled faces. 'That's what Uncle Garth always says when we ask him to do something. Only tomorrow never comes.'

'Shush,' said Georgie, forestalling Caro for the second time. 'You know that Mr Fitzroy always keeps his promises.'

'Always?' queried Annie, her eyes huge.

'I try to,' Jess told her. 'Now let me take your mama to my home. And when she has rested you may all return home in my chaise.'

'After tea? It *is* tea-time and I'm hungry,' said Annie. 'You gave us some nice Sally Lunns the other day.'

'Not me.' Jess smiled, waving his whip at them before he drove away. 'My cook—and we really must be off.'

'You are far too patient with them,' said Caro severely after Jess had driven her through the gates. 'They are much too forward these days. I put it down to Georgie's influence. They used to be so quiet and good before she came to live with us. But needs must…' she ended cryptically.

Now what exactly did she mean by that? Jess asked himself. He was beginning to wonder whether marrying Caro Pomfret would be a good idea after all. It was plain that the twins' affections were given to Mrs Georgie; if she were a little too informal in her manner with them, perhaps that was better than the loveless rectitude with which their mother tried to control them.

He thought this even more later on when Georgie and the children reached the house to find Caro installed on a sofa again and drinking tea.

'Oh, how jolly,' Gus exclaimed. 'May we have some, too?'

Their mother said in a forbidding voice, 'Augustus, you should only speak when you are spoken to and you should never ask questions of a grown-up. If Mr Fitzroy wishes to offer you tea then I am sure he would agree with me that, since he has no nursery, the proper place for you to drink it is in the kitchen.'

This severity rolled off Master Gus like water off a duck's back, as his old nurse would have said.

'Oh, good,' was his reply. 'I like eating tea in the kitchen. I don't have to worry if I spill anything and our cook always allows me to eat as much as I like—which I'm never allowed to when I have tea in the drawing room.'

This frank outburst set his mother tutting again and had Jess saying hastily, 'Perhaps, Mrs Georgie, you could take the twins to the kitchen. Cook will be sure to look after them—and you could warn her against over-indulging them.'

This tactful suggestion failed to silence the irrepressible Gus who now came out with, 'I say, Fitz, why do you call her Mrs Georgie? The grown-ups call her Mrs Herron and Mama calls her Georgina—except when she forgets and calls her Georgie, like us.'

'Augustus!' exclaimed Caro. '*Mr Fitzroy*, if you please, and in future you and Anne must call your aunt by her true name—Aunt Georgina or Aunt Herron.'

'Must we?' Gus appealed to Georgie.

'Yes,' she told him gently. 'She is your mama and it is your duty to obey her. Now, take my hands, both of you, and we'll be off to the kitchen.'

At the door she turned to Jess and said in her coolest voice, 'I am sure that you and Caro will agree that it might be as well for me to remain in the kitchen with them in case Gus persuades the cook to allow him to overeat. I promise not to overdo things myself.'

Jess, suppressing a grin, bowed his agreement, before pulling up a chair in order to seat himself opposite Caro and take tea with her.

On the whole, he silently concluded, he thought that he might have enjoyed himself much more if he had been able to join the children and their aunt in the kitchen rather than remain in the faded splendours of the drawing room with their mother to listen to her lamentations about the length of time which her brother, Sir Garth, was remaining in London.

And what a splendid mother Mrs Georgie would make, always provided that their papa—whoever he might be—added a little leavening of sternness to her kind regime.

Sir Garth's overlong stay in London was causing him as much annoyance as his sister. He kept presenting himself daily at the Home Office, only to be kept kicking his heels and then to be told that the Less Important Personage, one Courtney Beauchamp by name, was unable to see him that day owing to pressure of business.

His annoyance was not only at being kept waiting, but because he had to keep a constant watch for the duns and the bailiffs whom he had originally left London to escape. He had no mind to spend the rest of his days in the Marshalsea Prison where he would almost certainly be sent since he had nothing left with which to pay his mountain of debt.

Just when his patience was stretched to the limit, he arrived in Whitehall one morning to be told by some over-officious flunky, 'Mr Beauchamp will see you immediately, Sir Garth. Pray oblige him by not keeping him waiting any longer than you need.'

Which statement was a bit rich, was Sir Garth's opinion, when it was made to a man who had been kept waiting for days. Nevertheless, he followed the flunky into a large office where Mr Beauchamp sat in state. His clerk, in the corner of the room, was condemned to stand at his old-fashioned tall desk.

'Good day to you, Sir Garth. You came immediately when sent for. Most commendable. Most. I trust I see you in health.'

Sir Garth, irritated, had no time for pleasantries and told the man before him as much. 'And I don't like being kept waiting for several days, either. I would be obliged if you would inform me why I have been sent for at all.'

'I apologise for the delay—caused by affairs of state, I do assure you. The reason why I wished to see you is because I wish you to do the state some service in return for the favour done to you in a recent matter—which I am sure we need not go over again in here,' and he threw a warning look at the clerk in the corner.

An old name Beauchamp might have, but he possessed the manners of a bloody grocer, concluded an angry Sir Garth.

'I thought that was over and done with,' he grunted.

'In one sense, yes. In another, no. You were informed at the time, I believe, that some kind of future payment would be expected of you in return for the favour which you received.'

'Yes, indeed, but you know as well as I that I have no money with which to repay you.'

'Then repayment must come in another form, wouldn't you say?'

'Depends on what form,' Sir Garth ground out.

'Any form we choose, I think,' said Beauchamp, his airy manner never changing. 'Much better to oblige us, wouldn't you say, than rot in a prison cell?'

There was nothing for it but to agree. Sir Garth nodded his assent.

'Good, I'm charmed that we seem to have reached some form of understanding. What I have to ask of you is not difficult, I assure you. You are, at present, residing in Netherton at the home of your sister, Mrs John Pomfret. Is not that so?'

'With Caro, yes. What the devil has she to do with anything?'

'Patience, patience, I am coming to that. You have recently acquired a new neighbour, I believe. One Mr Jesmond Fitzroy, who has inherited Jesmond House and the remnants of its impoverished lands.'

'That's so. I have met him several times.'

'Ah, excellent. Then you will not find it difficult to keep a close watch on him—without him being aware of it, of course—with a view to informing us of any change in his habits—or of his associates—which might be of interest to the authorities. You will keep us posted by writing to us once a week, whether or not you have any information of interest.'

Sir Garth stared at the sleek man before him. 'Why in the world should you ask me to do such a thing? And what in the world am I to look for? Is he a criminal? And if he is not, what exactly is he, to exercise you so? In all fairness, you can scarcely leave me in the dark.'

Beauchamp smiled. A slow aggravating smile.

'No, he is not a criminal and what he is, is not your business. Your business is to watch him discreetly and tell us of his doings.'

'Bloody hell,' howled Sir Garth. 'I can tell you exactly what he's doing at this very moment: fascinating all the women in the neighbourhood, toadying up to Banker Bowlby—and doing up Jesmond House.'

'Excellent,' said Beauchamp approvingly. 'I see that you've already been keeping an eye on him. Carry on the good work, and may I remind you that it's not what he's doing now, but what he might do in the future. Report to us if his behaviour becomes in any way odd or suspicious.'

'And if I refuse to carry out this nonsense?'

'May I remind you that a year ago we saved not only your financial hide, but rescued you from a probable prison sentence when you and a minor member of the Royal Family misbehaved? This was done because the last thing we wanted was yet another scandal in high life. Refuse to do this for us and I cannot be responsible for your future. The Marshalsea is not a happy place for a man of your calibre to end up in.'

'And if I choose to go to a Radical paper and tell them of these shenanigans…?'

'That would be most unwise. I could not answer for your safety.'

Sir Garth grimaced, began to speak and then stopped.

At which Beauchamp leaned forward and said confidentially in a wheedling tone, all threats apparently forgotten, 'Come, come, now. You are being asked to do very little. Consider it payment for which, once made, the other will be forgotten.'

'Very well, then. I seem to have no alternative. I will do what you ask.'

'Excellent. Most wise of you. The clerk will give you an address to which to write. We cannot have you corresponding with the Home Office, can we? Good day, sir. I assure you that you will not regret this decision.'

I wish that I could believe that, thought Sir Garth morosely as he walked down Whitehall. By the sound of it, Jesmond Fitzroy might not be the happiest of men if he twigged that I was watching him on behalf of the Home Office.

And if he's not a criminal, what the devil can he be?

Beauchamp, on the other hand, was thinking that it was a good thing that a Bow Street Runner would also be in the district to keep an eye on Sir Garth as well as on Fitzroy!

All unknowingly, everyone was keeping an eye on everyone else. After Jess had waved goodbye to Caro and her train he sent for Kite to dine with him. Afterwards he interviewed Kite in the drawing room and not the library, which was already being refurbished. He poured out one glass of port for each of them—Kite resembled him in being abstemious—and, while they were drinking it, asked him if he had anything useful to report.

Kite was as short—and as informative—as usual.

'About Banker Bowlby, not yet. Some rumours and promising lines which are worth following up. Nothing substantial. If you had not required me to be discreet I might have discovered more immediately. As it is I have set an old friend of mine to continue investigating him. He had heard some tale of Bowlby being involved with moneylenders. He'll follow that up. If matters are as I believe we both think and you wish to move against him, we need hard evidence—which might be difficult to find.

'As for the other matter, that of Mrs Charles Herron, I was much more successful there. I have another old friend who knows all the *ton* and their country relatives to boot. He told me that Charles Herron had been a don at Oxford, Balliol no less. Around the age of fifty he came into money—he was the last of his line—left the University and decided to marry.

'He was a notorious freethinker and like Thomas Day, whom he had known in youth, he decided to train a young woman up to be his wife—after marriage rather than before. He believed, like Day, that if women were educated and properly treated they could be as clever as men. The Pomfrets were distant relatives of his and on a visit to Netherton he met Miss Georgina Pomfret, then seventeen, decided she would do and asked for her hand in marriage.'

He paused, and said a little slyly, 'Do you want all this, sir?'

Jess laughed at his impudence. 'Of course I do, you dog! Carry on.'

'Very well. Her father was delighted. The Pomfrets were on their beam ends as regards money and Herron was rich, never mind that he was an old man—fifty at the time. Once they were married he educated her—devoted his whole time to nothing else, friends said—but, alas, he succumbed to a syncope after only a few years of marriage and Mrs H. became a rich—and highly educated—widow.'

So that explained Georgie and her contradictions. She had been married off to a clever old man and he had made her as freethinking as he was. Had he loved her? Or she him? Had she been nothing but an experiment? Did she regret losing him? He must have been more of a father and a tutor to her than a husband.

'You've done as well as I expected,' he told Kite. 'Netting Bowlby may prove harder than discovering Mrs Herron's past. Discretion remains your watchword. No word of this must get out. Your man investigating the Banker is discreet, I trust?'

'As quiet as the grave, sir. And reliable. If there is anything to be found about Bowlby, be sure he will find it. I hired him because I took the liberty of believing that you would prefer me to return rather than remain in London indefinitely.'

'Indeed.' Jess finished off his port. 'There is work for you here. When Sir Garth returns I want you to keep an eye on him. The odour of rotten fish about his person is extremely strong—metaphorically, of course. He actually stinks of Rowland's Macassar oil—never mind that Byron calls it incomparable! I also need you to help me to restrain Parsons and the builders and workmen. I have no wish to be the owner of the most expensively improved house in England.'

'So noted, sir. Although I may need to go to town to receive a personal report from my friend. Speaking of Sir Garth Manning, I have to inform you that I have already kept an eye on him, quite by accident. I was in Whitehall, visiting my financial friend, when I saw Sir Garth entering the Home Office.'

'Did you, indeed? An odd place for such an idle fellow to visit, would you not say?'

'True—and bearing in mind that you wish to know more of him—a discreet note to my society friend, perhaps?'

'No "perhaps" about it—see to it immediately, Kite—and have another glass of port to celebrate some excellent work.'

'For once, sir, yes. If you will join me, that is.'

'So noted, Kite. Here's to both of us!'

And Mrs Georgie Herron, too, Kite thought, carefully keeping his face straight.

Georgie was having difficulty keeping her face straight that week—but not because she wished to smile. First it was Caro who troubled her. She came back one morning from a visit to Miss Walton, who was confined to the house with a rheumatic strain, to find Banker Bowlby leaving in his splendid new carriage.

Curious as to what he was about, she looked for Caro in the drawing room but she was not there. She enquired of one of the footmen if he knew where Mrs Pomfret was, only to be informed that she had retired to her bedroom the moment Mr Bowlby had left.

Had she, indeed? Remembering what Garth had told her of Caro's shaky financial situation, Georgie lost no time in running upstairs to Caro's suite at the front of the Hall.

She found her sister-in-law seated on her magnificent four-poster bed crying bitterly.

'What is, Caro? Whatever can be wrong?' Which was all a hum, really, for she was pretty sure what Banker Bowlby had come to tell her—but best not let Caro know that Garth had told her her secrets.

Caro turned a tear-stained face in her direction and wailed between sobs, 'Oh, Georgie, I can scarce believe it, but it must be true. Both John and your father managed the family's financial affairs very badly—as Mr Bowlby only discovered when he became my chief trustee. He has been so kind to me over the last few years, lending me money and trying to help me. But, oh, dear…'

A fresh bout of sobbing followed while Georgie sat down on the bed and put her arms around her sister-in-law. She had to confess to herself that she had never greatly liked Caro, but to see her like this touched her to the heart. All the loving kindness which she normally directed towards Gus and Annie was turned on their mother instead.

'Try to be brave, sister dear,' she said, rocking Caro gently, as though she were the baby she had once held in her arms. 'Tell me what he said today.'

'He said that we were quite ruined. That he was no longer able to assist us because our situation was beyond his help. We are facing bankruptcy if we go on as we are. He said that the only thing to save us would be to sell the Hall and the Pomfret lands. Most of it would go to pay our debts and what remained would provide us with enough to buy a small house in Netherton and buy an annuity which would be large enough to keep the three of us in a little comfort.

'Oh, Georgie, I cannot bear it! Why did John have to die and leave me to suffer this? Why were he and his papa so careless with their money that they have left me ruined? How can I face my neighbours when I am reduced to near poverty? I shall go mad, I know I shall.'

She flung herself face down on the bed and succumbed to a fit of hysterics.

Even though this outburst showed that Caro's selfishness had not been affected by what was happening to her, for she was not mourning for poor Gus's loss of home, lands and gentry status, but only for her own hurt feelings, Georgie could not help feeling sorry for her.

But feeling sorry would not help. As Caro's sobs turned into screams and she began drumming her feet and hands on the bed while she threw herself wildly about, Georgie was compelled to resort to sterner measures.

She put an arm around the flailing woman and dragged her upright before slapping her sharply on each cheek. 'Stop it, Caro, stop it at once! Reflect, you have Gus and Annie to look after and you cannot do so if you sink into madness.'

Caro, restored by this severity to some semblance of sense, fingered her reddened cheeks before faltering, 'You hit me, Georgie! You hit me! How could you?'

'Only to bring you back to a reasonable state of mind again. For example, you could tell me the details of your financial ruin. Perhaps I may be able to help.'

'What do you know of finance, Georgie? You're an innocent like me.'

'Not quite. Charles made me keep his accounts for him after he taught me how to do so. At least let me try. You do have your deeds and other papers here, I hope.'

'Mr Bowlby has most of them.'

'Then ask for them back.'

Caro gasped weakly. 'He might not like that.'

'That is of no matter. They are yours, after all.'

'But he took them when he made me my loan two years ago. He said they were…security…I think.'

'For a mortgage, I suppose—that does alter things. Then we may ask to examine them at the bank. He could surely not refuse that.'

'But he has been such a good friend, Georgie. Without him I might have lost the Hall long ago.'

'And now you have. Good friendship has only extended so far.'

'He has a bank to run.'

'Is that what he told you?'

'Today, yes. Oh, Georgie, what am I to do?'

'Listen to my advice, Caro, and act on it if it seems useful. It may not answer, but we could at least try.'

'Wouldn't it be better if I asked Garth to help? He is a man, after all, and these are men's matters.'

'Did Banker Bowlby tell you that, too?'

Caro did not need to answer. Georgie saw that it was hopeless. She would rather trust the Banker—who might, or might not, have ulterior motives—and the ineffably foolish and slippery Garth than her sister-in-law merely because they were men and she was a woman.

She rose. Caro seemed much calmer, almost resigned to her fate. 'Let me send for your maid,' Georgie said kindly, 'to help you to restore yourself a little. If you were to lie down for a while, you might feel better.'

'My maid,' intoned Caro tragically, 'and how long shall I have her, pray? I should never have married John. My poor mother was always against the match—she said I could have had an Earl at least. What a mistake I made. Look what it has reduced me to.'

How an earth did one answer that? It was no wonder that men thought that women were stupid if Caro's sole response to her ruin was to moan over what might have happened over twelve years ago rather than consider what sensible course of action she ought to take.

Ask Garth to advise her, indeed! One might as well ask Mr Punch from the Punch and Judy show to help her. On second thoughts, Mr Punch might be more useful.

On third thoughts, perhaps she ought to ask Fitz for help. It was not that she thought Fitz knew very much about such matters, but he seemed to be a man of the world in a sense which Garth could never be. It would mean taking private matters out of the family—but what of that, when poor Gus's inheritance was at stake?

At the worst, Fitz would merely shake his head in regret, at best, he might even know someone who could help them. Georgie thought that Mr Crane was hardly the man to go to. He had grown old and tired and would probably regard any cry for help from her or Caro as distrust of his friend and neighbour, Banker Bowlby.

Did *she* distrust him?

Georgie had no real answer to that question. Only that someone beside the Banker ought to take a look at the situation to see if it could be mended in a way which he had not visualised. She remembered something Charles had said once: 'Never trust anyone unconditionally, my dear. If it is foolish to live one's life trusting no one, it is equally foolish to live it trusting everyone.'

Odd that it was his kind voice she always remembered while she had almost forgotten what he looked like.

What would he have thought of Fitz? she wondered. I think that he would have liked him. Never mind that, she told herself briskly, you are as foolish as Caro if you spend your time thinking about what might have been or what never could be. That was another of Charles's maxims, she remembered, and he had made her translate it into Latin. To fix it in your memory so that you behave with sense when I am gone and can no longer protect you, he had said.

What neither of them had foreseen was how soon he would be gone...

The here and now was Caro's misfortune, Banker Bowlby's part in it—and Fitz. Yes, she would confide in him the next time they met—provided only that Caro was not with them. Well, that was easily accomplished, she thought, amused by her own ability to play the conspirator. I shall take a walk, alone, to Jesmond House's Park and hope to meet him. Gus says that he goes there most days to supervise the improvements.

For the first time Georgie acknowledged what a large part Fitz was coming to play in her life and thoughts.

Chapter Eight

Sir Garth was predictably furious when he arrived back at Pomfret Hall not long after nuncheon on the same day that Banker Bowlby had delivered his bad news to his sister.

'And that's it,' he exclaimed. 'You're ruined and will have to sell the Hall. How long have we got before the sale? I need to know.'

His fury arose from the fact that he might have lost his cheap base from which to watch Jess Fitzroy. His lack of sympathy for her plight not only distressed Caro but annoyed Georgie.

'Oh, Garth, how can you be so callous?' she exclaimed indignantly. 'Caro is losing her home and Gus's inheritance; you are merely feeling put out because you have lost a place where you can sponge on her.' She was well aware that when he stayed with Caro, which was often, Garth contributed nothing towards the upkeep of the Hall.

'You have no idea of what you are saying, Georgie,' he told her. 'Has this Banker fellow really given you an ultimatum, Caro? Is there nothing he can do to help you?'

'Nothing more,' wailed Caro. 'I was hoping that you might have some notion of what I ought to do to try to mend matters.'

'Who? I? Whatever gave you that notion? I'm neither a banker nor a solicitor. And you know as well as I do that our father left me virtually nothing. I can scarce keep my own head above water, never mind help you not to drown. No, I suggest that you go to solicitor Crane and see if he has anything useful to suggest.'

More than ever it seemed to Georgie that she ought to talk to Fitz—and soon. This very day, perhaps. There was little that she could say or do to comfort Caro, and Garth was beginning to annoy her so grievously she feared that she might snap something quite unforgivable at him. Which would certainly not help matters.

'I'm going for a walk,' she said abruptly in the middle of Caro's wailing and Garth's reproaches. He was damning her half-brother and her father for their carelessness and, like his sister, was groaning about lost opportunities in the past.

'I never thought that our father was over-wise to consent to your marriage with John Pomfret,' were the last words which Georgie heard when she slipped from the room. 'There were a number of men mad to marry you, but because you had a *tendre* for John Pomfret...'

The rest was lost as she closed the door, crossed the entrance hall and ran upstairs to put on her best bonnet. She had already decided that she would go straight to Jesmond House and ask to speak to Fitz. Ladylike dallying was not the order of the day and time was of the essence... Caro's distress and her own powerlessness to do anything about it were beginning to make her think in clichés.

To avoid Caro and Garth, as well as Gus and Annie, she left the house by one of the back doors and walked briskly across the park towards the footpath which led to the back of Jesmond House. The day was warm, but the sun was not oppressive and in happier times she would have enjoyed her walk.

But not today. She spent the time rehearsing in her head what she ought to say to Jess when she met him and trying not to hurry—it would never do to arrive perspiring heavily and looking flustered.

Oddly enough, it was her late husband's voice which was advising her. The oddness was that since his death she had tried not to think of him, but since she had known Fitz— a quite different man, when all was said and done—memories of Charles, and his tuition of her in life and letters, were coming fast.

She had half-hoped to come across Jess on the way, but no such luck, so she slipped through the wicket gate at the back of the park and walked round the house, past the gardeners who were restoring the flower beds to their former glory. Further on she passed a party of workmen who were erecting some scaffolding at the side.

When she reached the front door she found that the bell was out of order, but fortunately the door was open. She rapped on it, but nobody came, so she walked into the entrance hall which had been emptied of furniture. At the far end of it a workman, up a ladder, was stripping faded green paper from the wall.

Georgie coughed loudly. The workman turned slightly to look at her.

'What is it, miss?'

'Do you know whether anyone is at home?'

He climbed down the ladder and said, 'Yes, but they're all at the back of the house—including the butler. In the kitchen, I think.'

'Oh.' Georgie had a dreadful impulse to run away. This was all a mistake. Instead she held her ground and asked, 'Do you think that you could go there and inform Mr

Fitzroy that Mrs Herron has called and would like to speak to him—if that is convenient, of course.'

He thought for a moment, muttered 'Yes,' and disappeared through the door beneath his ladder.

Georgie sat down on the bottom steps of the main staircase and waited. Nothing happened. The workman did not reappear and she was just about to give up and go home, since God apparently did not wish her to speak to Fitz that day, when the door opened and a tall thin man dressed in black walked towards her, the workman following him.

'Do I address Mrs Herron?' he enquired, bowing.

'The same,' returned Georgie.

'My name is James Kite, I am Mr Fitzroy's secretary. He sends a message to you: That if you do not object to meeting him in the kitchen he will be happy to receive you there.' He bowed again.

So this was the mysterious Mr Kite.

And what could Fitz be doing in the kitchen?

Well, one way to find out was to assure Kite that the kitchen rather than the drawing room would certainly do.

He bowed again, saying as he straightened up, 'Follow me, madam.'

The kitchen was at the end of a long corridor, a huge gloomy room, its windows set on high. A number of workmen in their shirt sleeves were gathered in front of a huge empty hearth. A disassembled spit was lying on the ground: one of the workmen was kneeling before it, his back to her, examining it carefully.

Georgie looked around for Jess, but could not see him.

Kite cleared his throat. 'Ahem,' he said. 'Mrs Herron is here to see you, sir.'

The man kneeling on the ground rose, turned around and, bowing to her, said, 'Mrs Georgie, I knew that inviting you to the kitchen would have you here on the double. You will forgive my dishabille, I'm sure. One can scarcely take a large and sooty spit to pieces dressed as for Bond Street.'

Georgie nodded a dazed agreement. In a coarse linen shirt, yellow with age, and rough woollen breeches and stockings Jess showed to advantage rather than otherwise, even though his clothing was heavily soot-stained. She had not fully realised how powerful a body he possessed—nor the effect it would have on her.

'Of course,' she told him. 'But how came you to be involved...?'

'In such an ungentlemanly occupation? Come, come, you, of all people, should know that if a task needs to be done then it must be done properly. The man who should be engaged in dismantling the spit in order to repair it broke his leg yesterday and, rather than wait around either for another expert, or for him to recover, I decided that the matter could not be so complicated that an old soldier, who had turned his hand to many things, could not solve it.

'We had just succeeded in mending it when one of the men came to tell me that you had arrived. Your arrival was fortunate since it enabled me to send Kite to you and give me some respite from his tut-tutting. He has notions of what is proper and that I should turn mechanic is not one of them.'

'Parsons,' he said, addressing his agent who stood at a little distance, the only formally dressed man in the kitchen, 'I think we may safely conclude that the spit is in good working order again. All that is needed is to restore it to its old place after giving it a modicum of grease, start a fire, summon the boy who turns it—and see whether it behaves itself. In the meantime, I shall entertain Mrs Herron in a more suitable spot.'

He turned to Georgie again. 'Forgive me, Mrs Herron, I may not offer you my arm since it is scarcely fit for a lady to touch. Neither may I escort you to the drawing room in my present state. Dare I suggest that we venture outside where we may talk at our leisure? Otherwise I'm afraid that I shall have to both bathe and change myself—an operation which I fear will take some time.'

He was leading her out of the kitchen as he spoke.

Georgie said, 'Of course, unless you would rather I retired and returned another day.'

Jess shook his head. 'By no means, unless my present rough state is distasteful to you.'

Before she could assure him that it was not, he continued, 'I am of the opinion that a lady who assumes breeches to make her tasks more easy will not object to a gentleman doing the same thing when the need arises.'

'Exactly what I was about to say myself,' Georgie told him. 'And now that we are alone may we be Mrs Georgie and Fitz again?'

'By all means. I hardly know myself by any other name.'

'And now you are funning,' she told him.

'Indeed, not. I would never fun in your presence. I would not dare.'

His expression as he said this was so mischievous that Georgie began to laugh. They were now outside and Jess led them to a low stone wall by a flight of steps which gave on to a herb garden, long neglected, which was being restored by two workmen.

'I hope you will consent to sit here,' he said. 'I have ordered some benches for the terrace, but they have not yet arrived. Now, what is so urgent that you have walked over here to beard me in my den?'

'How did you know?' exclaimed Georgie, startled.

'That the matter was both serious and urgent? I have come to read you well, Mrs Georgie. Your face and your whole manner when I first saw you in the kitchen told me so. We're quits, you know, for I think that you can read me.'

That was true. However, she could not help riposting with, 'How did you know that I was not shocked at the sight of you, indistinguishable from your workmen?'

He took her clean hand into his grubby one and kissed it. 'Because you would not be shocked by such a thing. You are neither Caro, Garth, nor Mrs Bowlby—thank God. Nor will you go tattling round the village with the tale that Mr Jesmond Fitzroy knows no better than to play the artisan.'

Her face informed him of her agreement. He kissed her hand again, saying, 'Now, tell me why you're here. You have come on an important errand, I am sure.'

Georgie said faintly, 'I have, indeed, but how did you know that?'

'The manner of your careful dress, your stance, your serious face—and finally, I repeat, because I know you.'

'Mind-reading again,' she said, laughing a little because she was disconcerted. 'I once thought that it only happened in fairs.'

'In life, too. Now tell me what troubles you.'

She had feared that it might be difficult to inform him of Caro's sad story, but he listened to her so attentively that the longer she spoke the easier her explanation became.

'It is very apparent to me,' she ended, 'that neither Caro nor Garth have the faintest notion of what to do next. They appear resigned to ruin. It may be wrong of me, but I am of the opinion that someone from outside the family, who has no connections with Banker Bowlby, ought to examine their sad situation and see if anything might be done to rescue them. For a variety of reasons I didn't think that I ought to involve Mr Crane, and there is no one else in

Netherton to whom I can usefully speak—other than your-self, that is.

'If you think that this appeal to you is an imposition, I shall quite understand if you tell me there is nothing you can offer me in the way of advice.'

She fell silent, and for a moment Jess did not answer her. He was not sure exactly how much he ought to tell her. What she had just said had served to confirm his sus-picions that there was something fishy in Banker Bowlby's dealings with his clients in Netherton, and had strengthened his resolution to carry his investigations of him a stage further.

For his own reasons, however, he wished to say nothing that would inform Georgie of his knowledge of the world of business and finance. If he was to succeed against Banker Bowlby—assuming his suspicions were correct—it would be best that Bowlby continued to consider him an idle innocent. The fewer people who knew the truth about him, the better.

After what Kite had told him about her marriage he was not surprised that Georgie was more worldly-wise than Caro and her brother, but he also knew that it might not be safe to tell her the whole truth lest Bowlby somehow trick her into revealing it to him.

'Forgive me for taking so long to answer you,' he said at last, for the longer he had remained silent the more anx-ious her face had grown, 'but I have been thinking hard about the nature of the advice I can offer you. Whilst I have no first-hand knowledge of such affairs I know that Kite has friends in London who do. In order for us to con-sult them, we need a little time. Do you think that you could persuade your sister-in-law to ask Mr Bowlby for a month's delay before he acts? You need not inform her that the suggestion is mine—present it, rather, as yours.

'Advise her to point out to him that it would be a kind and neighbourly act for him not to move against her immediately the due date for clearing the loan has passed. He could not lose by it if her affairs are as parlous as they appear to be. If you will allow, I will immediately consult Kite—you can wait here for me, I shall not be long.'

'Oh, Fitz, I knew that you would think of something,' exclaimed Georgie gratefully. 'I shall certainly advise Caro to do as you say when I return home. I shall also be happy to sit here in the sun and admire the gardens which are being re-created while you are so good as to act on my behalf. You may take as long as you wish. I feel a little at ease for the first time today.'

It hurt him to deceive her, for of course he did not need to talk to Kite. It was Kite who carried out his orders and he who gave them. Nevertheless, he walked into the house, discovered that Kite had returned to the library and spoke to him there. What he had to say to him was brief and to the point.

'I have just received further news which points to the likelihood of Bowlby being dishonest. Tonight we'll have a discussion on the matter and this time I shall visit London. I need to talk to Mr Wolfe. You can look after matters here. You will give out that I have a fever and am confined to my room. We shall arrange matters so that the servants do not know of my absence. I shall not leave until a few days have passed. I do not want my journey to appear to have any connection with Mrs Herron's visit. Discretion must be our watchword.'

'And Mrs Herron?' asked Kite. 'Is she to know anything of this?' He was well aware that this new piece of information must have been acquired as a result of her visit.

'By no means—and for her own safety, that is. I have led her to believe that you are the man who has links with the City of London and will be able, through me, to advise her.'

Kite permitted himself a small smile. 'You seem to have covered your back as successfully as is your usual habit.'

'I have to hope so. I must leave you to return to Mrs Herron and tell her that you are willing to assist her.'

Georgie's thanks were heartfelt. 'So we are conspirators now,' she said, 'and must watch what we say when we next meet. We shall be dining at Mrs Firth's tonight, and I believe that you are also invited.'

'The cream of Netherton society under one roof—' Jess smiled '—and none of them are to know of our secret— particularly Kite's part in it! Now, may I offer you tea in the drawing room while I retire in order to turn into a gentleman again so that I may walk you home?'

'By all means—and if the spit is working I should like to see it in action.'

'And so you shall. May I also...' Jess hesitated for a moment, for what he had to say was a trifle daring, although he hoped that the freethinking Mrs Georgie Herron might not consider it so '...inform you that most afternoons I take a walk along the boundary between Jesmond and Pomfret lands and it might be useful if we could meet there—by accident, of course.'

'Oh, yes,' agreed Georgie, her eyes shining. 'By accident—of course.'

Her expression had changed so completely from the unhappy one she had worn when she had walked into the kitchen that Jess regretted more than ever that his sooty state was preventing him from making gentle love to her.

Which was perhaps just as well for he was not sure that he could confine himself to gentle love. Her care and compassion for her unworthy sister-in-law—whom he now had no desire to make his wife—were just two more bricks in the wall of admiration he was building for her.

Sir Garth Manning was writing a letter to Mr Beauchamp. It was the end of his first week back at Netherton. Much had happened during it, but little, he thought desperately, of any use to his master.

Caro had gained a stay of execution from Banker Bowlby. Someone had shot Miss Walton's dog—its body had been found on the path between Pomfret Hall and Jesmond House; Jesmond Fitzroy had fallen ill of a fever and was confined to his bed; the Firths' dinner party had been a success; one of the workmen had fallen from the scaffolding at Jesmond House and had broken his arm.

'I have little to report,' he wrote. 'Fitzroy behaves in an eccentric manner, to be sure, but there is nothing suspicious about it. Report says that when the spit in his kitchen failed to work he dressed in labourer's clothes and dismantled and repaired it himself. Half of the women in the parish think that they are in love with him—or his supposed fortune—although I understand that he claims that he does not possess one.'

When this missive arrived in Whitehall, Mr Beauchamp gave a great sigh and compared it with another which he had received on the same day. His spy in Netherton, neatly camouflaged and working at Jesmond House as an unskilled labourer, had reported all of the above, but also something more central to Mr Beauchamp's purpose.

'I have,' his agent wrote, 'to inform you of something suspicious. Fitzroy, under pretence of being ill of a fever and confined to his bed, has instead travelled to London in such secrecy that the only person who knows of it is his creature Kite. Otherwise I have little to report.'

Mr Beauchamp tossed both letters down. A secret visit

to London. Now that was not only suspicious, but slightly sinister, as was Fitzroy's claim to be fortune-less when Mr Beauchamp well knew that he was extremely well-endowed. So that ass Manning had told him more than he knew.

The only annoying thing was that there was no hint of why Fitzroy should need to visit London secretly—unless he was engaged in some dubious activity against the state of which he wished no one to know!

'The news is that Mr Fitzroy has recovered from his fever and is up and about again,' Caro told Georgie after nuncheon one fine afternoon. 'It must have been a nasty bout to last ten days.'

Little ears were listening to her. Gus piped up, 'Oh, Aunt Georgie, may we go the park this afternoon, and ask him for a game of cricket if we find him there?'

'Certainly,' said Georgie, who was eager to inform Fitz that Caro had visited Banker Bowlby and that he had reluctantly given her a stay of execution for a month. 'But you must not be disappointed if he does not feel up to it. We'll take the kite with us as well in case he simply wishes to sit and talk.'

'Oh, good,' exclaimed Gus, and ran out of the room to inform Annie that Aunt Georgie was going to take them for a walk.

'I wonder if I ought to come with you,' Caro offered, causing Georgie's heart to sink a little since she was also hoping that Fitz might have some news from Kite to pass on to her and would prefer to hear it before Caro did. She had made such a tohu-bohu before she had consented to see Banker Bowlby about the month's grace that Georgie was not sure how she might respond to even more difficult demands. If any were to be made of her, that was.

Fortunately, Caro decided that the day was too warm for her to risk her complexion by exposing it to the afternoon sun, so she and the children set off on their own.

'There he is,' cried Gus when they reached the park. 'He doesn't look too ill to play cricket.'

He was wrong, though. Jess, feeling that, in the interests of backing up his story of having been ill, he needed to make a show of resting a little, seconded Georgie's urgings that Gus and Annie fly the kite while he and she sat on the grass and admired the shining landscape.

'Ought you to be out so soon?' Georgie asked him, although she privately agreed with Gus that Fitz had never looked better. 'The *on dit* was that you had a severe feverish attack.'

'Oh,' said Jess, feeling a little ashamed of his deceit—even though it was being carried out for Georgie's sake, 'I am advised that if I take things easily a breath of fresh air will do me nothing but good. Simply to see you revives me.'

At least, he reflected unhappily, that last sentence was true.

Georgie coloured a little. 'Well, I'm happy to see you, and to inform you that Caro did as you suggested and asked Banker Bowlby for a month's delay—to which he agreed. Which gives us a breathing space in case Kite comes up with something.'

Jess nodded his head gravely. 'I don't want to raise your hopes too much, but he informs me that there is a strong possibility that where Bowlby's running of the bank is concerned, ''something is rotten in the state of Denmark''. However, more hard evidence is needed before he can be moved against. Suspicion alone is not enough.'

'You mean that what he is doing might be criminal?'

'Indeed, but it is of the utmost importance that you say nothing of this to either Caro or her brother. Neither of them strikes me as reliable. Everything might be lost if he has the slightest suspicion that Kite is on his trail.'

'Then I shall not say a word—but time is running out.'

'I know, but these matters are delicate. For example, I understand that if Bowlby were to be challenged in the wrong way then the bank might fail and all those in Netherton who have money in it might be ruined.'

'Everyone in Netherton has money in it,' exclaimed Georgie, horrified.

'I thought so,' Jess said ruefully. 'And that makes discretion absolute and the handling of the whole business enormously difficult. Bowlby must not suspect that anyone suspects *him*.'

Bright though the day was, Georgie shivered. 'It does not bear thinking about. I wholeheartedly agree that neither Caro nor Garth should be told anything. Neither of them could be trusted to keep quiet…' She fell silent.

'Yes,' said Jess, 'and any gossip might also cause a run on the bank which would be fatal, and Bowlby would not be the only one to be ruined.'

Fortunately for Georgie's immediate peace of mind at this point, Gus and Annie came running up, the kite flying high behind them. Their innocent faces, their lack of knowledge of how wicked the world might be, was some comfort to her, even though she knew that if matters went the wrong way their life was sure to be changed for the worst.

'You are not to worry overmuch, things are on the move in London. We shall have to be patient, ' Jess told her before she and the children returned home after he had shown Gus a few tricks with the kite to make up for not having played cricket with them. 'Another day,' he had promised.

After making arrangements with Georgie for them to meet again on the morrow—without Gus and Annie, who were being taken by their mother to a children's party at Mrs Firth's—he watched them until they disappeared around a bend in the path.

What he had not told Georgie, for she had enough to trouble her, was that another matter had come up in London which might, or might not, have some bearing on his investigation of Banker Bowlby.

He had refused to stay with Ben Wolfe while he was in town, although he had used his office in the City to work from.

'You and Susanna do not want a third wheel in the house in your first year of marriage,' he had told them. The real reason was that he wished to come and go as he pleased and he had taken rooms in a quiet back street where he had lodged before he had made his fortune. He had given up his London home when he had moved to Netherton.

On his second day, he had suddenly found himself aware that he was being watched. What alerted him, he never knew. A shadow, perhaps in a window, or over-familiar footsteps behind him. He had dodged into an alley once, and watched while an anonymous man in anonymous clothing walked by the alley's entrance, looking anxiously about him.

When, later, in another part of the City, he saw the same man staring in a shop window, pretending to be interested in the prints displayed in it, and later espied him in a cab rank—although he had no intention of taking a cab—Jess was sure that someone was on his trail.

What was interesting was that the someone was shadowing him by night as well as by day. Jess chose night for a confrontation. He had spent part of his day with a moneylender who, true to his trade, chose to tell Jess nothing of what he knew of Bowlby, although Jess's informants had told him that Bowlby had visited his offices more than once.

'I'm looking for paper to buy up,' Jess had told him, 'and I'm prepared to pay a good price. Something in the country—a nice little investment.'

He knew that moneylenders were prepared to sell the debts and securities—always known as paper—of those to whom they had lent money if they felt that the debts were risky.

The man, Clarke by name, had shaken his head. 'Nothing to sell at the minute,' he muttered.

'But if the price were right, and you wished to cut any losses, you know where to find me,' Jess had told him and had given him Kite's name and an accommodation address to which to write.

The man had nodded—and then had given him the address of another man named Smythe, who had also had dealings with Bowlby. 'You might find pickings there. He can't afford to take many risks with his clients,' he had added.

After that Jess had dined late in a small tavern and had appeared to drink well in order to fool his shadow who was sitting two booths way from him, secure in the false knowledge that he had not been twigged.

His meal over, Jess left the tavern and staggered off down a dark alleyway, his clumsy follower still behind him. This time he disappeared into a doorway and, when the man walked by, he caught him from behind in a cruel strangling grip and brought him to his knees.

'Now,' hissed Jess in the wretch's ear, 'tell me who is paying you to track me round London—and why—and I won't hand you over to the watch as a thief to go before the magistrate in the morning.'

'You're mad! I ain't follering you,' the man gasped.

'Two days,' said Jess. 'For two days I've had you as a shadow. It's Botany Bay for you, my beauty, if you don't do as I ask.'

'You'd not peach on me to the beaks,' croaked his victim. 'I ain't done nothing.'

'No? If I haul you before the watch, and then the magistrate, waving my purse and gold watch at them and say I caught you in the act, who will they believe, you or me?'

'You wouldn't do that—it's a lie.'

'Try me,' said Jess tightening his grip, and then loosening it again. 'Or tell me the truth, and I'll let you go.'

'I was told to follow you, your honour, report where you went, but I don't know who hired me, that I don't. I was asked by a pal who said that some nob wanted you followed and, seeing that he hadn't the time to do it himself, he let the job out to me—for a consideration.'

'And what consideration do I give to this tale?'

'That it's Gawd'strewth, so help me.'

His voice carried such conviction that Jess felt inclined to believe him.

'And you've no idea who the nob was?'

'None.'

'And you know nothing else?'

'Only that the news was that you was secretly in London and had come up from the country where you live. Said you was supposed to be ill, but was shamming. And that's it, as Gawd's my witness.'

So someone had been watching him in the country, too. And who might that be—and why? Jess asked himself once he had let the man go. Was it Banker Bowlby? He rather thought not.

Which meant that, once back in Netherton, he must be on his guard there as well as in London—but from what?

Chapter Nine

Georgie almost skipped along the path, looking out for Fitz as she hurried towards Jesmond House on the following day. Would he keep his word? Of course he would. Had he not always done so in the past?

Turning a corner she saw him, seated on the trunk of an old tree which had blown down in one of last winter's storms. He rose to greet her, punctilious as always. She sometimes wondered what it would take to disturb his lovely calm.

He was as neatly turned out as ever in clothing eminently suitable for a country walk and, after he had bowed over her hand, he invited her to sit next to him and enjoy the peace of the afternoon.

She needed no second invitation. 'It seems odd,' she told him, 'for me not to be worrying you over some financial nonsense or other, but until you have further news we may perhaps talk of better things.'

'So noted,' he told her, his blue eyes dancing.

'Which means?' she asked.

Jess explained. 'It's a clerk's answer to his employer when he informs him that he has understood his instructions and will carry them out. Kite is very fond of it.'

He thought that he might have given himself away a little with the last sentence for after all, in matters financial, he had pretended that Kite was his master and not himself, but Georgie had missed his slip for she was saying, 'What an apt name for him! Kite, I mean. Is not a kite-flyer someone who finds out things by speculating on them? I seem to remember my husband saying something of that order.'

'True,' Jess said. 'And he's very good at it.' He did not add that he was better and that his friend, Ben Wolfe, was better still. He decided to change the subject, which was a tricky one, for he thought that he might say something untoward which would give him away.

Instead, he began to ask her about Netherton. 'I've been here well over two months now,' he said, 'and I've still not met all the notables. Am I right in supposing that most of them rarely visit London? No one has yet spoken to me of the place other than in terms of awe.'

His comment arose from his determination to discover who, in Netherton, was spying on him. The only person he could think of was Sir Garth Manning, but that seemed almost too easy a guess.

'Come to think of it, you are right,' Georgie said, all unsuspecting of his true motive. 'I suppose I've always taken it for granted. At Nether Brington, though, most of the local gentry have town houses and go there for the Season. It's not entirely a matter of wealth,' she added thoughtfully, 'more one of habit and liking. Father and John detested the place, but I enjoyed myself there. We had a little house in Chelsea and my late husband loved to visit the British Museum.'

'Do you miss him?' Jess asked her gently.

'Not so much now, but when he first died, very much.' She shook her head determinedly. 'Regret and mourning become stupid after a time. It's wrong not to mourn and equally wrong to overdo it.'

'Sensible Mrs Georgie,' said Jess tenderly, leaning over and giving her a loving kiss. Afterwards he was to ask himself how such an innocently intended piece of comfort could have had such powerful consequences. He had thought he had seen unhappiness on her mobile face when she had spoken of Charles Herron and had wished to drive it away by a simple act of kindness.

However, his kiss, intended for her cheek, reached her lips instead as Georgie innocently turned her face towards his as he leaned towards her. The effect on both of them was dramatic. Ever since they had first met they had been gradually falling under the strong spell of a mutual attraction and the kiss became a catalyst which freed its power.

Jess's hands rose to cup her head as Georgie's rose to clasp him round the neck as the kiss, gentle at first, grew stronger and stronger. His tongue probed her mouth open and danced with hers, and then, deserting her mouth, he trailed butterfly kisses down the side of her neck while Georgie sighed and shuddered beneath his lightest touch.

By what logical progression they turned from a lady and gentleman sitting decorously side by side on a log to a nymph and a satyr celebrating their bodies on the grass beneath it, neither of them ever really knew. Long continence for them both might have had something to do with their sudden surrender to abandonment as well as the last few weeks which they had spent teasing and tormenting one another in a verbal dance of unacknowledged, unconsummated passion.

Later, Georgie was to remember what a parlour-maid, who had fallen pregnant by a married footman, had wailed at her, 'We never meant it, mum, neither on us. It just happened one day. It seemed right, somehow.' She could only be grateful that she had been kind to the girl, for how else could she now explain her own rapid fall from grace?

She could not even argue that Jess had seduced her. He had not needed to. The very first kiss which he had offered her had been sufficient to betray them both—if betrayal it were.

Lying there on the grass, clothes abandoned, commonsense abandoned, propriety and etiquette alike forgotten, they reached a release so powerful that Georgie thought that she was about to die, for nothing which she had shared with her late husband had equalled this, while Jess understood at last how strong and rewarding true passion is.

What neither of them knew was that they were being watched from a little distance. A man in workman's clothing had discreetly followed Jess from Jesmond House and was lying in some long grass, hidden from view.

So that was the way of it, was it? More grist to send to his master's mill in London—although what use it might be to him was doubtful. On the other hand, empires had fallen as a result of such apparently minor knowledge. He lay on his side once the main business was over, smiling at the thought that sir and madam thought themselves unobserved.

The reason for his good luck was because, for once, the caution which had ruled Jess's life since he had learned one of life's hardest lessons, when he was little more than a boy, had deserted him. Usually aware of unseen prying eyes, passion had overwhelmed him so that the only thing left to him was to celebrate it, all else forgotten.

How long they lay there, lost in an Eden of their own making, neither of them ever knew. Georgie slept a little in Jess's arms, watched by him until sleep claimed him also. A flock of birds cawing and calling in the trees overhead brought them back to the realities of life.

Awake again, Georgie could not for the moment remember where she was until returning memory flooded in on her.

Had she really fallen into the grass with Fitz to experience such pleasure as she had never known in her life before? And whatever would he think of her? To surrender to him so easily, without a struggle…to… She could not say the words even to herself. She, level-headed Georgie, always scornful of those who surrendered their reason at the sight and touch of a man, had fallen at last into Eve's age-old trap, lost to everything in a man's arms…

She flushed and sat up, suddenly aware of her discarded clothing. Jess, disturbed by her sudden movement, started from sleep to lie back, smiling at her as though it were the most natural thing in the world for them to have given themselves to one another in the open, the grass their only bed, with the sun shining and the birds calling…

All that she could think of to say as she groped around among the grass for her clothing, was the completely inadequate, 'Oh, Fitz, I never meant that to happen, did you?'

She looked down at the unclothed muscular strength of him, admiring almost against her will the powerful body which had given her so much pleasure.

'No,' he returned drowsily, 'but wasn't it splendid?'

What to say to that? She gave a little moan at which he sat up exclaiming, 'Never say that you regretted it?'

'No,' she returned distractedly, 'Of course I don't, but I've never done such a thing before, Fitz, believe me.'

The delightful lethargy which so often follows successful love-making caused Jess to be careless. His eyes caressing her, he said, unthinkingly, 'Darling Georgie, I believe you, although many would not, seeing what a freethinker your late husband was.'

He knew his mistake the moment the teasing words flew out of his mouth.

Georgie froze. She said, all the joy draining out of her face, 'Now, how do you know that, Fitz? I never told anyone—even Garth and Caro aren't aware of that. It is not common knowledge.'

And then, rising from their impromptu bed, agony written on her face, she began to pull on her lost clothing, exclaiming, 'Oh, I know. It was Kite, wasn't it? You had me investigated when he went to London, didn't you? Is that why you made love to me—because you thought I was like Charles and would lie down for anyone?'

'No,' Jess said, sitting up, suddenly aware of his nakedness and feeling at a disadvantage now that she was beginning to dress herself, although every movement of her shapely body was a delight in itself, 'No, believe me, Georgie, it wasn't like that, I...'

He was about to say I love you, but, pulling on her white cotton pantalettes, trimmed with pink ribbon, she broke in with, 'You're not denying it, are you, Jesmond Fitzroy? I know you—you did ask it of Kite, didn't you? Why, why?'

There was such anguish in her voice that Jess forgot his nakedness and rose to his feet to try to hold her to him, 'Listen to me, Georgie. It's Fitz speaking.'

She would have none of him. She pushed him away.

'Oh, I've been betrayed before, Mr Fitzroy, and I don't like the taste of it. Did you, or did you not, have Kite investigate me?'

'Not you particularly, he investigated everybody...'

Jess stopped speaking. He knew that it was no answer—or at least not one that she would accept. She wasn't everybody, she was Mrs Georgie who had come to trust him.

'So it was a business relationship all along, was it?' she said bitterly. 'Shall we leave it at that? Send your bill in,

Mr Fitzroy, when you have finished helping Caro and I will pay it. Goodbye.'

She was dressed now, had hidden away all the glories of her body, and she was leaving him.

In his distress Jess began to pick up his own clothing in order to dress and follow her, but she was running away from him, down the path, at top speed. He had lost her and like a fool he had never told her that he loved her.

And wished to marry her.

That knowledge stunned him.

He dropped the breeches which he had picked up.

Marry Georgie, who was the exact opposite of the kind of wife he had decided on for himself before he had met her?

Marry Georgie who had melted in his arms and given of herself so generously?

For one mad moment he considered running after her wearing only his breeches to try to tell her so, but returning sanity told him that he must not make bad worse. There would be time to speak to her again, to tell her that he loved her…to propose. Ah, there was a thought! That should convince her of his sincerity, should it not?

Comforting himself thus, Jess began to dress and, in the doing, recovered his normal cautious self, and for the first time felt that someone was watching him.

But when he looked around he could see no one and concluded that guilt and shame had misled him.

Across the park a workman ran towards Jesmond House, happy that at last he had something to report, even if his superiors thought that that something was nothing!

Georgie didn't think that her recent adventure was nothing. On the contrary merely to recall it was agonising. How could she have been so deceived in him? The worst of it was that, Netherton society being so small, she could not avoid him. And, even more distressing, she could not, without revealing something, deprive Gus and Annie of their games with him—although how she could face him without betraying her unhappiness was beyond her immediate conjecture.

Her first concern was that she should not appear at all overset by the time that she reached Pomfret Hall again. She stopped running once she was on Pomfret land, and strolled home so leisurely that no one could have guessed that she had just suffered a mortal blow.

Fortunately, Caro and Garth were seated together in the drawing room before the tea board and she was able to manage the nothings of tea-time conversation.

'Did you chance to see Fitzroy while you were out this afternoon?' Garth asked.

The lie flew, almost unbidden, off Georgie's lips. 'In the distance, only.'

'Gossip is he's doing more at the House than was originally supposed. Old lady Jesmond must have cut up for rather more than she was credited with—or he's even warmer than rumour suggested.'

'Really,' said Georgie, her voice suggesting a total lack of interest in Jesmond Fitzroy and all his works.

Garth shrugged. 'You know,' he said, looking hard at Georgie to see whether she would contradict him, 'I think that there's something odd about Fitzroy—something of a mystery man, don't you think?'

'The only mysterious thing about Jesmond Fitzroy,' offered Georgie as coolly as she could, 'is the amount of interest and gossip he seems to generate. It all goes to show how little happens in Netherton that he can create so much. And speaking of interest, Caro, has Banker Bowlby written that letter to you which he spoke of at your meeting with him? The one confirming the one month's stay of execution—without interest.'

This last comment was a piece of desperation on Georgie's part being engaged in only to turn the conversation away from Fitz.

Caro shook her head. 'No, but he did promise.'

'Only verbally,' Georgie said. 'Might I suggest that you and Garth go to see him tomorrow and persuade him to put it in writing immediately.'

'Oh, come, Georgie,' exclaimed Garth. 'Don't want the feller to think that we don't trust him, do we?'

'Charles had his faults,' she returned, 'but he always insisted that financial matters were put on a proper footing.'

'Can't hurt, I suppose,' conceded Garth. 'Go to the bank tomorrow, eh, Caro? Stop your sister-in-law from nagging at us. You're in danger of turning into a shrew, you know, Georgie? Doesn't suit you.'

Georgie put down her tea cup and stood up, secretly fighting off tears and the impulse to inform Garth that he was a spendthrift fool in danger of spending the rest of his life in a debtor's prison. Normally she could shrug his spite off, but coming on top of the revelation of Fitz's villainy his unkindness was almost too much for her to bear.

'Must go,' she announced as brightly as she could. 'Letters to write. I'll see you both at supper.'

Another thundering lie to blame on Fitz, she thought bitterly when she reached her room. The worst of it was that she would now have to worry until her courses arrived over the possibility that her folly of the afternoon would result in something more tangible than regret!

Jess was busying himself so that he might have no time for regret. Whilst he was away in London Kite had brought yet another large box of papers and documents down from the attic, and he decided to sort through it immediately. Like the others he had examined, it was probably only the rubbish of bygone years, kept lest it might be needed in a future which had come and gone, leaving them like worthless flotsam cast up by the sea on to the shore.

Half an hour and a frayed temper later, all that he had found was a pile of rubbish, fit only to be burned, when he came across a large yellowed envelope with his name written on it in his great-aunt's hand.

'For Jesmond, when I am gone,' he read.

His curiosity aroused, he opened the letter with some little hope that the envelope's contents would be more interesting than the old dress and upholstery bills which he had been examining. He drew from it a document folded into three which he opened and read with mounting astonishment. It was of such a nature that he wondered whether it was the reason for his being followed in London.

He was reading it again, staring at the seal at the bottom, when Kite came in. Instinctively, without conscious thought, he refolded it hastily and thrust it back into the envelope.

Kite, who was carrying papers of his own, said in his cold voice, 'Want these burned, do you?' pointing at the pile of rubbish.

'Yes,' replied Jess abstractedly. 'Nothing of importance there, old bills and uninteresting letters from long-dead Jesmonds.'

He added, as Kite skirted the papers to lay some letters for him to sign on the table before him, 'The day I find something interesting out of the attic you may fire a gun or run up a flag—your choice.'

Now this was yet another lie, and like Georgie he was beginning to regret how many he was telling these days, but the document concerned him alone, and it was of such a nature that it was not for anyone else to know that it existed—so the lie was inevitable. It was plain by the condition of the box and the papers that Kite had not touched them—which was all to the good.

'I could go through them for you,' Kite offered, 'but most of the stuff so far has been personal, relating to the family, and it's difficult for me to judge what to keep and what to destroy.'

'Um,' said Jess, 'I agree, stupid to do the job twice. You did find something useful in the first batch you looked at— but I've found nothing since.'

'You mean the manorial deeds?' Kite said.

'Indeed, and we must keep them to ourselves. I've no wish to stir up a hornets' nest by trying to prove that the Jesmond Family owns the manorial rights to Netherton and not the Pomfret family, since I haven't the slightest desire to be the Lord of the Manor of Netherton. On the other hand, if Banker Bowlby does succeed in ousting the Pomfrets, then I shall use them to stop him from claiming the title—which is partly, I think, why he wants to bankrupt them and take their lands over.'

Jess began to read and sign the letters, correcting one of them before handing them back to Kite to be posted. After Kite had left the room, he congratulated himself on retaining his normal composure despite the two-fold shocks of his rift with Georgie and the discovery of the document which his great-aunt had left him.

He would have been surprised to learn that he had not fooled Kite, who was busy asking himself what could have occurred to distress a man who normally allowed nothing to touch him.

Probably that woman from Pomfret Hall, was his conclusion. Well, he could do worse…much worse. She seemed to have more sense than most women—which wasn't saying much.

Caro Pomfret was too indolent and too selfish to notice that Georgie was very *distraite* these days and that the frequency of the occasions on which she and the children met Jess had lessened. Sir Garth, on the other hand, wondered what had occurred to diminish her usual effervescent manner. She was strangely quiet these days, not at all her usually lively self.

Georgie frantically thought up a variety of explanations to persuade Gus and Annie not to visit Jesmond Park to invite Jess to play cricket with them, but fortunately they were not needed, for the weather, which had been warm and sunny for weeks, suddenly turned cold and wet, confining them all to the house, so her flimsy excuses were not put to the test.

It was easy to evade him when she met him at any of the soirées and dinner parties to which they were invited. Sir Garth, indeed, began to think that his luck with her might have changed since she constantly used him as a shield to prevent herself from being alone with Jess.

Unfortunately for her peace of mind, she underrated Jess's ingenuity. Miss Walton, having recovered from her rheumatic strain, invited everyone of any consequence in Netherton to supper to be followed by a musical evening provided by the guests. Georgie was particularly asked to bring her guitar along and favour them with some songs.

She had scarcely sat down before the assembled company, and had begun tuning the guitar, when she became aware that Fitz—to her annoyance she could not stop herself from using her nickname for him even now, when disillusionment had told her to think of him formally, or not to think of him at all—was seated at the end of the front row, his bright blue eyes firmly trained on her as though she were the most important thing in the world.

She was so distressed that she almost dropped her guitar, and then common-sense took over. What a weak-willed thing she was to allow a man to overset her. She would not be overset, not she! On the contrary, she would show him that her life without him was quite satisfactory, and that he could stare at her as much as he liked, but she would not be either daunted or disturbed.

To prove it, once tuning was over, she launched into a blazing version of the old North country ballad 'Bobby Shafto' which set everyone's feet tapping. She followed it with a lively song in which a maiden rejected her importunate lover, ending with a chorus which ran 'Oh, no, John! No, John, no!'

To her delight her voice had never sounded more bell-like, more true—and more defiant.

A wave of appreciative applause followed. Someone cried 'Bravo!' and it was Jess, of course.

Answering him, she said sweetly, 'Would you care for me to sing that again, it came from the heart?' to receive a cry of 'Encore, encore' from him and others.

Well, if he could enjoy himself as though nothing had happened, so could she, never mind the pain which the sight of him was giving her. Her hands trembled, but the resolution which had carried her through the early days of her strange marriage enabled her to behave as though all was well with the world.

She decided that her next song would be a sentimental one so, mastering herself, she launched into 'Sweet Afton,' her head bent over the guitar, and her voice, low and sweet, gave full value to the beautiful words. Immediately after she finished silence fell, to be followed by full-blooded applause—particularly from Jess, who did everything but blow her a kiss.

Miss Walton, clapping her hands together, exclaimed, 'That was delightful, my dear. May we impose on you by asking you to play for us again before the evening is over?'

Georgie, prey to the most conflicting emotions, quietly agreed to do so. She had never been so aware of Jess before. Divided from him though she was, both in mind and body, she could almost feel his presence, even when she sat down as far away from him as possible.

It was as though they were joined together by a chain so strong that she could not break it. Was that what one mad afternoon on the grass had done to her? And did he feel the same? Useless conjectures, for she was determined not to speak to him however much it hurt her not to do so.

He, on the other hand, was determined to speak to her. Miss Walton was ending the evening with a night-cap. Footmen passed among the guests, carrying trays of hot rum toddy. Georgie accepted hers, and even as she lifted the glass from the tray she saw Jess approaching her, his glass raised in salute.

'You will allow me to compliment you on your playing and singing, Mrs Georgie?' he asked, as though the last time that they had spoken he had not been naked and she had not been reproaching him for his deceit after they had been making passionate love on the grass of his park.

'If you must,' she said pleasantly, even managing to smile at him, for she was well aware that in Netherton everyone watched everyone else and, since her recent manner to him had been so warm, to be too cool now might occasion unwanted gossip.

'Oh, I must,' he told her, his manner unchanged from the one which he had used to her since they had become so friendly. 'You must be aware that your performance was quite professional. Do I infer that you were taught by one?'

It was plain that he was determined to make her talk, so she answered him, 'You infer correctly. I take it that you admired my songs. Particularly the second one,' she added provocatively, 'where the lady says "No".'

'Oh, indeed. You have had some practice at saying "No" yourself, I presume?'

'Not so often as I should have done in the recent past,' she told him, knowing full well that he would take her meaning.

He did.

'Oh, brave,' he said. 'My advice, should you wish to accept it, is that you should say "Yes" more often. It makes for a happier life. May I ask you to allow me to visit you tomorrow afternoon? I have a particular question to ask of you.'

Georgie took a recklessly long swig of her rum toddy. It scorched her throat. 'Alas, no. I have a previous engagement.'

'The afternoon after that, then?'

She took another gulp before replying, 'Do you know, it's odd, but I have yet another engagement then, and on the day after that, too.'

The blue eyes looking at her steadfastly were sorrowful. 'You are determined not to allow me to visit you at all, I collect.'

'You take my meaning exactly, sir.'

'Then I am tempted to ask my question now—and to the devil with etiquette.'

Jess's expression when he came out with this was a wonder. Panic-stricken, Georgie took another swig of her rum toddy—and overdid it!

Gasping and spluttering, her eyes watering as an excess

of hot liquid scalded her throat, she found that Jess's arms were around her once again. He was muttering, 'There, there,' and patting her back. Miss Walton, hands upraised, was exclaiming, 'Oh, Mrs Herron, did I overdo it with the rum toddy? Pray accept my excuses. I thought it would be a splendid end to the evening.'

'And so it is,' murmured Georgie, disentangling herself from Jess and half-grateful for the commotion since it had ended their verbal duel which he had been winning. 'It was my stupidity in forgetting that the liquid was hot which did the damage.'

In the face of Miss Walton's concern Jess was compelled to stand back and allow her to take over. She ordered a tumbler of cold water to be fetched for Mrs Herron after she had led Georgie to a sofa and told her to put her legs up. The reason for this last command was lost on Georgie, but she dutifully did as she was bid by her hostess.

The only untoward thing which happened after that was when the tumbler of water arrived, Jess, who had advanced to her side again, took it from the tray and, giving her a wink, handed it to her.

Oh, the wretch!

'Did I overset you, Mrs Georgie?' he said for her ears only. 'Don't be frightened of me. I love you.'

What a time and place to tell her! And, of course, he was only teasing her, as usual.

She took the water and turned her head away from him.

'You are not to speak to me so, sir,' she said frostily. 'I have not given you leave.'

His only answer was to shake his head and to bow. 'Not now,' he said in a low voice. 'I was wrong to raise such a matter here. Later—at another time and another place.'

Any answer she might have made to him was impossible,

for he had moved away from her to tell Caro to look after her and make sure that she arrived home safely.

And who made him my keeper? Georgie asked herself furiously—and could make herself no answer.

Chapter Ten

Beauchamp, the Less Important Personage, was reading an ill-spelled letter, and smiling as he did so. The information inside it not only amused him, but would enable him to administer a rebuke to a man whom he thought deserved it, and whose own ill-scrawled and uninformative letter he had just put down.

Picking up his quill pen, he dipped it into an ink-pot in order to scrawl a letter of his own.

'Tompkins!' he called peremptorily.

A harried clerk jumped to attention and exclaimed, 'Sir?', eager to show that he was always ready for action. He took the piece of paper his master handed to him and began to read it.

'Turn that draft into a letter, Tompkins, to be addressed to Sir Garth Manning, Baronet, Pomfret Hall, Netherton, Nottinghamshire, and submit it to me when you have done so.'

Beauchamp smiled to himself while he watched his clerk begin to write. His reprimand to Sir Garth had been, he thought, sufficiently strong to prod that idle fool into some useful action. Exactly what kind of useful action he couldn't imagine—knowing Sir Garth, the action might not even be useful—but so long as it stirred things up in south Nottinghamshire, what matter?

Everything had been far too quiet there for far too long and, if he were not to be harried by his master after the same fashion that he harried his own clerk, it was time he had some information to show him.

The devil of it was that he was privately of the opinion that there would never be any information, and that, contrary to official belief, Jesmond Fitzroy was not involved in any kind of minor treason or conspiracy against the Crown.

But who was he to disagree with his masters? He was paid to do as he was told and not to ask questions—other, of course, than those he addressed to his inferiors.

The arrival of the post at Netherton was always an event since life there was so quiet and even. The Luddite and other riots which had plagued the north Midlands had passed them by. The rick burnings and bread riots of East Anglia had been events to read about, not endure.

Consequently, any news from the outside world was gratefully received, and the more interesting letters from London were often passed around for the amusing gossip they contained to be enjoyed by a wider audience.

At Pomfret Hall the butler always brought the letters in and laid them on the breakfast table to be read and enjoyed either then or later. Sir Garth Manning rarely enjoyed his letters. They consisted mostly of bills and demands from his various creditors, with an occasional note from a crony asking to know when he was going to return to the capital.

This morning's post was no exception. While Caro retired to the drawing room to read a letter from her sister whose sole news consisted of the information that she was breeding again—her eighth—Sir Garth read his over his coffee and rolls. He had enjoyed a hard drinking session at an all-male dinner at the Bowlbys' the night before, and he bypassed the cold beef and ham and the dish of eggs on the sideboard with a disgusted grimace.

The grimace reappeared when he began to read his letters. On reaching the last one, not only did his grimace enlarge into a rictus, but he jumped to his feet with an oath, waving the offending piece of paper in front of him before he rushed into the drawing room to question his sister.

'Where the devil's Georgie?' he demanded rudely.

'Really, Garth,' moaned Caro, all petulance, 'how can you speak to me so? I am neither a servant nor one of your bully boys from town. Ask me a civil question and I shall give you a civil answer.'

'To hell with all that claptrap,' he returned coarsely. 'Where is the bitch?'

Caro clapped her hands over her ears. 'Oh, Garth, how can you? Such language! You can see for yourself that she's not here. She rose early and went for a ride before breakfast.'

'Did she, now? On her own? Or with that Johnny-cum-lately brute from nowhere, Fitzroy? And what sort of ride is she having with him, I ask you? Or is he giving her one—and not on a horse?'

'I shall faint, I know I shall,' exclaimed Caro, falling back against her cushions. 'No one has ever spoken to me like that before. How can you?'

'Easily,' said Sir Garth, waving his letter about.

The letter said in plain terms: 'May I remind you that your future safety depends upon your sending me complete and reliable information about the doings of Mr Jesmond Fitzroy. I shall be compelled to call off our bargain if you continue to neglect your duty to me and to your country.

'Immediately after reading your letter, which assured me

that you had nothing of importance to report, I was the recipient of another, which informed me that your sister-in-law, Mrs Georgina Herron, has formed a liaison with him and is in the habit of meeting him in his park for the purpose of making love.

'This information may not have seemed worthy of report to you, but it is not your business to judge what we deem to be important or not. One more dereliction of duty of this nature and you may no longer take our protection for granted.'

Fright, wounded pride and jealous rage warred within Sir Garth's none-too-reliable bosom. He had lusted after Georgie himself—and not only for her money. To learn that she had become Jesmond Fitzroy's mistress after refusing his own honourable proposal was the outside of enough.

And to think that her illicit goings-on might ruin him almost brought him to the verge of a syncope. He had to calm himself down, to remind himself that he must not betray from whence this information had come or he might be doubly ruined if she then passed on the news to Fitzroy.

What the devil could the man be doing to cause all this brouhaha?

He had no time for further self-questioning for Georgie, flushed and fresh from her morning ride, walked into the drawing room. She was wearing her boy's clothes again, damn her, which was enough to rouse a man at any time, but particularly after he had just discovered that she was apparently available to anyone, but not to him.

He thrust the letter into his pocket and keeping his voice steady, said, 'Good morning, sister-in-law. I trust that you enjoyed your morning ride.'

He heard Caro give a low moan of 'Not now, Garth,' but ignored her.

Georgie, who had enjoyed her ride—it had invigorated

her immensely—knew at once that something was wrong. Caro had raised a lace handkerchief to her eyes and was wailing gently into it. Sir Garth was staring at Georgie as though she had just grown another head.

'What is it,' she asked, sitting down by Caro, 'are you ill? Shall I send for a doctor?'

Before Caro could answer, Sir Garth said savagely, 'No, she's not ill. She's just succumbed to yet another fit of the vapours, and no wonder. I was about to tell her of your infamous conduct when you came in. Just to begin has reduced her to this state. I can't imagine how she will behave when I inform the pair of you that I know that you have become Jesmond Fitzroy's mistress and have been seen making love with him in the open in his Park, no less.'

Georgie, her face white, stared back at him, and said, unwisely she afterwards thought, 'Would it have been no more if I had been making love with him somewhere else? Indoors, in my bedroom, perhaps?'

Caro let out a shriek and fell forward on to the floor, sobbing gently into the carpet.

'Oh, Georgie, how can you say such things? Think of the scandal. And, Garth, how could you say this to her before me? How could you?'

'I offered you marriage, madam, and you scorned *me*.' Sir Garth was incandescent with rage. 'Scorned me in order to behave like a servant with her lover. To become that man's mistress. Well, I scorn *you*.'

Georgie did not answer him. She fell on her knees beside Caro, saying urgently, 'Do not take on so. There's really no harm done, you know, unless Garth tattle-tales this story about Netherton. And I really am not Jesmond Fitzroy's mistress, that I do assure you. Besides, what I care to do— or not do—is no concern of Garth's.'

Even Caro, in her muddled state, grasped that Georgie

had not denied Garth's accusation. She sat up and wailed, 'Suppose people find out? Whatever will they think?'

'No one will think anything if Garth holds his tongue, and I'm sure that he will.'

'Indeed, I shan't,' he threatened.

'Then I shall have to inform Netherton of the truth about *you*, shan't I?' said Georgie, her voice quite steady. 'Of how you are no longer received in any house in London, or any club, because not only did you cheat at cards, and renege on your debts, as a consequence of which you were compelled to resign your commission in the Guards, but that you also forged a note to obtain money to which you were not entitled.

'I'm not sure how you escaped the attention of the law for your varied crimes—but you have certainly been exiled from London because of them.'

Sir Garth, his face now as white as Georgie's had been, was too astonished to discover how much she knew about his past to do other than bleat feebly, 'How…?'

'How do I know? You forget who my husband was, I think. No, Sir Garth Manning, do not try to ruin me—you have too much to lose yourself.'

She knew that she sounded braver than she actually felt.

Caro, now back on the sofa, asked fearfully, 'Is this true, Garth?' And then, 'No, do not answer me, I see by your face that it is.'

'You see,' Georgie finished sweetly, 'the pot cannot call the kettle black, Garth, can it? I think I'll have my breakfast now, if you will both excuse me.'

Georgie didn't want breakfast—in fact, her appetite had quite disappeared. She drank coffee desperately, busily thinking over what had occurred. Well, that was a turn-up, was it not? And thank God for the fact that her late husband had kept little from her—including his knowledge of Sir Garth Manning's misdeeds.

The worst of it was that she would have to go herself to Jesmond House and tell Jess that they had been seen. Which brought her to the key question related to Garth's denunciation of her: who was it who had seen them and had told Sir Garth, not immediately, but a fortnight after she and Jess had enjoyed their Arcadian tryst?

Jess, unaware of the bombshell which Sir Garth had thrown at Georgie, had been asking himself some different questions of his own. Who was it who had hired someone to watch him? And for what purpose? Since he had returned from London he had kept a look-out himself, for there had undoubtedly been a spy in his camp if the London watcher had been telling the truth.

Either his instincts had deserted him or the man had been lying.

He wasn't happy with either explanation. It was more likely that the local watcher was a cleverer spy than the London one.

He had written to Ben Wolfe, telling him of the incident and asking him to make discreet enquiries in London. Like the inhabitants of Pomfret Hall, Jess often read his letters over breakfast and that morning one of them was an answer from Ben.

Very briefly it said that he had nothing to report. Jess's guess, made in his letter to him, that the major spy was in Nottinghamshire, was the most likely explanation, he thought. So that was a dead end.

Jess had wondered once or twice whether Sir Garth Manning might be involved, but the man was such an ass that even when—as at Banker Bowlby's all-male dinner the night before—he had asked Jess several pointed questions about his past, he could not be sure that it was other than idle curiosity which moved him.

He had just been fetched by the master carpenter to admire the refurbishment of the drawing room when Craig came to tell him that Mrs Charles Herron had arrived and wished to speak to him on a matter of some urgency.

Now what the devil could that be? By her behaviour the other night at Miss Walton's, she had made it plain that she had done with him, did not even wish him to visit her, and now here she was, asking to see him.

He could not deny that his heart leaped at the thought. He had never been so obsessed by a woman before and when he had taken her in his arms at Miss Walton's musical evening it had been hard work to let her go, she felt so delectably right there.

Of course he would see her and, when Craig ushered her in, the sight of her was like water in the desert to a man dying of thirst. For once she was dressed as though she were about to ride in Hyde Park: she even wore a little black top hat with a green cockade on it to match her eyes. Her boots were spotless.

Jess was not to know that she had deliberately changed out of her boy's clothes so as not to challenge him in any way when she met him.

He bowed low over her hand, and told her, his voice full of such love and admiration that, had Georgie not been so occupied with her undesirable news, she would have heard it and known how much he cared for her.

As it was she said a trifle breathlessly, 'I'm sure that you must be surprised to see me here.'

'Not at all,' he told her. 'What more natural than that you should wish to speak to me again.'

The quirk of his right eyebrow when he came out with this amused Georgie mightily despite her inward distress.

'Oh, Fitz,' she exclaimed, laughing, 'how like you. You're never surprised, never overset, are you?'

'Except once,' he answered her, 'recently—as you well know.'

She nodded and bit her lip. 'It's about that I've come. Something rather dreadful has happened. That afternoon— we were seen.'

Jess's expression changed. He became instantly alert.

'Who saw us? Is it general knowledge?'

She shook her head at him. 'As to who, I have no idea who it was. And no, it is not, I believe, general knowledge. But this morning, out of the blue, Sir Garth Manning told me that we had been seen making love—in the open.'

'Sir Garth Manning?'

Georgie nodded. 'He accused me before breakfast. In front of Caro. I thought that you ought to know so that we both tell the same story—if we have to tell one, that is.'

'In front of Caro? That must have set the cat among the pigeons.'

What a comic picture that summoned up!

Georgie could not help herself. She began to laugh. 'Indeed, it did. I think that it was a help to me, though—it created such a splendid diversion. If I couldn't think what to say to Garth, then I attended to Caro.'

'Tell me, Mrs Georgie, did you admit that this dreadful accusation was true?'

'Not in so many words. I didn't deny it, either. I'm afraid I did what Charles advised me to do if ever I was in difficulties—I equivocated.'

'Do forgive me,' Jess said, 'if I tell you that I wish that I had been there. Seeing that you said neither yes nor no, is your ass of a brother-in-law going to broadcast our shame all over Netherton?'

Georgie shook her head again. 'I rather think not,' and,

when Jess raised his brows at her, added, 'You see, I then blackmailed him.'

'You did? How did you manage that?'

'Not long before he died Charles told me about Sir Garth's past. I think that he did so to prevent me from marrying him. Why he thought that I would ever do so, I can't imagine. I've always detested the man.'

'What excellent taste you have, Mrs Georgie. May I know of his past?'

'Indeed, you may,' and Georgie told him.

'A liar, a rogue, a loose fish and an embezzler,' said Jess thoughtfully. 'That interests me.'

'The trouble is, Fitz, if Garth knows, who else might know?'

She was calling him Fitz again, a good sign, and she had not rebuked him for calling her Mrs Georgie. In between having these cheering thoughts, Jess's brain was busy working in quite another direction.

'Tell me something, Mrs G. You said this happened before you had breakfast—had the post come?'

'Yes, it had, and there's an odd thing, Fitz. Later, after I had tried to eat some breakfast, Caro sent for me and actually apologised for Garth's behaviour. She said that it was most strange. He hadn't mentioned our affair—he called me your mistress—while she breakfasted with him. It was only later after she had gone to the drawing room that he came in shouting about us and waving a letter.'

'Did he, indeed?'

'Could someone have sent Garth a letter which said that we had been seen—and, if so, who? After all, we were quite a long way away from either the Hall or Jesmond House, and we never saw anyone the whole time—or heard them. I met no one on the way home. And why should they tell Garth?'

Jess said thoughtfully, 'I had the feeling, when I was dressing, that someone might be watching. I looked about, but I couldn't see anyone, either—which doesn't prove that there hadn't been someone spying on us.'

He couldn't tell Georgie that he knew that he was being watched—he wanted neither to worry her nor to make her a target of whoever was trailing him. He was certain now that there was a spy in his camp—but why, and for what purpose, should that spy inform Sir Garth that he had seen him and Georgie making love?

She looked so anxious, his poor darling, that he said, 'Let me ring for Craig to bring us some tea and some Sally Lunns. From what you have told me, I don't think that this will go any further and, if it does, why, you can always marry me and then we may make love where we like.'

'Don't fun, Fitz,' said Georgie, a trifle reproachfully. 'And yes, I would like some tea and Sally Lunns—I couldn't eat any breakfast after Sir Garth's imitation of Othello accusing Desdemona. You know, I really said some terrible things to them both—but it did answer.'

'More than ever I wish that I were there. You have a nice line in invective, Mrs G. And, bye the bye, I wasn't joking when I asked you to marry me. I really meant it.'

'Oh, Fitz, don't think that you have to make an honest woman of me, just for one afternoon's piece of folly. Not that I *am* a dishonest one. Indeed, Charles once said...'

She stopped, her face losing the gay insouciance which it had worn while she had told him her news, so that Jess did not ask her what Charles had once said. Nor did he repeat his offer. For some reason, perhaps some kind of self-protection, she was not taking him seriously, and when all was said and done this was not a propitious occasion on which to make her a profession of undying love—however much he wished to do so.

She was such a gallant creature, so unlike most of the women he had known—other than Susanna Wolfe, that was. He was about to tell her so when Craig and a footman arrived with tea, Sally Lunns and something which Georgie informed him were Bosworth Jumbles.

Up went his eyebrows again. 'Bosworth Jumbles, eh? What are they, and why have I never been served them before?'

'A very tasty sweet biscuit,' Georgie told him, and added, laughing, 'I expect that the servants save them for their own consumption—I know ours do.'

'Then these must be a tribute for you,' Jess said. He already knew from something that Craig had said that the servants both at the Hall and Jesmond House liked Mrs Herron. 'Very considerate where the staff are concerned,' Craig had told him so smoothly that Jess had wondered whether there had been any purpose in his chance remark.

Georgie had arrived with a high colour and a distracted manner, but sitting eating an impromptu meal with Fitz, exchanging gently mocking words with him, her colour lessened and her manner became less disturbed. Jess had been so cool about the whole business that she had almost begun to think that she was making a fuss about nothing.

And yet...

And yet... Some instinct, as old as Eve, whispered to her that Jess's calm was on the surface only. The same instinct told her to say nothing to him. He had joked with her while they ate, but when he had drunk his last cup of tea he had set it down before saying more seriously, 'Pomfret Hall was not the only place to be exercised by His Majesty's Mails. I have to tell you that some useful news about Banker Bowlby arrived by today's post. You will forgive me if I do not pass it on to you, but it is essential that no one, absolutely no one, but Kite and I know of it.

All I can say is that your sister-in-law's worries may be over in the near future—but do not tell her so.'

'Indeed, not,' replied Georgie with one of her infectious grins. 'Had you seen her this morning you would know that it is not wise to tell her anything.'

'"Where ignorance is bliss, 'tis folly to be wise,"' quoted Jess, matching Georgie's grin.

'Unkind but true,' Georgie agreed. She decided to change the subject to something less serious. 'Have you been invited to supper at the Firths' this evening?'

'My invitation was delivered to me by the fair hand of the lady herself. I understand that her brother is visiting Netherton and she wishes to have the privilege of introducing him to us, or us to him, I wasn't quite sure which of us was supposed to be the more privileged. I understand he is a very learned gentleman, Dr Maynard Shaw by name.'

Georgie's mobile face changed its expression yet again. Something almost of distaste rode on it.

'You didn't know,' Jess asked, 'that Dr Maynard Shaw was in Netherton?'

'No,' said Georgie. 'I didn't. Had I—' She stopped, and then continued, 'Had I known, I would not have accepted the invitation—pleaded a megrim…or something.'

'You know him, then?'

'Too well,' said Georgie simply. 'I can't cry off, Fitz, not now that I have accepted. It would be cowardly of me.'

'My Mrs Georgie is never cowardly,' Jess declared. 'May I know why you wish to avoid him, or would you prefer not to tell me?'

She hesitated again, and then hesitated no more. After all, she and Fitz had shared the ultimate which men and women could, and for all her distress over his apparent betrayal of her, she loved him still, and loving him, perhaps she ought to trust him a little.

'He is a bad man,' she said simply. 'He shared Charles's freethinking ideas—particularly those which relate to women being as free to love where they please as men, not considering their duty to their parents or their husbands. Worse than that, I have reason to know that he is treacherous.'

For a moment her eyes shone as though tears were about to fall.

Jess put a hand out to take hers. 'Suppose that I were to promise to protect you tonight, Mrs G. If so, you could go to the Firths' knowing that I would be there to act as your knight—you could give me that pretty handkerchief which you carry at your belt as my favour.'

'Oh, Fitz,' she sighed, 'your kindness makes me ashamed of my cross words to you on our fatal day. But I have to inform you that he is such a snake that you might need to protect yourself as well as me. You know, in Shakespeare's *Hamlet*, Hamlet says "that one may smile, and smile, and be a villain". That describes Dr Maynard Shaw precisely.'

'I am warned,' said Jess, 'and shall be ready for him.' He was not mocking her. He was beginning to respect Georgie's judgement. If she disliked Dr Shaw then she had good reason. And if she were not telling him why she disliked Dr Shaw, then he was not telling her of the nature of the evidence with which he shortly hoped to snare Banker Bowlby—so they were quits.

When he had first met her he had dismissed her as an impulsive creature, frank and free, always giving way to the mood of the moment. But the more he knew of her the more he realised that she had depths which the outward woman never revealed. He now knew that she could practise discretion as well as frankness—if the occasion demanded it.

Moreover, from the few references she had made to her husband and to her marriage, he was beginning to grasp that it had been a difficult one, which was not surprising, after all, given the discrepancy between their ages. There was no doubt that Dr Charles Herron had educated his young wife as though she were a boy whom he had been tutoring for a degree—but in what other ways had he educated her, or tried to educate her?

Again, this was not the time or the place to find out. Instead, he took from her the handkerchief for which he had asked, and which he kissed and tied into the buttonhole of his superfine navy-blue jacket.

'And I am forgiven, I hope,' he said gravely, 'for prying into your affairs. Believe me, it was as much for your protection as for anything else.'

Georgie had risen and was looking shyly at him. 'Yes,' she said simply, 'I forgive you, but that does not mean that we can behave again like we did that afternoon—not only was it morally wrong, but it was also—as events have proved—dangerous.'

The look which she gave him when she finished speaking was so winning that it nearly destroyed all Jess's good resolutions. He was hard put not to take her in his arms again. He was saved not only by the caution which ruled his life, but also because he did not want any rash action of his to hurt her.

He wanted to propose to her, but in her present mood that might be fatal to all his hopes. She was not prepared, after their love passage, to take his offer seriously, thinking that he would only be doing so in order to protect her good name and not because he truly loved her. Jess had learned patience in a hard school and now he was having to practise it in order to win his love when the time was ripe for him to propose.

So he placed his unruly hands behind his back lest they betray him again, and escorted her to the front door, saying, as he threw her up on to her horse, 'We shall meet again this evening, I hope—and, remember, I shall be wearing your favour.'

Georgie flourished her whip at him in salute and rode off down the drive. She had not brought a groom with her and the journey back to Pomfret Hall was a short one. If Jess, watching her ride away, was happier than he had been since she had left him alone and naked in the Park, Georgie also was recovering much of the joy in his company which she had temporarily lost on that unhappy afternoon.

Only when the turn of the bend in the drive hid her from his sight did Jess make his way back into the house in order to ponder on what she had told him about Sir Garth Manning—and she had told him more than she knew.

There was no doubt in his mind that the information about his and Georgie's love-making had come from the local spy in his camp of whom his follower in London had spoken. It was plain, given the lapse in time between the event and Sir Garth's reproaching Georgie with it, that it was not he who had seen them. He was not the kind of rogue who would have kept the information to himself but would have confronted her with it immediately.

This reading of his character was supported by the fact that Caro had told Georgie that Sir Garth had lost his temper with her after reading a letter which had only arrived that morning. Consequently, the questions which occupied Jess were three in number. Firstly, who was it who had informed Sir Garth? Secondly, why had they done so? And thirdly, what was Sir Garth Manning's role in this odd business?

He had never been so puzzled in his entire life, for he could not think of any reason why any person or persons should need to keep watch on a man who had retired from the hurly-burly of City life in order to turn himself into a country gentleman living on his acres.

The only current business in which he was engaged was the business of Banker Bowlby; he could not bring himself to believe that such a relatively minor matter lay behind the vast conspiracy against him which this was turning out to be.

The only immediate action he could think of would be to suborn Sir Garth in some way and twist the truth out of him about the origin of the letter and why it had been sent to him. How, though, could he do that without causing gossip and scandal? And what a foolish question that was, to be sure, for had he not spent much of his life in the City solving exactly such problems?

He was sitting at his desk in the library when he reached this point in his musings, Kite was working at a table behind him, and the noise of hammers was coming in through the windows where the workmen were erecting scaffolding at the side of the house prior to painting the woodwork.

Inspiration struck—he would attack Sir Garth through his weaknesses. He laughed aloud at the thought of reverting to the buccaneering days of his early work for Ben Wolfe. The true man who lay behind the mild mask which Jesmond Fitzroy had assumed when he came to live in Netherton would reappear for a moment in order to frighten Sir Garth Manning into submission.

Kite looked up as Jess's laughter rang out and he immediately recognised its nature. A smug smile crossed his face before it disappeared as quickly as it had arrived. So— Mr Jesmond Fitzroy was going to hunt big game again, was he? Whose head was he going to hang as a trophy on the walls of his mind this time?

Chapter Eleven

The evening was warm and at Highcross House, the Firths' new-built mansion on the outskirts of Netherton, all the windows in the supper room had been opened to let in the night air. A long table had been laden, picnic fashion, and guests were invited to fill their plates and to sit down where they pleased, either inside or outside where wooden seats were ranged along a flagged walk which skirted beds of flowers and sweet-scented herbs.

This was after a small reception had taken place during which the assembled Nethertonians were, one by one, introduced to Mrs Firth's distinguished brother, Dr Maynard Shaw. The guests knew that he was distinguished because Mrs Firth had so informed them when making her invitations. Only Georgie knew what the true nature of Dr Shaw's fame consisted of; from what Mrs Firth had said when she had given Georgie her invitation, she was quite unaware of it.

Certainly she was unaware that he was a freethinker, a great friend of many whom she would have regarded as infamous. His intimates included the devout follower of Rousseau, William Godwin, whose wife Mary Wollstonecraft had written in revolutionary terms of the Rights of

Women, and who was the father-in-law of the poet and extreme radical, Percy Bysshe Shelley, who had run away with Miss Mary Godwin, the Godwins' young daughter, while he still had a wife alive.

All this Georgie knew, but she had never said anything of it to her family who knew nothing of the true nature of her life with Dr Charles Herron.

Dr Shaw smiled greasily at her when Mrs Firth introduced her to him. He bowed low over her hand, reluctantly offered in return for his. 'Oh, my dear sister,' he intoned, 'Mrs Herron needs no introduction to me. Many is the time that I have dined with her and her late husband. I cannot say how great is the pleasure with which I renew my acquaintance with you, madam,' and his greedy eyes devoured her.

Jess, who was next in line after Georgie to be introduced to the great man, took instantly against him. He rightly read the Doctor's lubricious stare and saw Georgie's slight shiver when he had clutched her hand to his bosom. The rest of the company saw only polite admiration, particularly when he went on to say, 'I trust that, after supper, I may have the pleasure of a longer conversation with you, my dear.'

What could Georgie do—well aware that every word they uttered could be heard by the whole assembly—but give a brief and graceful assent? Neither Jess's presence, nor his wearing her favour, could assist her here in this quiet, civilised room. They were not living in the Middle Ages where, at a word from her, Jess would have attacked the good doctor with his broadsword. Indeed, it was immediately apparent when Jess was introduced that any attacking would be done by the Doctor using his tongue on Jess!

Both Georgie and Jess were later privately agreed that

Mrs Firth must have informed him before the party began that Mrs Herron and Mr Fitzroy were good friends for, on being introduced, Dr Shaw said thoughtfully, 'Jesmond Fitzroy, eh? An interesting surname, yours. I believe that it was often given to the illegitimate offspring of the Royal House. Was there not a Miss Anne Jesmond who was a great…friend, shall we say…of Frederick, Prince of Wales, the father of the late King George III?'

'Possibly so,' replied Jess coolly, as he heard a collective gasp from all the other guests except Georgie who, as Charles Herron's pupil, was more used to such plain speaking, 'but she is no concern of mine, I do assure you. My family name originates from the Welsh Marches and goes back to the Middle Ages. I may, perhaps, be the descendant of a Plantagenet bastard, although I think not, but I am scarcely a Hanoverian by-blow.'

He felt safe enough in telling this thundering lie for the Jesmonds had never boasted of their illegitimate Royal connection and had never used it to gain—or lose—favour from any quarter. So far as he knew from his examination of Miss Jesmond's archives, all but one of the papers relating to his ancestress and the Prince had been destroyed, so he felt safe in telling it. Miss Jesmond had been particularly ruthless in determining that the family name should not be sullied by the association.

'Interesting.' The Doctor smiled. 'I do so hope that my question did not disturb you. I meant no offence by it, particularly as I consider that the whole business of marriage and legitimacy is an absurd invention designed to fetter the natural instincts and behaviour of men and women, thus rendering them unhappy.'

'Rest assured that you have not rendered me unhappy,' returned Jess smoothly, 'although I am not entirely certain how I would behave if I gave vent to my natural instincts in answering you. Were I to do so, you might not be so sure that exercising our natural instincts is always either wise or beneficial.'

If Dr Shaw—and the company—was aware that he had been given a polite and elaborate rebuke he gave no sign of it, and nor did they. Only Georgie was stifling her giggles in her handkerchief and telling herself gleefully that Jess would certainly have given Dr Shaw a mighty blow with his lance or broadsword if they had been living in the Middle Ages and the Doctor had informed the company that he was the descendant of a Royal bastard!

One of the guests, on hearing the mention of a Miss Anne Jesmond and of Jess's possible connection with the Royal family—which he had denied—grew exceedingly thoughtful. Sir Garth Manning immediately asked himself a question. Was that the reason why the authorities wanted Fitzroy watched? If so, whatever for? It all seemed very distant, but perhaps Fitzroy was engaged in activities which might be dubious if it were known that he had this backhand connection with the ruling house. Like more than one of Jess's hearers, Sir Garth was sure that he was not telling the truth about his origin.

After that small burst of scandalous excitement matters grew a little duller, except that Jess was aware that more than one of the guests was staring at him in order to try to trace any resemblance to the Royal family in his face. Mrs Firth, a little troubled by her brother's tactless remarks, approached him when all the introductions were over and the party was streaming in to the supper room.

'Take no notice of my brother, Mr Fitzroy,' she trilled at him. 'He means nothing by his frank manner. You must understand that to these great men matters which we try to avoid are the very staple of life and discussion.'

'Oh, indeed.' Jess smiled back at her. 'I take no note of

him, no note at all. Stale and idle gossip, whether it comes
from a fool or an eminent scholar, should never be dignified
by being heeded, don't you agree?'

Like Dr Shaw before her, Mrs Firth was not sure whether
she was being rebuked or not. Jess appeared to be his usual
mild and charming self, smiling at her as he spoke.

'Oh, yes, I do agree,' she told him after a short pause
while she collected herself. 'And now, pray, do enjoy yourself in the supper room. The chef has excelled himself tonight and we must repay the compliment he has done us
by eating heartily.'

She turned to a passing footman, snatched two glasses
of white wine from his tray, handed one to Jess and trilled
at him again, 'Let us drink to your arrival in Netherton, sir,
and may your stay here be long and happy.'

Georgie came up to him when Mrs Firth had taken herself off, still trilling desperately. 'You know, Fitz,' she told
him, her face alight with mischief, 'I think that we made a
mistake this afternoon. *You* should have given *me* a favour
so that I could have defended you from my *bête noir*. That
wretched man made a dead set at you, and I have been
asking myself why, and the only answer which I can think
of is that Mrs Firth told him that we are great friends and...'

She paused and coloured a little. 'You will think me
conceited, I know, but while Charles was alive he pursued
me assiduously and ruthlessly. I do believe he's jealous of
you.'

'My thought also,' replied Jess wryly.

'But you gave as good as you got. Rather better, in fact.
I was proud of you. He usually wins exchanges like that.'

'Um,' said Jess, 'but remember that he couldn't go too
far in being frank before his rustic audience. He was a bit
daring as it was.'

'I won't ask you the question which everyone is dying

to put to you,' said Georgie naughtily, 'which is: were you telling the truth about your ancestry?'

'And I shan't answer you—or rather, I shall refer you to the one I gave to Dr Shaw.'

'You know, Fitz, I have misjudged you, I think—and so has Netherton. I do believe you're a very devious person. Sometimes, I think that I know you very well—and then I think that I don't know you at all. Very worrying.'

'I could say the same of you,' countered Jess, 'but I won't. Mrs Firth tells me the food is superb. Shall we repair to the supper room while there is still some left?'

'With pleasure, sir, if you will allow me to take your arm.'

Two jealous pairs of eyes followed them as they walked along, smiling and talking. Dr Maynard Shaw and Sir Garth Manning had only one thing in common—a deep desire to make Georgie either their wife or mistress, and an equally deep desire to do an injury to Jesmond Fitzroy, her apparently favoured escort.

Jess had scarcely filled his plate before someone tapped his shoulder from behind. It was Banker Bowlby, already scarlet in the face from over-eating and over-drinking. 'Interesting, that, Fitzroy. Often wondered where the name came from, now I know. No offence meant, I'm sure.'

The smile which he offered Jess on coming out with this was such a knowing leer that Jess regretted that he could not indulge himself by displaying the natural instincts of which Dr Shaw had spoken and knock it off his face.

'Happy to hear that you learned something this evening, Bowlby. Not usual on such occasions.'

'No, indeed,' Bowlby agreed, bringing his fat face so close to Jess's that his proposed victim was almost overwhelmed by his foetid breath. 'Thought about what we discussed at our last meeting, Fitzroy? Expected to have heard from you by now. Kite proving difficult, eh? How about a little discussion of our own on the matter? Could advise you on how to deal with him.'

Georgie, standing by, holding a full plate in one hand and a glass of white wine in the other, and who had over-heard and resented Bowlby's impudent hectoring of Fitz, put in her oar.

She said cheerfully, echoing what he had earlier re-marked to Jess, 'Mr Bowlby, no offence meant, I'm sure, but if it is business which you are proposing to discuss with Mr Fitzroy, this is neither the time nor the place in which to do it. The bank parlour would appear to be a more nat-ural venue. My husband, Dr Charles Herron, the Duke of Durness's cousin, always declared that discussing money in any other place was the height of bad manners. I thought that you might like to know that,' she finished brightly with the air of one offering useful and necessary advice.

Banker Bowlby glared at her, fortunately unaware of Jess's grin which grew broader with every word Georgie uttered. He had always disliked Georgie. He thought that she was a bad influence on Mrs Caroline Pomfret and would have disliked her even more if he had known that she had set Jess on his trail. Had Jess not been present, he might have tried to give her a savage put-down, but some instinct warned him that it might be unwise.

He swallowed and came out with, 'Oh, ladies never un-derstand business, do they, Fitzroy? Their pretty little heads were not made to cope with such difficult matters. That is doubtless why your late husband said what he did.'

'On the contrary,' Georgie declared after drinking down some of her wine, 'he made a point of ensuring that I *was* able to cope with such difficult matters.' She sighed sen-timentally. 'His manners were always perfect, though, and it distresses me when so many forget themselves these days. It is then that I miss him most.'

Had she possessed a free hand she would have pulled out her handkerchief to wipe away a tear each time that she mentioned Charles, but had to make do with bending her head slightly and looking distressed instead. Banker Bowlby, harassed, aware that he was being baited but unable to think of any suitable response, looked wildly about him, saw his wife in the distance and announced that it was time that he looked after her, Mrs Herron must excuse him.

'Indeed I will,' was Georgie's parting shot. 'I'm always ready to excuse you, Mr Bowlby.'

Jess choked over his wine, and said to Georgie when Bowlby was out of earshot, 'Am I to believe all that piff paff you were talking, Mrs G? Or was it simply your way of putting down that fat, dishonest fool?'

'Partly,' she told him as he guided her to one of the benches in the open. 'Charles did teach me double-entry book-keeping and how to read a balance sheet. He was very far from being one of your unworldly clerics and he made the fortune which his father left him even greater, rather than frittering it away as many do.'

'A regular female Rothschild, are you, Mrs G? I think that I shall come to you for advice the next time I need any.'

'Which will be never, Fitz. I think that I have smoked you out. You needn't answer me if you don't wish to, but I do believe that you use Kite as a diversion—but don't worry, I shan't tell Banker Bowlby!'

She was even shrewder than he had thought and his respect for her grew. At the same time, the knowledge that he couldn't take her into his arms and tell her so—with trimmings—was beginning to distress him physically. There, in the moonlit garden, as he watched Georgie's green eyes shining in the dark, and her delectable scent filled his nostrils, his arousal was so great that it was painful.

'Witch,' he exclaimed hoarsely. 'I don't know when I desire you most: either when you are exercising your wit on fools, or when you are doing nothing but sitting by me, simply being Mrs Georgie in the moonlight. Either way you tempt me to follow the natural instincts of man of which the greasy Doctor spoke and have at you immediately, forgetting decorum—and the outrage of my fellow guests if I should do any such thing!'

Georgie, her plate and glass now empty, began to laugh. 'Oh, Fitz, how did I manage to live without you? I am right, am I not? What you are, and what you appear to be are two quite different things. You are so damnably clever that I, for one, don't believe in that cock-and-bull story about your ancestress and the Prince of Wales!'

Jess took her hand and held it gently between his own, even though to touch her was painful. 'Now, dear Mrs G., do you think a clever man would ever tell you the truth if to do so was unwise? That being so, don't expect me to answer that last question of yours. If you are truly the clever woman I think you are, you already know the answer.'

If he was having difficulty in preventing himself from falling on her, Georgie was in similar difficulties with him. She withdrew her hand from his and said, imitating her late husband when tutoring an undergraduate, 'To answer with an evasion, sir, is no answer at all. Propositions and plain statements only, if you please.'

Jess began to laugh. 'Is that what I would have been put through if I had gone to Oxford or Cambridge.'

'Oh, yes. Charles was very good at it. Guaranteed to frighten the wits out of every young man he tutored.'

'And what about his one young woman?' riposted Jess.

He was letting her know how much he had discovered about her life with Charles Herron and hoping that this time she would not hold it against him.

She didn't.

Instead she looked steadily at him and said, 'I wasn't clever enough to be frightened of him. That came later. To begin with, it was all wonderful. Keats wrote of being like Cortes and seeing the New World for the first time. That was exactly how I felt…'

'And later,' prompted Jess as she fell silent.

'Later—well, when I had, in Charles's words, graduated from the simpler knowledge of life—he introduced me to its more complex aspects. And after that he no longer found me a model pupil.' She stopped again.

'Why was that, Mrs G.? You appear to me to have an excellent grasp of life's complexities.'

Georgie decided to be truthful. 'The complexities to which Charles wished to introduce me were not those of which I could approve because they offended against my moral sense.'

'Ah,' said Jess thoughtfully. 'Like Dr Maynard Shaw, among other things, he wished to free you from following the absurd conventions which prevent men and women from following their natural instincts.'

'Exactly. I can't talk about it, Fitz. I had been so happy, you see, enjoying my new world and pleasing my master, and then I couldn't.'

Her voice had grown very low. Jess decided not to ask her any more questions and they fell silent for a little time. The empathy which had grown up between them was so strong that Jess could almost feel her misery. He wanted to put an arm about her to comfort her, but daren't. Instead he said, his voice low and tender, 'You know that I do love you, Mrs Georgie, and I would never ask you to do anything which would offend against your strong sense of what is fitting.'

He felt her quiver and she turned towards him, her eyes brimming with unshed tears... They had reached a watershed in their relationship and Jess was on the point of achieving his heart's desire when Caro Pomfret's petulant voice broke in on them. 'Oh, there you are, Georgie, we wondered where you had hidden yourself away. Apparently you promised to renew your friendship with Dr Shaw after supper, but you were nowhere to be found.'

'Quite so,' echoed Sir Garth who had been escorting his sister.

Georgie's eyes flashed dangerously. 'Hidden myself away,' she repeated incredulously. 'Mr Fitzroy and I have been sitting here in the open, in full view of everyone, quietly eating our supper. And, if Dr Shaw is so desirous of speaking to me, I wonder why he has not come looking for me himself.'

'Quite so,' said Jess maliciously, but managing to look angelic even as Sir Garth shot an inimical glare at him.

'Well, now that we have found you, you may accompany us to the rose garden where Dr Shaw is waiting for you.'

'By no means,' said Georgie, making no attempt to rise and join them. 'Dr Shaw may wish to renew his friendship with me, but I have no desire to resume my acquaintance with him. I would rather leave at once.'

'Should you need any assistance, I would be glad to drive you home,' interjected Jess.

'Certainly not, Fitz, although I thank you for your kind offer. I came in my own carriage—and I have no intention of leaving. I am enjoying myself immensely and intend to continue doing so! I was about to ask Fitz to accompany me to the supper table in order to refill my wine glass, and that still remains my immediate intention.'

'Only too happy to oblige, Mrs G. I'm a little thirsty myself. Do stand aside, Manning, and allow Mrs Herron to pass by you. You are in her way.'

He was, indeed, one arm extended towards her and saying earnestly, 'I am sure that your sense of what is proper will convince you that you ought to accept my offer to walk you to the rose garden...'

Georgie, enraged by this impolite blackmail, and aware that they were beginning to attract curious glances and raised eyebrows, pushed by the importunate baronet, saying in a low, but determined, voice, 'My sense of what is proper instructs me to avoid Dr Shaw at all costs. Fitz, your arm, please. I am most exceedingly thirsty.'

Jess shook a rueful head at the brother and sister as if to say, *You see how things are*, and did as Georgie bid him.

'Was that wise?' he asked her when they were back in Highcross House again.

'No, it wasn't, Fitz. But Caro and her brother are not my guardians. I have no notion why they were so insistent on me meeting that dreadful man, but I am beginning to wish that I had taken the coward's way out and pleaded a migraine this evening. I dislike Sir Garth Manning nearly as much as Dr Shaw, they have both in their different ways contrived to make my life miserable. Garth, I can hold off for he is a fool, but Dr Shaw is a clever, cunning man—as you must have guessed from the manner in which he tried to cut you down.'

'Agreed on both counts. And, Mrs G., I will not think you a coward if you wish to leave at once. You may plead a headache, the vapours, or anything you wish, for I don't like to watch you being bullied when I can do little about it. I hope that you will allow me to take you home, for I don't care to think of you being alone on the journey back to Pomfret House. I came in my curricle and I think a drive in the open will blow the cobwebs away.'

Georgie surrendered. She made her adieux to the Firths, resisting their efforts to make her say farewell to the Doctor—'he will be so sorry to have missed you'—and she was not happy again until she sat in Fitz's new carriage, bowling along in the moonlight.

What would it be like to sit in his carriage for life, as it were? Was she a fool to refuse him simply because she wasn't sure whether he was proposing to her out of pity? She looked at his strong profile, at his firm mouth and his determined chin and wondered why Netherton had fallen into the trap which he had set for them—the trap which said that he was an indolent country gentleman of so little steel that Banker Bowlby thought that he could bully him!

Neither of them said a word until Jess pulled up before the front entrance to Pomfret House.

'I think that you enjoyed that,' he said, for he had felt her breathing change and her body relax as she sat by him.

'Oh, yes, I did, and I have to thank you, Fitz.'

'It was nothing, Mrs G. I was happy to rescue you from the harpies. Before I leave you, I must tell you that in a few days' time I shall have to go to London on some business which Kite cannot do for me. Will you miss me, Mrs G.?'

'Oh, Fitz, you know I will.'

'Good, and remember this—' and he took her hand as he spoke '—I love you, Mrs G., and one day you will believe me, and then...'

He stopped and smiled down at her.

'And then, Fitz?' she asked shyly.

'And then, Mrs G., we shall see what we shall see. And now let me assist you to alight and to kiss the back of your hand before I leave you, for that is the most that I dare do for propriety's sake.'

So she held out her hand to him and the footmen, coming forward to light her in, thought what a splendid pair they made—and what in the world was Mr Fitzroy thinking of not to have proposed to her already!

Chapter Twelve

Decidedly, Jess told himself, he needed to do something about Sir Garth Manning—and soon, before he went to London. If he could discover what Manning was up to, he might then be able to kill two birds with one stone when he visited the capital.

He swiftly concluded that subtlety was out—strong-arm tactics might be best with such a cur. He knew that Sir Garth played cards every Friday night at the small gaming hall which formed part of the little Spa's amenities. It opened off a rotunda beneath which Netherton society drank water drawn from a well nearby, convincing themselves that in so doing they were improving their general health.

The stakes were so petty that Sir Garth could not ruin himself—in any case, he had done that already! Playing whist for shillings with rustic gentry gave him the illusion of still being a dashing actor in life's game. He drank heavily, too, something which Jess had already noticed, and was beginning to acquire debts which he had no means of paying, small though they were.

The evening over, Sir Garth invariably walked back to Pomfret Hall—he had no carriage of his own—and Caro's parlous financial situation had compelled her to reduce the size of her stable. He had tried to persuade Georgie to lend him her gig, but she had refused—Sir Garth had a heavy hand with horses.

Jess showed himself in the Spa's rooms that night. He played whist and was careful not to lose or to win too much. Sir Garth lost, but not heavily, and drank rather less than usual: he was probably beginning to worry about his growing debt.

At last he rose, announced, 'The devil's in the cards tonight,' emptied his glass and walked out. After a short interval Jess followed him—he had been seated on his own, reading the *Morning Post* as though it interested him mightily in order to ensure that no one came up to chat with him.

Outside there was a waning moon, half-covered with clouds. He could see Sir Garth ahead of him, walking slowly along, his head bent, the picture of dejection. Nothing, Jess thought, could be better. Sir Garth was already half-lost in himself and consequently would be unaware that he was being tracked. He followed his prey for about a quarter of a mile until he reached a bend in the road at the end of the village where a footpath led across fields.

Here was his opportunity. He ran quickly and quietly until he reached Sir Garth, when he flung an arm around his throat from behind and dragged him helpless off the main road and ran him down the footpath, gasping and spluttering, until they were out of sight and sound.

Once there Jess released him and stood back. Sir Garth, trying to recover his breath, was too frightened to run. He was clutching at his throat which was hurting him too much to shout. Between shock and fright and in the semi-dark he had not yet identified his attacker.

He pulled a purse from his pocket and thrust it at Jess. 'Take it,' he croaked. 'It's all I have, and let me go.'

Jess leaned forward and grasped Sir Garth by his cravat, pulling him until they were eye to eye. 'I don't want your damned money, Manning. I want something much more precious: information.'

'Fitzroy! What the devil do you think you're playing at? Release me at once and I'll not inform the constable, otherwise—'

'There *is* no damned otherwise, Manning. You won't say anything to anyone about this, I know too much about you.'

He twisted the hand which held Sir Garth's cravat until Sir Garth rose on his tiptoes, choking again, before he released him.

'Oh, by God, Fitzroy, you've gone mad,' he said when his voice returned at last. 'Have you been drinking?'

'No,' said Jess grimly, 'and I'm eminently sane. I'll let you go, relatively unharmed, if you'll tell me several things. Who was it who wrote the letter which told you about Mrs Herron and myself will do for a start?'

Sir Garth gulped. 'What letter?'

'Don't take me for a fool, Manning. I know all about the letter,' Jess lied, 'but I want to hear about it from you— and this is *my* otherwise...' He grabbed Sir Garth's cravat again and began to strangle him, quietly and efficiently.

Sir Garth's hands rose ineffectually to try to break Jess's grip. Somehow he managed to choke out, 'Let me go and I'll tell you. It was Beauchamp.'

Jess loosened his grip and stood back, saying, his voice a rapier in itself, 'Which Beauchamp, and why? Why the devil should he be writing to you about such a thing—and how did he come to know what I was doing in Netherton?'

'Courtney Beauchamp, at the Home Office. He said it was an affair of state.'

'What? What Mrs Herron and I should choose to do—

or not do—is an affair of state? That beggars belief, it really
does. Tell me more or I'll throttle you again.'

Sir Garth clutched at his abused throat. 'No…yes,' he
babbled. 'I'll tell you everything if only you won't touch
me again. He sent for me some time ago—I owed him a
kind of debt, you see. He threatened me with ruin if I didn't
keep a watch on you and then write to him, telling him of
everything you did. I didn't know about you and Georgie,
so of course I couldn't write to him about it—and then he
sent me a letter, renewing his threat to ruin me because I
wasn't aware of your affair, and giving me details about
what you got up to in the Park. He said I wasn't doing my
duty by my country by not keeping a proper watch on you.'

'Did he, indeed?'

'Yes, you see, he and m'lord Sidmouth, his master, have
another man here, keeping watch on you, but they thought
that I'd know more. But, dammit, Fitzroy, you never *do*
anything out of the ordinary, do you? And I can't invent
anything, they'd soon find me out if I did because of that
other man here and they'd know I was lying. For God's
sake, what *are* you getting up to, man? They seemed to
think you might threaten the State. Oh, God, I'm sure
you've done some permanent damage to my throat,' he
ended pathetically.

Jess was suddenly sure that the poor fool was telling the
truth—he was too frightened to do anything else.

'And that's all?'

'As God's my witness, yes! Has everyone run mad, Fitzroy, you included, tell me that?'

'No,' said Jess slowly, light breaking in.

The only thing about him which might worry Britain's
rulers was his descent from Frederick, Prince of Wales. He
was sure that was what lay behind this ridiculous farrago
of spying and conspiracy. He also thought that he knew

what Beauchamp and m'lord Sidmouth were frightened of, and he intended to do something about it—soon.

Sir Garth was staring at him as though he were the devil. Who would have thought that Jesmond Fitzroy, that rather indolent and mild-mannered man, would turn into something resembling a demon out of the pit—his pitchfork being the only thing lacking to complete the picture. Banker Bowlby had been so amusedly contemptuous of their new neighbour that everyone had followed his example in thinking him slightly lacking where wits were concerned.

Now Sir Garth, at least, knew better.

'For your information, although God knows why I should tell you,' said Jess slowly, all threat having left his voice after he had turned himself once again into the man that Sir Garth and Netherton thought they knew, 'I'm not getting up to anything. Some of our masters see conspirators in every corner of every room and under every bed. I assure you that I'm not a conspirator, in the past, now or in the future.

'Listen to me carefully. You will say nothing to anyone of what has passed tonight. You will continue to report to that ass Beauchamp, and I shall tell you what to send him. Tomorrow you will write a letter informing him that I shall be in London by the week's end, and that I'm quite excited about it. Oh, and that I had a bit of an argument with Dr. Maynard Shaw—that will give them something to think about.'

'Yes, yes, anything,' babbled Sir Garth, 'anything you please.'

Jess stepped back. 'If I need you again, I shall not hesitate to use you. And if I find out that you have breathed a word to anyone of any of this, then God help you, because I won't. I do hope you take that threat seriously, Manning.'

'Oh, I do, I do, Fitzroy. You do understand that I only

became involved in this wretched business because they threatened me with ruin if I didn't. I've nothing against you personally.'

Jess offered him an evil grin. He thought that it might be more intimidating than half-strangling the poor wretch again. 'Well, I've a great deal against you personally, Manning, and don't you forget it. One more thing. Stay away from Mrs Herron. If I hear that you have been persecuting her, you're cat's meat. That's all.'

Sir Garth backed away from him slowly.

'I can go now?'

'By all means. Your company is far too unpleasant for me to be able to stomach much of it.'

Jess watched him bound up the road before he began to laugh. It had been even easier than he had expected to gouge the truth out of him, and the whole business had the added bonus that Sir Garth Manning wouldn't trouble Mrs Georgie again.

And now he knew why Kite had seen Sir Garth in White-hall entering the Home Office.

Georgie, eating breakfast the next morning, was half-listening to Caro retailing Netherton gossip over coffee and rolls. 'Apparently Mr Fitzroy is leaving for London early tomorrow. His man Kite told Forshaw that he is visiting his tailor to be measured for new clothes. Did you know that he was going, Georgie?'

'He mentioned something to that effect the other night when he drove me home from the Firths, yes.'

Sir Garth, sitting opposite to them, was drinking coffee, an agonised expression on his face. Before him was a dismal concoction of bread and milk. He had developed, he had told them, his voice barely audible, a nasty case of laryngitis and could eat only invalid food.

'I do wish you'd let me call the doctor, Garth,' said Caro worriedly, 'you do look ill. I'm sure that he would give you something to ease the pain.'

'No, no,' he croaked hurriedly, thinking of the bruises on his neck about which any halfway competent physician would surely question him. 'No need, no need. I don't like being mollycoddled.'

There was something so desperate in his voice that Georgie, looking across at him said, feeling sorry for him for once, 'Caro's right, you look ghastly. You really ought to let the doctor examine you.'

Part of his extreme pallor was caused by his hearing that that devil Fitzroy was going to London. Was he going to peach on him to the Home Office, in order to add insult to injury? He rose hurriedly from his chair to prevent his officious relatives from bullying him further.

'I think that I'll retire to my room and rest a little,' he croaked. 'Best not to talk, eh?'

The moment that the door closed behind him Caro leaned forward to say confidentially to her sister-in-law, 'I think that something more than laryngitis is troubling him, you know. Ever since he came back to Netherton he's not been at all himself. He was a man who never worried about anything, but he really does look haunted these days.'

Georgie, who had little time for Caro's brother, nevertheless felt compelled to agree with her. Garth's insistence on refusing the ministrations of a doctor was most unnatural behaviour in a man who, despite what he had said earlier, had always coddled himself.

It was a pity that Fitz had taken himself off to London: she would have valued his opinion on the matter.

Every time Jess returned to London he liked it less. The place smelled vile, for one thing. The smoke pall over it could be seen from any approaching coach for many miles before one reached its boundary. In summer, the Thames reeked, and in winter it looked as though it was composed of oil, not water, on which floated unrecognisable objects which one knew one ought not to try to recognise. The reek of humanity in its crowded streets, largely unnoticed when he had lived there, was almost overwhelming to someone who had recently been breathing the purer air of Netherton.

Oh, the country had its smells, too, but they were of the earth, part of the common inheritance of man since the time of Adam. It also had the sweet scent of flowers, hedges and herbs, and even in London's many parks and open spaces the miasma of the town was never very far away.

This summer there was the added discomfort caused by the constant presence of the mob which supported Queen Caroline. They had now resorted to stopping coaches and passers-by and demanding that they shout 'Long live the Queen', threatening them if they refused to do so. They had already threatened the Home Secretary, Lord Sidmouth, when he was leaving a Cabinet meeting, and the Duke of Wellington had been compelled to supply him with an armed guard to protect him on his way home.

Jess's first port of call was Ben Wolfe's office in the City, for it was a letter from him, received before he had wrung the truth from Sir Garth Manning, which had made his journey essential.

'You were right,' Ben told him when they had shaken hands, 'to ask me to follow up both Clarke and Smythe over Banker Bowlby's possible debts. My latest informa-tion is that, despairing of ever recovering much of the money he had lent him, and fearing that if the bank failed he would get nothing, Clarke finally sold all Bowlby's debts and securities for a smallish sum to Smythe, who is one of the sprats of the usurers, picking up farthings where others pick up pounds.

'The word was that no one else was willing to touch them, so I contacted Smythe on your behalf—as you had asked—and he was only too happy to offload Bowlby's papers on to you for a sum which we agreed was fair to both parties.'

Ben named a price which Jess privately thought to be more of a bargain to him than to Smythe—who was doubt-less relieved to get anything for paper which was com-monly agreed to be worthless.

Jess nodded. 'My thanks,' he said briefly. 'You have saved me a deal of trouble.'

His friend's returning smile was a sardonic one, pro-voked by the fact that Jess was looking uncommonly mag-nificent—dressed to kill, in fact.

'Think nothing of it,' he said, 'and, by the by, I hope you're not going to visit Smythe togged out as though you were going to an audience with the King. He's sure to try to up the ante if you do.'

'Oh, I'm not visiting Smythe today. Today I shall go to Coutts to obtain a banker's draft for the sum you have negotiated. Tomorrow will do, and while I'm not going to an audience with the King your guess is not far off the mark.'

'You intrigue me, Jess, but I see by your expression that you aren't going to tell me what you're up to now. The best of luck in both your ventures, anyway. Country living not palling yet?—I thought that it would have bored you back to town by now.'

'Bored!' exclaimed Jess, laughing. 'No, I'm not bored, far from it, and do not expect to be.'

'And the ladies, Jess? Any Mrs Fitzroy in sight yet?'

Jess sobered immediately. 'Perhaps—and that's all I

shall say. I have hopes but I'm not inclined to bank on them yet—and nor should you, you old dog. I know that you and Susanna are dying to marry me off. Rest assured that when the right time comes I shall be at the altar ready and willing, but I don't think that the right time has arrived yet.'

'Good,' said his mentor. 'Caution still your watchword, I see. Well, best of luck with all your ventures—particularly today and tomorrow.'

Well, I shall certainly need some luck today, thought Jess in the hackney cab which was taking him to the Home Office in Whitehall, particularly as I'm going to be about as subtle with the Government as I was with Garth Manning the other night! If they let me in, that is.

Of course they would let him in, that was why he was dressed up like the dog's dinner, looking for once the rich man of power he actually was.

'I wish to see Mr Beauchamp, the under-secretary,' he drawled at the porter at the door, fetching out a quizzing glass on a gold chain and peering at him through it. 'Tell him that Mr Jesmond Fitzroy wishes to speak to him on a matter of some urgency.'

When told that he needed an appointment, he brought the quizzing glass into play again, and said wearily, 'No, I don't have an appointment, but, as I said, the matter is urgent; he would not thank you for denying me entrance.'

His entire manner was so haughty that the porter gave way and allowed him in—calling an attendant to take Mr Jesmond Fitzroy to Mr Courtney Beauchamp's office—at once.

Jess followed his guide down long corridors until they reached the office. His guide said, 'A moment, sir, if you please,' and vanished inside—to return a moment later saying, 'Mr Beauchamp will be pleased to see you immediately, sir.'

Will he, indeed? thought Jess with a wicked internal smile. I wonder if he will be quite as happy after I have finished with him? But he said nothing aloud and walked into a largish room where a smallish man was seated at a medium-sized desk.

The smallish man rose, walked round his desk and bowed at Jess. 'Mr Jesmond Fitzroy, I believe. What may I do for you, sir?'

Jess smiled, bowed back at him, pulled out his quizzing glass again and inspected the smallish man closely with it before saying in a languid, world-weary voice, 'There is little that you can do for me, sir, but I have an idea that your master, Lord Sidmouth, could do a great deal. Pray take me to him. I understand that he is in his office today.'

'Alas, sir,' said Mr Beauchamp, giving Jess a condescending smile. 'Lord Sidmouth only sees people by appointment, and then only those who are of the utmost importance. All others I am left to deal with. Pray state your business and I shall be delighted to either enlighten or assist you.'

'Would you, indeed?' returned Jess, waving his quizzing glass about. 'But I shall not be delighted to do business with you. I understand that my private affairs are considered by the Home Secretary to be so important that I am favoured with a constant and impertinent watch as ''a matter of state''. I believe that was the phrase used. That being so, I have not the slightest desire to be fobbed off by an underling. Please take me to him at once.'

He saw Beauchamp's face change when he quoted the words which Sir Garth had used, but he continued to hold his ground.

'Really, sir, I am at a loss to understand to what you are

referring. That being so, I cannot trouble Lord Sidmouth with your supposed affairs. You could, of course, submit your request to him in the form of a letter, but all that would achieve would be a reference back to me to speak to you—which you are already doing. Unless you raise some matter of real substance with me, I must ask you to leave. Should you refuse to do so, I shall call the guards who police these premises and ask them to remove you by force.'

Jess walked forward until he was standing directly before Beauchamp. 'You know quite well to what I am referring,' he said, 'and since you have made of my name and my family's origin something for the state to investigate I have come here to clarify certain matters for Lord Sidmouth, and to him, and to him alone, will I speak of them. For the last time, will you take me to him? I am told that his office opens off yours.'

'I dislike repeating myself, Mr Fitzroy—' Beauchamp began, his expression haughty, but he got no further, for Jess, pocketing his quizzing glass, had leaned forward and bent down a little until he was eye to eye with Beauchamp, saying in a conversational and chatty tone,

'Don't do so, then.'

'Allow me to finish, sir…'

Jess first raised his hand before his face in order to inspect it, saying, as though he were discussing something neutral like the weather, 'Useful things, cravats, and not just for wearing round one's neck, either—as, for example,' before using it to seize Beauchamp's cravat exactly as he had seized Sir Garth Manning's. He twisted it sharply, so that, like Sir Garth, Beauchamp gurgled with pain and fright.

'Unpleasant, isn't it?' queried Jess amiably. 'Don't trouble yourself to answer. Just lead me through that door into

Lord Sidmouth's room and I promise to release you at once. Otherwise…' and now he had both hands on Beauchamp's cravat '…otherwise—I don't think you'd like my otherwise.'

'You'll hang for this,' panted Beauchamp as Jess relaxed his grip a little so that he might speak.

'No doubt but, being dead as a door nail, you wouldn't enjoy the spectacle any more than I would. Just do as I say, there's a good fellow.'

'Under duress—and I shall see you suffer for this.'

'I think not,' Jess told him. 'Now take me in—and tell m'lord to dismiss his clerk.'

There was nothing for it but to do as he was told. Moaning gently and fingering his bruised throat Beauchamp knocked at Sidmouth's door, obeyed the command to enter and walked in, followed by Jess.

Lord Sidmouth, a serious-looking man of middle age who, years before, had been Prime Minister of England for a brief time, looked up from his desk, making no attempt to rise, and said irritably, 'What is it, Beauchamp? I told you that I was not to be disturbed.'

'It's Jesmond Fitzroy, m'lord. He manhandled me until I was compelled to bring him to you. I told him that you were busy and that he could do his business with me—and then he attacked me. I demand that the guard be sent for and that he be arrested.'

Before Sidmouth could answer, Jess said, 'I think, m'lord, that that would be most unwise. What I have to say to you would be extremely damaging if it became common knowledge. Send your two flunkies away and allow me to speak to you in private. You won't regret it, I promise you. Otherwise I shall go to the Radical press and provide them with information of the most inflammatory kind. The London mob would be happy to hear of it, too.'

He paused and added significantly, 'I am sure that you know of what I speak.'

Lord Sidmouth rose and walked towards Jess, examining him as Jess had examined Beauchamp. Inspection over, he said, 'I also see that you mean what you say. Very well, my two flunkies, as you call them, may leave.'

He stared Beauchamp's protests down and said coldly, 'Pray be silent, sir. I must also inform you that your silence must be absolute. Neither of you will say anything of what has passed today. Mr Fitzroy has not visited me. He saw you, Beauchamp, and was satisfied with what you had to tell him of the minor matter on which he came. You understand me?'

M'lord had spoken. Beauchamp and Sidmouth's clerk gave sullen assent and departed. Once they were alone, Lord Sidmouth said to Jess without offering him a seat and remaining standing himself, 'Now tell me at once what you have come here to say, and if the explanation for your cavalier conduct is not sufficient to satisfy me, I shall not hesitate to see you roundly punished for it.'

'Most proper,' said Jess. 'And when you have heard me out we shall be in agreement, I am sure, that nothing I have said will leave this room. Furthermore, you will call off your spies and agents who have been following me and fob Beauchamp off with some explanation which might not satisfy him but which he will not be able to challenge. You will agree never to contact me again, nor shall I again approach you. Furthermore, you will take no further action against me and mine after I have given you certain guarantees.'

Lord Sidmouth's face was a picture. 'You must surely understand that I cannot agree to all your proposals until I have heard you out. I can scarcely buy a pig in a poke. If, however, what you have to say is such that I can agree to what you wish, then I shall do so. I cannot say fairer than that. Other than that, I am all agog to hear what you have to tell me which is so important.'

Jess shook his head, 'Oh, no, m'lord, you are not. You know, or think you know, what I am about to prove to you.'

He took the piece of paper which he had found among his aunt's documents and handed it to Sidmouth.

'Read that, m'lord,' he said roughly, and stood back to look out of the window to m'lord's right which offered a view of Whitehall and its surrounding offices. A small crowd had gathered waving banners which proclaimed 'God save Queen Caroline'.

There was silence in the large, beautiful room from which England's internal affairs were run. Jess swung round to find Sidmouth staring at him.

'Yes,' said Jess in a low voice. 'It is what you think it is—or what you feared that it might be. It is a marriage licence: a record of a ceremony properly, though privately, conducted which married Frederick, Prince of Wales, to Miss Anne Jesmond. A legitimate marriage that was made before the Royal Marriage Acts were passed, which made the consent of the monarch mandatory before any member of the Royal Family could marry. The marriage was, and is, therefore a legal one and since Anne Jesmond did not die until long after Frederick married the Princess Augusta, the late King George III and all his descendants were, and remain, illegitimate, and my line is thus the true one.

'Is this the affair of state which troubled you, m'lord so that you had me watched and followed? Were you fearful that my Cousin George, who is unpopular and scarcely worthy to be King, could be dethroned if I were ambitious enough to make public this document—which you knew might still exist because rumour said that it did—and with

it try to claim my rightful inheritance to the joy of the mob
which hates him, thus raising the spectre of revolution
again? A spectre which, bearing in mind the conduct of the
London mob which has gathered outside this very office,
might suddenly acquire a body and power.

'You know that the situation of England is extremely
volatile, for I have been informed that when you go abroad
in your carriage you carry two pistols with you to defend
yourself from attack by the mob—an odd position for the
Home Secretary to be in!'

Sidmouth nodded.

'I believe that you were aware that Prince Frederick had
made this marriage, partly to spite his father, and that in
some way Anne Jesmond was later bought off—either by
money or by threats—but somehow she managed to keep
her marriage licence. It was a state secret so dangerous that
you never told Beauchamp or any of your flunkies of it.
You also knew that I am a man with a ruthless reputation
like that of my patron, Ben Wolfe, and feared that I might
therefore choose to exploit this knowledge.'

Sidmouth nodded again, still clutching the paper.

'Know this, then. I have not the slightest wish to dethrone, or try to dethrone, Cousin George. I would not be
a member of the Royal Family if you paid me. When I was
young and foolish this knowledge might have tempted me,
but now I am older and wiser and I am happy with my life.
I have made myself a rich man by my own efforts—and
when I found that piece of paper it changed nothing for
me.

'Now hand it back to me, please. It is mine.' There was
something of his Cousin George IV's arrogance in Jess's
speech as he said this, and for the first time there was a
hint of a resemblance to the Royal Family in his face and
bearing so that Sidmouth instinctively obeyed him.

Jess gave a rueful smile. 'What I am about to do may put me in danger, for it leaves me with no hold over you and may thus render me vulnerable, but I don't give a damn—I intend to live a quiet life in private with the woman I love. I am trusting you to keep to the terms of my proposed agreement with you because I believe you to be a man of honour.'

He walked forward purposefully. Sidmouth backed away from him. There was a fire burning in the grate opposite m'lord's desk. Jess walked by him, tossed the marriage licence into it and watched the flames consume it until it turned to ashes.

For a moment he stood there, head bowed. He was Miss Jesmond's heir and he knew that she would have approved of what he had just done and that was the only reward he wanted.

Sidmouth stared first at the ashes in the grate and then at Jess…and said nothing.

Jess bowed and said, 'You have nothing to fear from me, m'lord. Anne Jesmond's story is over. I shall leave now, and you will not hear from me again. Neither, I trust, shall I—and my descendants, if I have any—be troubled by you and those who follow you. I shall never speak of the matter again to anyone—indeed, I have already recently and publicly denied any connection with the Royal Family: a statement made *after* I had found the marriage licence.'

Sidmouth said, still staring at Jess, 'You may leave, confident that the state secret of which you spoke is no more, and that you may resume your life in peace, without interference from us. Your country is grateful to you, sir, for sparing it civil strife.'

He gave a small smile, hesitated and asked, 'Before you go, pray tell me one thing. How did you compel Beauchamp to admit you to my room?'

Jess's smile was sweet. 'Why, m'lord, I began to strangle him with his own cravat—a useful trick which the Spaniards first practised, and is often employed by thieves in London—it's known as garrotting. With Beauchamp it wasn't necessary to finish him off, of course, just to frighten him.'

Sidmouth, who had never been known to laugh, simply broadened his smile. 'I'm glad you spared him. He's conscientious, but he has no vision.'

Jess asked, 'I may leave now?'

'Indeed, and you have my word that this is the last you will hear from me.'

Jess bowed and turned to go. He had his hand on the door knob when Sidmouth spoke to him for the last time, addressing his back.

'Your Royal Highness, I think it a pity that a man of such undoubted resource is not to rule England.'

Chapter Thirteen

The whole world looked strange and different: walking towards Smythe's dingy office in the City, the morning after his visit to the Home Office; Jess even felt different himself. All his life he had been the dubious descendant of an illicit affair between a member of the Royal Family and a gentlewoman of easy virtue. Suddenly he had discovered himself to be of impeccable lineage, the descendant of princes and a claimant to the throne of England.

Lord Sidmouth had addressed him as Your Royal Highness even after he had thrown the proof that he bore that title—and any other which he might have claimed—into the fire in a massive act of renunciation.

Who was he now? Why, he was none other than Jesmond Fitzroy, Esquire, a country gentleman of good birth, whose pedigree, whatever others might think, bore no taint of illegitimacy to smirch its honour, who needed neither to defend nor to regret what his great-grandmother had done. She might rest in peace at last.

He would never know how she had been persuaded to dub herself wanton and her child a bastard, nor did it now matter. Only he and Lord Sidmouth knew the truth of the matter and once they were dead and gone, no one at all would know of it, and that was of no consequence either, for sooner or later everything is lost in the past.

In the long reach of time, not only the small but the great are forgotten: their names and deeds are distorted or turned into myths of which no one knows the real truth. That Troy fell is a fact, but how and why is conjecture, as are Helen, Paris, Achilles and the rest who did not necessarily possess any more reality than the Gods of Olympus who were reputed to have fought over their destiny.

What mattered was the here and now, the Jesmond Fitzroy who was on his way to right a wrong, to prevent the weak from being exploited by the ruthless.

Smythe's office was exactly what he had expected it to be: small and dirty with a bald clerk standing at a high desk in the corner, driving a quill pen along. Smythe stood up to meet him, bowing and smirking. There was a pile of documents on the desk before him.

'Honoured to do business with you, sir. I have heard of you and of your associate, Mr Ben Wolfe. Your reputation for fair dealing has gone before you. Pray be seated, sir. Benson, pour Mr Fitzroy a glass of port.'

Jess was amused by all this obsequiousness. It was plain that Smythe was falling over himself in his delight at getting rid of Bowlby's worthless paper. He had doubtless been in a lather of suspense that the bank might fail before he rid himself of it, in which case he would have lost everything. Now he knew that he would recoup some of his losses, which was more than he had thought possible until Jess and Ben Wolfe had appeared on the scene.

The port poured, Jess and Smythe toasted one another. 'Living at Netherton, now, are you? Going to run the bank yourself? Not coming back to the City?' Smythe asked.

'Perhaps,' said Jess, who believed in giving away as little

of his plans as possible, caution always being his watch-word. The port was rather better than he had expected, and when, after a little more financial chit chat, they had finished it, Smythe produced the necessary papers for Jess to sign and Jess produced a banker's draft, drawn on Coutts, for the price already agreed through Ben Wolfe.

At the last moment Smythe suddenly had doubts about selling Bowlby's debts when two such tigers thought it worth while to buy them, but it was too late for him to renege on the deal, particularly when he was so short of the ready himself.

The banker's draft clutched in his hand, he watched Jess leave his office, and wondered precisely why my fine gentleman was spending so much money on nothing. He immediately revised that judgement.

If Jess Fitzroy was buying Bowlby's Bank, he must see a profit in it for himself somewhere.

Georgie was on her own—Caro and Sir Garth were visiting a distant relative of theirs who lived in the next village, taking Gus and Annie with them. She had declined to join them, preferring to spend an afternoon alone.

She was not destined to be alone for long. Shortly after the little party had driven off, Forshaw came in to inform her that a Dr Maynard Shaw had called and would like to renew his acquaintance with her, she being the widow of his oldest friend.

For a moment Georgie considered telling Forshaw to say that she was not at home, but she remembered what she had told Jess about not being a coward, and changed her mind immediately. She was sitting on the terrace, the day being a fine one, her canvaswork in her hand, and a new novel nearby if needlework began to pall.

'Tell him I will receive him and bring him here, Forshaw—a pity to waste a fine day by frowsting indoors.'

Why she should make such a banal confidence to Forshaw she couldn't imagine! Possibly because she didn't really wish to see Dr Shaw when she was alone, but thought that she ought to for the sake of remaining on good terms with the Firths, who obviously believed that for anyone to know him was a privilege.

He seemed larger and more intimidating than ever when he walked on to the terrace after Forshaw. Even offering him a seat on a bench opposite to her didn't make his presence seem any the less overwhelming. Nor did his first words serve to reassure her in any way. She wished to keep their social intercourse as impersonal as she could, but he soon made it plain that he was having none of that.

'May I say that you look particularly charming this afternoon, my dear! Many women are not seen to advantage in a pastoral setting, but it suits you admirably.'

Now what could she say to that? What she would have liked to say was, I am not your dear, nor do I wish to be, and no, you may not say that I look charming when, in your presence, I feel quite the reverse, particularly when I remember the nature of our last meeting before poor Charles's death.

What she actually said was, 'I thank you, sir. The only drawback of the current bout of hot weather is that it makes one feel uncommonly thirsty. Would you care for me to ring for a pitcher of lemonade?'

'Indeed, yes. Most refreshing—if it is of no trouble to you. I would never put you to any trouble, my dear Georgina.'

The correct answer to that was, I am not your dear Georgina, either, and it's of no trouble to me, only to Cook and my servants.

What she actually said was, 'No trouble, I assure you,' and rang the small bell that stood on the table which held her sewing basket and bade Forshaw, when he arrived, to ask Cook to send them a pitcher of lemonade and a plate of ratafia biscuits.

After that they made conventional small talk for a few moments until the lemonade arrived. Georgie asked him what he thought of Netherton and he answered that he thought the miniature Spa delightful. He said that he was sorry that he had not visited it before and how long had she been living with her sister-in-law?

'You must know,' he said earnestly, leaning forward to gaze into her eyes, 'that after your husband died your disappearance from the circle which you both graced in his life was so absolute that we were all distressed. Particularly as we had no notion as to where you had gone. I was particularly overset, the more so when my dear wife died of the chest infection from which, as you know, she had always suffered. I would have valued your presence as a form of solace of which she would have approved. Indeed, on her deathbed, she urged me to seek you out with a view to marriage.

'Judge of my delight when my good sister wrote in one of her letters to me of a Mrs Charles Herron who was living at Netherton with her sister-in-law. That news, and that news alone, led me to beg her for an invitation to Netherton, although, of course, I found the little Spa itself to be a most salubrious and charming spot which I shall hope to visit again.'

He paused. Georgie said, 'Here comes the lemonade.'

She had even less wish to entertain Dr Shaw now that she knew that he was a widower. Mrs Shaw, being an invalid, had never travelled with her husband so that her absence on his visit to Netherton had not alerted her to the fact that she had died, particularly since after her husband's death she had severed all ties with what Dr Shaw had called his circle.

Indeed, had she known that he was a widower, she would never have consented to entertain him on his own.

'Delightful,' exclaimed Dr Shaw of the lemonade. It seemed to be his favourite word, to be used regardless of whether it was Georgie, Netherton, or a cooling drink to which he was referring.

He set down his glass, leaned forward again and regarded Georgie with soulful eyes. 'My dear Mrs Herron, you have already had ample proof of the tender regard I have for you, so it will not surprise you to learn that over the years I have never ceased to think of you, and with my dear wife's approval of you to sustain me, I am encouraged to ask you to consider my proposal to you seriously.'

So saying, he flopped on to his knees before her and tried to grasp the hand which lay in her lap, but Georgie, as quick as he, pulled it away. Nothing daunted, he picked up the hem of her dress and caressed that instead.

'What proposal, sir?' she said, willing herself not to knock his intrusive hands away. 'A dishonourable one like that which you offered me when my husband was alive, or an honourable one? Which?'

'Now, now, my dear,' he murmured reproachfully, 'you know perfectly well that I could not make you what you would describe as an honourable offer when my wife and your husband were still alive, but now that they are, alas, dead, I am hopeful that you will accept my offer of marriage—if that is what it will take to ensure that you become my partner in love. Marriage, my dear, so far as I am concerned, is merely an empty ceremony, but I am willing to go through with it for your own sweet sake.'

He sickened her, he really did. It was really his own sweet sake he was thinking of, and not hers.

Georgie rose so sharply that he was flung back on his heels, to stare foolishly at her as she walked to the door on to the terrace to fling it open.

'I think, Dr Shaw,' she told him, 'that you had better go. My answer to you is the same as the one I last gave you. I have no wish to be your partner in anything, least of all your so-called love. I trust that this time you will not try to take by force what I would not willingly give.'

She picked up the bell. 'I am going to ring Forshaw to tell him that you are ready to leave, and you will gratify me exceedingly if you say nothing of this to anyone. Furthermore, I must ask you not to attempt to make such a proposal to me again. It does neither of us honour…'

'Oh, honour,' he exclaimed, his face ugly. 'Another outmoded notion.'

'Nevertheless, it is one which I try to live by.'

So saying, she rang the bell. Dr Shaw tried to rise rapidly to his feet, but age and lack of activity betrayed him. He was unable to do so. His face agonised, he clutched at the seat of the wooden bench before him, but alas, even that did not answer, it gave him no help.

'You rang, madam,' said Forshaw, arriving to stare at the unhappy Dr Shaw.

'Yes, indeed, Forshaw. As you see, Dr Shaw stumbled and fell when he was leaving and is consequently unable to regain an upright position. Perhaps you could assist him, if necessary calling a footman to help you, and then ensure that he reaches his carriage safely.'

'I believe that he came here on foot, madam,' enunciated Forshaw, his face bland. He had a good idea of how Dr Shaw had come by his present plight, but wild horses would not have made him admit it—not until he told the servants' hall later, that is.

'In that case you may assist him to the sofa, then ring for my carriage to return him to the Firths with whom he is staying.'

'Would you care for me to send for the doctor, madam?'

'No,' groaned the unhappy Dr Maynard Shaw, 'I don't need a doctor, just help me up, you fool. I shall be better directly.'

'Very well, sir.'

It took Forshaw only a moment to haul the unhappy wretch to his feet. After making sure that he had suffered no vital damage, but found walking difficult, Forshaw helped him to the sofa where he sat mumchance, trying to avoid Georgie's eye.

For her part, Georgie was trying to avoid Forshaw's. Silence reigned until news came that the carriage was ready to return him home.

Before the footmen arrived to help him to it, he said through his teeth to Georgie in a low voice which no one could overhear, 'You may be sure, madam, that I shall say nothing of what has passed this afternoon, but rest assured that I do not accept defeat easily. You will hear from me again.'

'Oh, I do trust not,' said Georgie earnestly, before handing him over to the footmen.

'That will be all, madam?' Forshaw enquired when they had gone.

'Not quite,' said Georgie, looking up at his impassive countenance. 'I would much prefer it if you did not entertain the servants' hall with the details of what passed here this afternoon. I know perfectly well that you overheard most of it, and it is, I agree, something of a pity that such a good story must go untold.

'On the other hand…' and she picked up her reticule which lay on the table before the sofa and took from it a guinea '…on the other hand, your nobility of character by losing such a splendid opportunity to keep your fellows happy by discoursing on the follies of their masters is not going unrewarded by me.

'Here,' and she pressed the guinea into the hand which he had extended the moment she had picked up her purse, looking at the ceiling as he received it. As she had said, he regretted the loss of his good story, but the guinea would more than make up for that.

'That will be all,' she said.

His answer was brief and to the point. 'You know that you may always trust in my discretion in these delicate matters, madam.'

So saying, he slipped the guinea into his breeches pocket—and left.

Courtney Beauchamp was writing a letter to be delivered to Sir Garth Manning, post haste. His expression as he wrote it was not a pretty one. A vain little man, he was only too well aware that he was the least brilliant member of a brilliant family which had served England for generations. For that reason he had bitterly resented the easy way in which he had been humiliated by Jesmond Fitzroy that morning.

After Fitzroy had departed his humiliation had been further compounded when his master, Lord Sidmouth, had refused to explain why the Fitzroy business was to be dropped—merely saying that a mistake had been made and consequently all the agents who were spying on the man were to be called off at once.

'Write some nonsense to Manning to go off by express post today, telling him to forget the whole matter—he'll be

only too relieved to have us off his back. No need for any
explanations, the less said the better.'

When Beauchamp opened his mouth to protest at such
cavalier treatment, he added impatiently, 'And I don't want
to hear Fitzroy's name mentioned again, and that's flat.'

The less said the better. Well, damn that for a tale,
thought the fuming Beauchamp, it wasn't his cravat which
had been used to half-strangle him and make him take orders like a bloody footman. He would obey Sidmouth's
command to the letter; he wouldn't explain anything to
Manning about why he was being called off. He would just
give Manning his *congé*.

After he had done that, though, he would also tell him
some home truths about Jesmond Fitzroy's background and
career which Manning might find useful and which might
damage Fitzroy if he was trying to set himself up as a
gentleman in Netherton. This gratuitous piece of spite
cheered him up no end.

It was most unlikely that m'lord would ever find out
what he had done, and it would be some sort of salve for
his wounded pride and his bruised neck.

Georgie was eating her breakfast the morning after Dr
Shaw's disastrous proposal. She was alone: Caro had taken
to breakfasting in her room and not rising until midday.
Where Sir Garth might be was a mystery into which she
did not wish to enquire.

One trouble with being alone was that it gave her too
much time to think, particularly when her thoughts these
days were centred on one person and one person only—
Fitz.

The one thing which Georgie wanted more than anything
else in the world, after the scene with Dr Shaw, was to talk
to him. She could never have anticipated how much she

would miss him. She wondered if he would miss her as much, but perhaps not. After all he had gone to London on business and she guessed that he would have little spare time in which to moon about Georgie Herron, even though she spent much of hers in mooning about him! Men had a life outside the home which more than filled their long days, while women were prisoners in it with acres of spare time in which to think and worry about men.

It was surprising, though, how often she found herself thinking, I must tell Fitz that the next time that we meet— he'll be sure to see the joke. The only thing she didn't want to tell him about was the scene with Dr Shaw. Not because he wouldn't see the joke, but because she felt shy about telling Fitz something which bore so closely on her life with Charles Herron—she didn't think that the time was right for that yet.

Suppose he was serious when he had told her that he loved her? His manner had been so different from that of Dr Shaw when he had made his wretched and demeaning proposal that she began to think that she might have been mistaken to refuse him. From the very first moment that she had met Fitz she had misunderstood him.

Oh, she could feel superior to the good citizens of Netherton because they had misread him, and continued to misread him, but might she not be doing the same? Why should she disbelieve his professions of love? By doing so, was she not in danger of losing him to another woman who might be kinder to him, but might not love him as much as she did? Not, she hastened to reassure herself, that she had ever been really unkind, but she *had* refused him rather cavalierly.

Oh, dear…oh, dear…she wailed to herself, for her lively imagination had Fitz meeting some remarkable and charming London beauty who would turn her big eyes on him

and offer him all the worship which she, Georgie, had refused him!

It was not to be borne—the very idea of another woman
in his arms was enough to induce her to behave like Caro
and have a major fit of the vapours. Fortunately, the sturdy
common-sense which Jess so much admired came to her
rescue. For if Jess could be so easily lured by a London
siren, then he was not worth the love—and think it, Georgie—the passion which she now felt for him.

Like Jess, though she told herself sternly to go on living
in the here and now, not in fairy land. One thing in the
here and now was beginning to loom very large in her
mind: the month's grace which Banker Bowlby had extended to Caro was almost up, and so far Kite did not seem
to have found any way to help them. She couldn't ask Fitz
if there had been any progress until he returned from London—and how soon would that be?

No, she had never thought that she would miss anyone
so much as she missed him—and for such a variety of
reasons.

Forshaw ghosted in with a plate of hot toast and a pot
of fresh coffee on a salver on which also reposed a letter.
He carefully placed the toast and coffee before her, saying,
'Mr Kite from Jesmond House called this morning with a
letter for you, madam. It seems that Mr Fitzroy returned
from London late last night, his business there being concluded, and asked that it be delivered to you as soon as
possible this morning.'

With the same ceremony with which he had arranged the
toast and coffee on the table he laid the letter before her,
adding, 'Mr Kite did not wait for an answer. Mr Fitzroy
had assured him that one would not be necessary.'

He bowed and left.

Georgie snatched up the letter—her first from Fitz!—and

broke the seal, to discover that the message inside was a short one.

'Dear Mrs Georgie,' it said, 'I have just arrived from London, and to blow the London cobwebs away I shall take a walk this afternoon about three of the clock on that fatal path which runs between our lands. Would it be possible for you also to stroll in that direction at that hour? Not only do I have some important news for you, but I also cannot wait to see my dear Mrs Georgie again—and alone—with no prying relatives present to spoil our mutual joy.

'That you will agree to this is the hope of your everloving servant and cavalier, Fitz.'

Would she agree?

Of course she would agree.

Was he, then, missing her as much as she was missing him? From the tone of the letter he was. And that reference to the 'fatal path' must be to the time when they had misbehaved themselves after they had met there!

So excited was she that she was ready to bound upstairs and dress herself immediately in order that he might see her at her best. Which was a most ridiculous course of action to take, was it not, at ten in the morning with five hours still to live through before she saw him.

It was the longest five hours of Georgie's life. Even longer than the eight days which Fitz had been away. Her appetite at luncheon had disappeared quite. Caro remarked upon it disapprovingly before asking her to accompany her and the twins and their new nurse-cum-governess, Miss Havisham, on a drive to Frensham Park where a fête day was being held.

Given her inability to eat her lunch, Georgie could convincingly reply, 'Alas, I am a little under the weather. A carriage drive is quite out of the question for me in today's heat; a quiet afternoon on the sofa will be as much as I dare undertake.'

Caro, who had wanted her sister-in-law's company so that she might save herself from having to look after the children, said sourly, 'I do hope that you're not sickening for anything serious. It's not at all like you to be unable to eat—your appetite is usually quite remarkable.'

The only thing which I'm sickening for, thought Georgie, as she reassured Caro that her indisposition was only a mild one, is Fitz. Only I mustn't tell her so. After all, it was not so long ago that everyone, including herself, had thought that Fitz would make a dead set at Caro. Indeed, when he had first arrived in Netherton, gossip had married her off to Sir Garth and Caro to Fitz in double-quick time.

Well, those cocks didn't fight, she though inelegantly. I can't stand Sir Garth and it's patent that, once he had spent some time with her, Fitz felt the same about Caro.

From her bedroom window she watched Caro drive off not long before she readied herself to meet Fitz in as demure an outfit as possible. In a white dotted Swiss dress, with a pale green sash, a chip bonnet with strings of the same colour, and white kid slippers, she had never looked less like the hoyden in breeches on whom Fitz had first set eyes in late spring.

A light shawl and a parasol completed the ensemble.

On the way out she met Forshaw, who rushed to open the front door for her. Nothing in his face showed that he thought that she had made a remarkable recovery since luncheon when she had lounged about trying to look wan.

'I'm feeling much better, Forshaw. I thought that I'd go for a walk.'

He nobly refrained from saying, 'Towards Jesmond land, madam?' Instead, he rather naughtily asked if her she would care for a footman to accompany her and hold her parasol.

'Not at all. The parasol is no burden, I assure you. I hope that I shall not be too long. Do not send a search party out for me before midnight.'

Forshaw watched her cross the lawns towards the path which led to Jesmond lands, his eyes knowing. Back in the kitchen again, where the staff were enjoying an idle hour with Missis away, he said cheerfully, 'Mrs H. is off to meet *him* again. Got back last night, didn't he? Sent her a letter this morning, didn't he? She allows as how she's not well enough to go with the mistress to Frensham riding in the carriage, but a half-hour later is well enough to walk nigh on a mile to meet him.'

'Reckon it'll be a match?' asked Cook.

'Aye, sure of it. He's a pretty gentleman and no mistake. The fools round here think *he*'s a fool. Kite does nothing to correct them, but if Miss Jesmond's heir is a fool I'm a Mohawk Indian, that's for sure.'

'Which you ain't,' snorted Cook, laughing. 'Pour Mr Forshaw a cup of tea, Jenny, and pass him one of the Sally Lunns. Got the recipe from her at Jesmond House. Right popular place that is, these days. Can't say I'm sorry that Mrs H. has no time for Sir Garth—I haven't any, either.'

General laughter followed this sally, almost loud enough for Georgie to hear while she trotted along towards her rendezvous with Fitz. She had just reached the bottom of a slight dip in the path when she saw him coming towards her, down the other side.

The very sight of him was enough to set her heart hammering. He was dressed informally for once, his long legs in cream pantaloons, with a cream shirt open at the neck, no cravat, and a loose green jacket. The slight wind had blown his blond hair into curls which she had never known he possessed and, all in all, he looked so handsome that Georgie felt like swooning at his feet.

To cap all, he broke into a run the moment he saw her and when he reached her, regardless of her parasol, he threw his arms about her and swung her round and round, the parasol flying from her hand to lie unheeded on the grass.

'Oh, Mrs G.,' he exclaimed, kissing her soundly on each cheek, 'it is I who am the wild one today, and all because I have missed you so. I trust that you have missed me—although you do not look ready to sink into the grave. Quite the contrary—you look blooming.'

'And so do you,' Georgie gasped when he set her down again.

'I? I never look blooming—that is for the ladies. Gentlemen look in fine fettle.'

'Like their horses,' retorted irrepressible Georgie.

'Oh, Mrs G.,' he exclaimed again, leaning forward to kiss her on the cheek again—it was the only part of her which he dared to kiss, since saluting her lips had had such a dreadful effect on them both—'now I know why I missed you. That naughty tongue of yours—I found nothing like it in London.'

There was something different about him, Georgie thought. He had always displayed a cool seriousness, even when he was joking, or enjoying her jokes, but today he was as wild and free as he had so often asserted that she was. It was almost as though a burden had been lifted from his shoulders.

'Now we must behave ourselves,' he said, taking off his coat and spreading it on the grass for her to sit on. 'Not only because virtue demands it, but because I have no wish for you to be the subject of gossip.'

'I fancy,' sighed Georgie, 'that we are already a little

scandalous. Forshaw, for one, has suddenly developed a most knowing eye. This afternoon, after I had refused to go with Caro to Frensham Court on the grounds that I had a malaise, he caught me leaving, and he virtually twitted me about my sudden recovery. Not that he said anything, you understand, just looked. He has a most magisterial look. I fear that we may be a subject of entertainment for Caro's staff.'

'No doubt,' said Jess, sitting down beside her. 'The servants not only live their lives, but they live ours, their own being so narrow. We must always remember that.'

Fitz's kind and perceptive feelings about those who served him was one of the reasons why Georgie loved him. She knew, from their speech and behaviour, that Caro and Sir Garth, and many others of her acquaintance, considered that servants barely qualified to be regarded as human beings. One of the good things which Charles Herron had taught her was to act considerately towards those of inferior station.

'They have feelings just like we do, Georgina,' he had once said, 'but none of our advantages.'

So Fitz, who was, in many ways, quite unlike Dr Charles Herron, shared at least one thing with him. One day she might tell him so.

Today she merely said, 'You wrote in your letter that you had news for me. I trust that it is good.'

'Very good,' he told her lazily. 'You need not trouble yourself about Caro any more. She is no longer in any danger of losing her home and fortune, but I must ask you not to tell her this yet. A little time is needed.'

'Speaking of time,' said Georgie anxiously, 'the month's grace Banker Bowlby extended to her has almost run out.'

'No need to trouble yourself about that, either,' said Jess. 'It is of no consequence now. Tell me, Mrs G., what have you been doing whilst I have been hard at work in London?'

'Very little compared with you, I'm sure. Except for one thing, which wasn't, strictly speaking, my doing. It was someone else's.'

'How so?'

What a relief it was to describe Dr Shaw's preposterous proposal to Fitz, and to hear him laugh, and at the same time, to hear him roundly condemn the doctor for the insensitive nature of his approach to her.

He was quick to pick one thing up from her account: that this was not the first time that Dr Shaw had made such a proposal to her, and that that other proposal had been, in essence, dishonest.

'If you don't feel that you can tell me when and why the greasy doctor badgered you before, I shall quite understand, but judging by your manner when you spoke of it, it still troubles you. Would you feel any better if you confided in me?'

Georgie looked away from him. 'Yes, it does trouble me, but not because of Dr Shaw. It was Charles, you see, my husband. It hurts me to think of it—perhaps if I did tell you, I might forget it.'

Jess put an arm around her and held her against his heart. 'Let me hold you, dear Mrs G. I am always ready to be a refuge for you.'

Georgie closed her eyes and began to speak in a low voice. 'You must understand that, when my parents married me to Charles, I was seventeen and he was nearly fifty. He told me after the ceremony that the reason he married me was because I was young enough for him to be able to educate me and to transform me into a suitable wife for him—a woman to whom he could discourse on any subject. He didn't make me his true wife at first; instead, he tutored me as though I were a boy. He had resigned his post at Oxford to settle down and raise a family.

'I found that I enjoyed being educated by him. He was like a kind father, you see, and he was overjoyed to find that I responded to him better than most of the young men he taught. I was so willing to please him, you see. Even when he made me his wife at last he was such a considerate and loving husband that the age difference never seemed to matter.

'The trouble was, though, that Charles was a follower of William Godwin, the freethinker. At first that wasn't something which worried me. Very soon after we became truly husband and wife I found that I was breeding. Charles was overjoyed, he couldn't do enough for me. We had a dear little boy.'

Georgie stopped and began to cry into Jess's broad chest. 'Oh, Fitz, when he was six months old there was an epidemic of a killing fever in our part of London. William—he was named after Godwin—died within twenty-four hours of showing the first symptoms. We were inconsolable. Charles said that as soon as our grief had died down a little we could have another baby, but, alas, he suffered a stroke which, although it was not severe enough to kill him, meant that he could never be a father again.

'He was overwhelmed with misery. Then, one day, he brought Dr Maynard Shaw home with him for dinner. Dr Shaw's wife was an invalid, Charles said, and we must be kind to him. Unfortunately I took a dislike to him and told Charles so. It was the first time he was ever unkind to me. He said that I was stupid to dislike such a brilliantly clever man who could do us a great service, one which I would appreciate.

'I had no idea what he meant, until one afternoon, after visiting us several times, Dr Shaw called when Charles was

out, and tried to seduce me. I refused him, and then he told
me that I was following outworn notions of virtue and chastity, that he had Charles's permission to approach me, because his wife was no wife and Charles was no husband.
Consequently, he would enjoy the delights of the marriage
bed with me, and together we could give Charles the son
which he had always wanted. Thus our liaison would be of
advantage to the four of us.

'I didn't believe that Charles would consent to such a
thing and told him so. When I grew extremely distressed
he gave up trying to persuade me to become his mistress
and left, telling me to ask Charles about the agreement
which he had had with him, and that Charles had arranged
to be absent on this visit. I asked Charles to tell me the
truth when he came home and he confirmed every word
that Dr Shaw had said.

'He told me that I was being a silly naïve child, clinging
to outmoded values, and that by doing so I was depriving
us of what we most wanted, a child of our own. If he did
not mind not being the child's real father, why should I
babble about chastity and sin?

'My happy life with him was over. He could not bring
himself to allow Dr Shaw to make me his mistress using
violence, but neither could he forgive me for my unwill-
ingness to carry out his wishes. After six months of anguish
he had another stroke, an even more severe one, and died
within the week, leaving me a widow.

'Judge of my distress when Dr Shaw visited me a short
time after the funeral and renewed his pleas for me to become his mistress, in memory of Charles. The child could
be acknowledged as his, he said, and we could live a discreet life together after he had put his wife into an asylum.
To get away from him I left London and returned to Pom-

fret House to live with Caro, away from London and its wickednesses and away from Dr Shaw.

'You may further judge how unhappy I was when he arrived in Netherton. But I am no longer the deluded child who was Charles Herron's toy, and I was able to hold him off. The sad thing was that Charles taught me so much that was good and true, and yet, in this one thing, he wanted me to betray everything by which I thought that I was living.'

Georgie was crying so hard now that Jess began to rock her. 'He was such a good little baby, Fitz, and when he died, my happy marriage died too.'

Jess stroked her hair and comforted her, his own tears not far away. 'There, there, my love. If it's babies you want, then I want them, too. Let *me* give you one, Georgie. Marry me and let us be happy together, for I don't believe that either of us is truly happy apart.'

'Oh, Fitz, do you really mean it? You aren't saying that just to comfort me or feel that it's necessary to marry me because you have bedded me?'

Jess caught her by her chin and tipped her face up so that he could look deep into her eyes. 'Dammit, Mrs G.,' he said, half-laughing, 'I love you—why do you find that so hard to believe? As for sharing you with another man, I think I might be tempted to kill anyone who made me such a proposition. You'd better keep the ineffable Dr Shaw out of my sight if you don't want him to meet with a nasty accident!'

Georgie's tears had dried up. She said, her voice a little shaky, 'You really do mean that, don't you, Fitz? You're not funning, are you?'

'No, Mrs Georgie, I'm not funning, and my strictly honourable proposal does not need a dusty answer. Yes, or no, please, and on the double, as the drill sergeant says.'

Georgie turned her head to kiss the hand which held her face towards him. 'Oh, Fitz, it's yes, of course it's yes. Even if it's only because it's so different from the grease which Dr Shaw poured over me! Will that do?'

'Of course it will do,' he exclaimed rapturously. 'I never thought I'd receive anything but a *bon mot* from you. I should think you were ill if you simpered at me *à la* Caro, or came out with a plain no!'

His high spirits intrigued Georgie. They even made her feel a little shy. She released herself gently from his detaining hand and sank back against his chest again, murmuring, 'What happened to you in London, Fitz? You've changed. Where has all your solemnity gone to? Am I going to marry the man I thought I knew—or someone different?'

He kissed the top of her head in reply. 'Oh, Mrs Georgie, you're a witch. Yes, something did happen—but I made a promise which I must honour that I would never speak of it, so I can't explain what it was, even to you. Which is, I know, a poor way to begin our married life together—but you held to your honour when your husband and Dr Shaw challenged it, so you must respect me for holding to mine.

'What I can say is that it's as though a great burden has fallen from my shoulders, leaving me free for the first time in my life. Oh, I shall have new ones—indeed, there's one in the making at the moment, but today I am able to love my Mrs Georgie without stint, even though we must remain chaste until the wedding—or be as hypocritical as Dr Shaw.'

'The wedding…' sighed Georgie '…and when will that be?'

'Ah,' he said, 'you raise another problem. Having bullied you into accepting me, I must now ask you to keep our betrothal secret for the time being. I have things to do in

Netherton this week which might spoil the simple joy I wish to feel when we tell the world that we are to marry. Will you trust me and agree to that, my love?'

'I will agree to anything,' she told him, 'for love is about trust, is it not? Which is why I felt so betrayed when Charles wished me to become that man's mistress. Only—' and she pulled a tragi-comic face which had him loving her the more '—do not let the waiting be too long. That I couldn't bear.'

'Nor I, either,' he promised. 'For I know that I dare not give you more than a single chaste kiss, lest I become carried away—and I think that you feel the same, my love, which will make the waiting harder, I know. But loving will be all the sweeter when we finally become man and wife. I only live to call you Mrs Fitzroy instead of Mrs Georgie.'

Her heart was so full that Georgie could only nod at him. And there, on the grassy bank, comforted and held in the arms of the man she loved, and who loved her, she fell asleep, having reached safe harbour at last.

Passion could wait. They had a lifetime before them.

In the interim, though, there were rocks and rapids ahead of Georgie in the river of life. Flushed and happy, she walked into the drawing room at Pomfret Hall to find Sir Garth waiting for her. Caro was with him, looking serious, and sitting in a chair for once.

He knew immediately where she had been. If she did not wear what the poet Blake called 'the lineaments of satisfied desire' on her face, she still looked like a woman who had been with her lover. That knowledge enraged him even further.

As once before he was holding a letter. Beauchamp's letter. He did not deign to rise when Georgie came in, an omission of courtesy which was so blatant that Georgie knew at once that he was about to ring another peal over her.

'Yes, Garth, what is it?' she asked him wearily, sustained only by the knowledge of Fitz's love and her acceptance of his proposal.

'I see that you have been with him again,' he began.

'If, by *him*, you mean Jesmond Fitzroy, yes,' she said. 'And what is that to you? You are not my guardian or my husband.'

'And that is the meat of the matter, madam,' he told her savagely. 'For I offered you not only marriage, but an honoured name. And what is he offering you, pray? A dubious lineage, to say the least, the descendant of a whore, a man who is no gentleman, who served only in the Company army in India, the hanger-on of an East Indian trader whose own family is equally dubious, who has been compelled to defend himself in a court set up for that purpose. A court which chose to find for him in the face of incontrovertible evidence. Both men, Wolfe and Fitzroy, are merchants who exploit and make money from the misfortunes of others, using dubious practices to say the least.

'No, do not shake your head at me, madam, I have this— and more—on the most impeccable authority, that of a man who serves the present government and looks after the interests of honest men in society. Persist in your immoral *affaire* with this man and my sister will have no alternative but to ask you to leave Pomfret Hall so that she may retain her own good name, since you seem determined to sacrifice yours.'

Georgie did not answer him. Fitz had asked her for silence, so silent she would be. Instead she said to Caro, who sat there suddenly white-faced as she saw Georgie's financial support disappearing, 'Is this your wish, Caro?'

Caro stammered, 'Yes...no...I don't know.'

'If so,' Georgie said slowly, 'I will leave. Garth will be happy to support you, I'm sure.'

Garth said sharply, 'Have you no answer for *me*, madam?'

'None,' Georgie told him. 'Only to refer you to what I said earlier. You demean a good man who is trying to help your sister in her present difficulties. What are *you* doing to help her—other than try to turn out of her house someone who is?'

Fitz had also asked her for silence over his immediate intentions to save Caro, so she could not silence Garth by telling him of them.

'Oh, you have a ready answer for everything, madam, but you would do well to take heed of what I say. I have good reason to be aware that he is a most violent man.'

'Yes, I know,' returned Georgie irrepressibly. 'He has already threatened mischief to any one who would dare to injure or persecute me in any way, so you would be well advised to keep your unwanted advice to me at a minimum.'

Sir Garth did everything but actually gnash his teeth at her. He rolled his eyes before he raised them to heaven for assistance, before saying, 'I see that you are determined not to be warned, madam, so there is no point in my pursuing the matter further.'

'How very wise of you. We shall deal very much better together if you would refrain from criticising my conduct at every turn—'

She got no further. Sir Garth, seeing that he had so far lost every exchange with her, stormed out of the room, slamming the door violently behind him.

Caro said mournfully, 'You are being most unkind to him, Georgie. He is only trying to help you.'

'Forgive me, Caro, for criticising your brother, but he is not. He is trying to help himself, which is quite a different matter. The sooner you both grasp that I have not the slightest desire to marry him the happier we shall all be. And now let us speak of other things.'

For once Caro could think of nothing to say other than, 'Did Mr Fitzroy say anything to you this afternoon about my business with Banker Bowlby? The month he gave me is almost up.'

'Oh, we talked of other things,' Georgie replied, not willing to tell a direct lie even to relieve Caro's troubled mind.

For the first time her sister-in-law was beginning to grasp the gravity of her financial situation, for she continued, 'Oh, Georgie, I am so worried, and you are correct if you suppose that Garth does not fully appreciate that only the contribution you make to my finances since you came to live here is keeping me afloat. Do not leave me, I beg of you. I am grateful, even if he is not.'

This was the first time that Caro had thanked her for bailing her out of her difficulties. She was about to say more, but Gus and Annie came running in. They had heard that Aunt Georgie had returned from her walk and wished her to play cricket with them.

For once, Georgie refused. She thought that their mother needed her company more than they did. She rang for tea before trying to comfort Caro by talking Netherton gossip to her, wishing all the time that if Fitz were going to save Caro he would do so soon.

Not only for Caro's sake, but because then they could formally declare their love before all the world.

Chapter Fourteen

'We are going to carry out our business with the bank as discreetly as possible,' Jess told Kite the following morning. 'I hope that everything will go off quietly, but in case there is any trouble Mr Wolfe has lent me Tozzy.'

'Just like old times,' grinned Thomas Jarvis, always known as Tozzy. He was a large man with the build and skills of a prize-fighter, who could be depended upon to terrorise anyone from His Majesty King George IV downwards. In Netherton he would only be called on to terrorise Banker Bowlby—if that were necessary.

Jess could have done that for himself, but he wanted no scandal. He had carefully arranged it so that Sir Garth dare not reveal the strong-arm tactics he had used to intimidate him. Publicly terrorising Banker Bowlby would not be a wise thing to do if he wished to settle down in Netherton with a reputation as a peaceful citizen. Tozzy, though, had been a professional tipstaff and knew all the tricks of his trade.

'So, this is the plan. We take the chaise to Netherton. I shall briefly visit Mr Crane, the solicitor, before we go to the bank. You will both accompany me in, and from then on I shall improvise and you will follow my lead. You both understand me?'

Both men nodded. 'It'll be exactly like old times,' said Tozzy, grinning again. 'You're sure that you wouldn't like me to stay on and work for you?'

Jess shook his head a trifle regretfully. He knew that Tozzy's rather limited skills would not be needed in Netherton after Banker Bowlby was disposed of.

'Sorry, old fellow, but I promised Mr Wolfe I'd be sure to return you safe and sound. He wouldn't thank me for poaching you.'

'S'pose not.'

'Very well. The chaise is waiting outside, so we might as well begin our business immediately.'

Jess was not wearing his casual clothing of the day before. He was decked out like a London dandy, his clothes perfection: his cravat was a masterpiece and his boots had been polished with champagne. Kite was almost as grand, although he was all in black while Jess sported cream buckskin breeches above his boots. Tozzy looked like the Bermondsey bruiser he was: even his top hat was raffish and his Belcher neckerchief was scarlet with large white spots, and the ends of it were flying in the wind.

Jess understood why Tozzy wished to stay. They were once again—and possibly for the last time—the formidable trio who had been Ben Wolfe's outriders until Jess had made his fortune and struck out on his own.

He had sent a note to Solicitor Crane the previous evening, informing him that he proposed to visit him on business around ten of the clock and hoped that this would be convenient. It apparently was. Crane was in his office, seated behind his desk when Jess was announced and greeted him with a low bow.

'Delighted to see you, Mr Fitzroy. What may I do for you?'

Jess doubted that Crane would be quite so delighted by the time that their meeting ended, but he smiled and said, 'I want nothing from you today, sir. This meeting is for information only—principally yours.'

'Indeed, sir. Pray what have you to tell me?'

'This, sir, and what I have to say is confidential and must not leave this room. I have recently acquired full knowledge of the depredations of Mr Bowlby, which have reached such a pitch that the bank which bears his name is on the point of failing. I have good reason to believe that you were, and are, aware that he has been robbing his clients ever since he first made heavy losses by selling all his stock at the time when the market fell before Waterloo. He mistakenly believed that Napoleon would win.

'After that, he continued to gamble on the Stock Exchange in an effort to recoup his losses, but as a result of his continuing losses he has only kept himself, and the bank, afloat by selling his clients' good stocks and informing them that they had become worthless.

'The consequence of this was that, when their income collapsed, or disappeared, they only survived by taking out a mortgage, thus borrowing money from him at an exorbitant rate of interest, in exchange for his holding the deeds to their property as security—he representing to them that he was doing them a favour. When, inevitably, they failed to be able to pay the interest on the loan, he foreclosed, took over the property, evicted them and, using their deeds as security, borrowed money from London usurers to stay afloat himself. Alas, the further he advanced into the mire, the worse his affairs became since the rates of London's usurers are even more exorbitant than his.

'He was about to foreclose on my aunt, Miss Jesmond,

when unfortunately for him she died. He is by now a desperate man and his next victim is Mrs Caroline Pomfret whose month's grace before he forecloses ends next week...

'Are you following me, sir? You do understand that he has now reached the point when the bank must surely fail—and you, sir, knew of his illegal activities, although I believe that you may not have known the full extent of them. By keeping silent, however, you have betrayed those of your clients who banked with him—which, I understand, means virtually all of them—and all of whom will also be ruined should the bank go under.

'Would you like me to ring for a glass of water for you, sir, or something stronger? You look pale.'

Indeed, he did. Jess hoped that he was not about to suffer a stroke. Not because he cared about the health of a man who had connived at the ruin of a whole community by saying nothing, but because it would not suit his plans for saving that community.

'No,' Crane murmured. 'Is that all you have to tell me? What are your intentions?'

'If you mean, am I going to hand you and Bowlby over to the Criminal Courts to pay for your combined crimes—for you owed a duty to your clients which you did not fulfil and of which the law would not approve—so that you either end up on the gallows for embezzlement or are transported to Botany Bay, then the answer is no.

'Oh, not because I have any pity for his crime or your dereliction of duty, but if I did any such thing then the bank would inevitably fail, with dreadful consequences for everyone who lives in Netherton and has money in it—including yourself—unless, like me, you bank at Coutts! I see by your expression that you do, which does not make me like you the more.'

Jess paused. He had known that he would have no need of either Kite or Tozzy to help him when he confronted Crane, for he was sure that the solicitor would be overcome when he learned of the extent of Bowlby's villainy and only too ready to agree to whatever he wished. So shocked was Crane that he was finding it difficult to speak. Jess waited for him to recover himself and offer some sort of justification for his conduct before going on to inform him of his own intentions.

'You must understand,' explained the solicitor hesitantly, 'that, when I first realised what Bowlby was doing, I thought that it would be a temporary expedient, that he would recoup his losses, repay the bank's clients, and that no one would ever be any the wiser. But when he sank deeper and deeper into debt I felt helpless—for speaking out would have ruined not only a man who had been my friend but, as you say, the whole of Netherton. Consequently I was helpless. You do understand that if you are a man of business, which I now assume that you are.'

'No,' said Jess, 'I don't. I was trained by a man who was the soul of honour. True, he was hard, but he never cheated anyone honest—only the cheats who preyed on the weak, as Bowlby preyed on my aunt and Mrs Pomfret and others, among them Farmer Unwin who is at present on the verge of ruin. What I have done is buy up all of Bowlby's paper which was going begging—relatively speaking—it having been cornered by a man who specialises in bad debts. I have thus recovered all the securities which Bowlby stole, together with the deeds to the bank itself which he surrendered in order to finance his final attempts to save himself from ruin. Attempts which failed.

'In effect, I now own Bowlby and the bank. He is mine to do as I please with and I do not please to do anything to him which would ruin the bank. He will hand over to me any moneys, stocks and securities which he still owns in order to avoid the gallows—he is certain to have hidden something away to help him to survive whenever ruin might overtake him. I shall leave him with enough to enable him to leave Netherton, telling what story he pleases as to why he is disposing of the bank.

'Or he can do a moonlight flit, saying nothing to anyone. Either way, his remaining assets, however large or small, will go towards relieving those who are still in his toils— like Mrs Pomfret. They will be informed that a mistake has been made and that they are in no danger of bankruptcy. Those he ruined in the past I cannot help. What, if anything, is left over after that will belong to the bank.'

'*You* have bought the bank,' said Crane, dazed. 'But with what money? Miss Jesmond left you virtually nothing.'

'I have both Coutts Bank and Mr Ben Wolfe, a nabob of whom you may have heard, as securities for the bank should there a be run on it when Bowlby goes, until, with the help of my man Kite, and anyone else I may care to employ, it is placed on a sound footing again.'

He said nothing of his own fortune which would also go into the pot, but with Coutts and Wolfe's help he was risking little. The less Crane knew about him, the better. Let him think that he was only a minor backer—which in some sense, of course, he was.

Crane said, 'What do you expect me to do?'

'To support me and the bank—to which you will transfer your holdings at Coutts as a guarantee of your future honesty. To try to stop gossip about why Bowlby has sold the bank and why he should be leaving Netherton. To tell everyone that I have powerful friends in the City of London who are buying and backing the bank, and that I am merely their agent. My man Kite will run the bank on my behalf

for the present. Only you and Bowlby will know the truth—
and for your different reasons you will say nothing.

'Do I have your word on that, sir? You remained silent
in the face of Bowlby's dishonesty. Will you have the
goodness to remain silent in the face of my honesty?'

'I have no alternative. Of course I will do as you wish.
Not only to save myself, but to save Netherton. All depends
on Bowlby's consent, however.'

'Oh, that is not in doubt,' said Jess cheerfully. 'It's either
do as I wish or face the full majesty of the law. Besides, I
not only have powerful friends in the City, I have another
powerful friend who will be sure to make Bowlby see reason—if I have to use him, that is. I hope, however, to settle
matters peacefully.'

Crane gave a laugh which was half a sob.

'And Bowlby thought you an indolent fool! I became
aware that you were not when we attended his dinner party.
I nearly told him to be wary of you. I don't know whether
to thank God that I didn't, or curse myself for not warning
him!'

'Thank God,' said Jess briskly. 'Had you warned him
and I had found out, then I would have made sure that you
went down into ruin with him. I had half a mind to do that
anyway when I thought of Bowlby's treatment of my aunt,
Mrs Pomfret and many others—but I decided that downing
two birds in Netherton with one stone might look a trifle
odd. This way people may wonder about Bowlby's departure, but they will have no real notion of why and how he
went.

'I am an agent, only. Remember that.'

'You're a ruthless devil.' Crane sighed.

'But an honest one,' returned Jess, 'even though my
methods may be devious. Remember that, too. And I al-

ways keep my word, since I once saw what not keeping it could do to a man.'

It was over.

Crane said, 'For what it is worth, you have my word that I will back you to the utmost. I take it that you are on your way to the bank to deal with Bowlby now that you have seen me.'

'Certainly. I always prepare my ground carefully. By visiting you first and seeing Bowlby immediately after I have left you, I am giving you no opportunity to warn him. Remember what I said about transferring your money to the bank—see that the transaction is completed by the middle of the next week lest you strain my mercy.

'I bid you good day.'

The door closed behind him. Solicitor Crane leaned back in his chair, and if he had never pitied Banker Bowlby before, he did so now.

'Went well, did it?' asked Kite when Jess returned to the carriage.

'Very well. I needed neither you nor Tozzy. But you will accompany me in to the bank. Bowlby will be a tougher nut to crack than Crane, who was merely weak and foolish. Though not so foolish as to leave his own money in Bowlby's bank!'

Kite laughed and was still laughing when the chaise drew up at the bank's imposing doors. He was carrying a large leather satchel: Tozzy was carrying nothing. Merely to be his large and threatening self would be enough, Jess thought.

A clerk came to meet them. 'What may I do for you, Mr Fitzroy?'

'You, sir,' said Jess, smiling, 'may do nothing for me. I wish to speak to Mr Bowlby immediately.'

The clerk smirked insolently at him. 'Why, Mr Fitzroy, I believe that will be difficult. To begin with, I assume that you have made no appointment to see Mr Bowlby who therefore might not be able to fit you in today, and secondly, he has not yet arrived. I suggest that you call again this afternoon.'

Tozzy said cheerfully to Jess, 'Do you want me to settle this for you, master?'

'No need,' said Jess and, turning to the clerk, he said in his most reasonable voice, 'I have not the slightest desire to waste my time doing any such thing as you suggest. I will wait for him in his office. Pray escort me there.'

By now most of the bank's small staff was staring at them and grinning as the clerk continued to try to put Jess in his place.

'Oh, Mr Fitzroy,' he said, 'you must understand that I have no authority to do that, none whatsoever. I must ask you to leave.'

'You misunderstand me,' said Jess negligently, 'that was not a request. It was an order. Lead the way, Tozzy.'

Tozzy duly did, sweeping the astonished clerk to one side, before opening the door at the end of the public room, on which a large metal nameplate told the world that here was Mr Bowlby's office, so that Jess might enter it.

Inside was much as Jess remembered it. A large and imposing desk stood beside a large and imposing fireplace. A large and imposing portrait of Mr Bowlby hung on the wall above it. Large and imposing ledgers stood in a large and imposing breakfront bookcase. On a large and imposing sideboard decanters of various spirituous liquids stood, as well as a pitcher of water and glasses. The carpet on the floor was an expensive thing of great beauty. Bowlby might be descending into ruin, Jess mused, but he was doing so in grand style.

More prosaically tin boxes, on which were painted the names of Netherton's most favoured sons and daughters, stood on shelves around the room. Jess, seeing Caroline Pomfret's name among them, wondered sardonically how many of them contained papers of any value in view of the large number of deeds and documents which filled Kite's satchel.

He sat down in the imposing armchair behind Bowlby's desk. Tozzy, looking longingly at the decanters, lounged against the breakfront bookcase. Kite took up a position before an old-fashioned desk of a type at which the clerk stood to do his duties, laying the satchel carefully on the desk's frayed leather top.

'And now we wait,' said Jess.

Opposite to him a grandfather clock, with the signs of the zodiac painted around its dial, loudly ticked the minutes away.

'I could do with a drink, master,' said Tozzy hopefully.

'Water?' offered Jess, while Kite snickered.

Tozzy shook his head ruefully. 'You will have your joke,' he grumbled.

Silence fell again, broken suddenly by noise outside. The door was flung open by Bowlby, his clerk trailing behind him and excusing himself for having allowed Jess to enter the Holy of Holies.

Bowlby stared at the intruder seated at his desk. 'What the devil do you think you're doing, Fitzroy? Get out of my chair at once, do you hear!'

'In a moment,' Jess said, making no effort to rise, 'when you've dismissed your clerk, I'll tell you what I'm doing.'

'And supposing I tell him to stay and you to leave, what then?' demanded Bowlby belligerently.

Jess rose and strolled towards Bowlby, Tozzy watching them both keenly, saw him bend down, whispering so that the clerk might not hear him, 'I wouldn't do that if I were you, not unless you wish your destination to be Botany Bay or the gallows.'

Bowlby paled visibly. He looked from Jess to Tozzy, who had stopped lounging against the bookcase and was now at Jess's shoulder, and at Kite who had opened one of the tin boxes—to find it empty.

He snarled back at the clerk. 'On second thoughts, resume your duties, Fentem. I'll send for you if I need you.'

'Are you sure—' began the clerk, to be interrupted by Bowlby bawling at him,

'You heard me, Fentem, back to work. On the double.'

'Very wise of you,' commented Jess, when the clerk had gone and he had taken Bowlby's chair again, 'now we may get down to business.'

'I don't know what game you're playing, Fitzroy, but I don't like it.'

'I'm sure you don't,' agreed Jess. 'Never mind, it will soon be over.'

Bowlby stared at him. 'I can't think why you're here, Fitzroy.'

'Can't you, Bowlby? My little hint about Botany Bay didn't tell you? I'm here because I now own the bank, and I'm sitting in my chair.'

For one moment Jess thought that the stroke which he had feared for Crane was about to overtake Bowlby. He turned yellow, recovered himself and tried to bluster. 'I'm sure I don't know what you mean, Fitzroy. How can you possibly claim to own the bank?'

'I mean, Bowlby, that having discovered that you have been robbing the bank blind for years and covering up your near bankruptcy by borrowing in London on the strength of the securities you stole from your clients, I went to London and bought up everything you had pledged—at quite a cheap rate, fortunately, your credit being nil—among them being the title deeds to the bank.

'Show him, Kite.'

Bowlby waved a helpless arm at Kite as he walked forward, the bank's title deeds in his hand.

'That swine in London sold them to you? He promised not to do that without consulting me.'

'That's the sort of thing swine in London do, Bowlby. They trust you as little as I did when I first walked into the bank. You could offer him nothing. I could, and cash down, too.'

Bowlby bared his teeth. 'Well, you've bought damn all, Fitzroy. The bank's damned near failing, and now you'll be responsible for that, not me.'

It was a good attempt to deter him, Jess conceded, or would have been if he had not had Coutts and Ben Wolfe behind him.

'That's my worry, not yours. You do understand that if I had cared to do so, I could have set the law on you, and you know as well as I what the end of that would have been. Fortunately for you, I could not punish you for your misdeeds in that fashion without also bringing the bank down once the whole world knew what you had done. Most of Netherton would have been ruined, which would have profited nobody.

'Instead, I propose to allow you to escape your proper punishment by pretending that you have sold the bank to me and to my backers, Coutts and Ben Wolfe, in proper form. No one need know of what you have done, no one will be ruined—other than you. You will hand over to me any monies and securities you had hidden away against the bank's failing, and I will see that they go into the accounts of those whom you were in process of ruining. You may care to know that I discovered your villainy when I examined my aunt's affairs when I inherited.

'The other condition I have to make is that you leave Netherton immediately, giving any excuse you care to invent to explain your sudden departure.'

Bowlby said desperately, 'Have you no mercy, Fitzroy? You are leaving me—and my family—ruined and penniless. What shall I do? Where shall I go?'

'Mercy?' said Jess. 'What mercy have you shown to your victims? Those whom you ruined before I came to Netherton I can do nothing for. You pillaged my aunt's fortune when she was helpless and dying—what mercy did you show her? Those whom you were in process of ruining, Mrs Pomfret and Farmer Unwin among them, I can save without them knowing of your villainy. Had the bank failed, all Netherton would have been ruined, as other small towns and villages have been when their banks failed either through wickedness or incompetence—so don't prattle to me of mercy.'

It was useless: Bowlby could see that quite clearly. He had misjudged Fitzroy from the moment he had arrived in Netherton. He had never for one moment thought that Fitzroy would be able to discover that he had cheated his aunt or would be able to do anything about it.

He said, although he knew that he was whistling down the wind, 'Suppose I don't agree to your terms, what then?'

Jess leaned back in his armchair and surveyed him coldly. 'Two possibilities are open to me, Bowlby, neither of which you would like, and neither of which would profit you. In the first, I set Tozzy here on you to—shall we say—try to persuade you to change your mind. I think that you know what I mean. Neither of us would like that—although Tozzy would, but we are not here to please him, are we?

'The second possibility is that I hand you over to the law

and you either hang, or are transported to Botany Bay. That way you gain nothing, and your family is left without anyone to support them. True, Netherton is ruined, for the scandal of your trial would end the bank forever, but what would that profit you? It wouldn't damage me, either. I can quite easily recoup any losses I have made by buying your paper.

'Whereas, if you give way now and agree to my terms, we are all saved, including yourself. You are not a fool, you could try to make an honest living. It might go against the grain, but you wouldn't spend your life in a stew of fear that your villainy might be discovered. You really have no choice, have you?'

'None, damn you, Fitzroy. I agree, of course I do. Now get out of my chair. I'll have the contents of this office picked up, ready to leave with the rest of my possessions.'

'Tell him, Kite,' said Jess. 'I'm tired of talking.'

Kite moved from his desk to confront Bowlby.

'I must remind you that all your assets are now legally the property of Mr Fitzroy and that includes your house and its contents, as well as the bank and its contents. He is allowing you to keep the contents of the house, and a small sum of money, but nothing else. When your house is sold, the proceeds will go into the bank's coffers to assist it to become solvent again. Netherton, of course, will be unaware of that.'

Bowlby's head drooped. He had lost, and now had to pay the price of his double failure.

Kite said, 'Mr Fitzroy will require you to sign a document in which these conditions are set out as proof that you agree to them. That, too, will remain secret, but it is necessary, for your word will, we fear, not be enough. I have the document here, and you will sign it now. When you have done that you will leave, after telling your staff that you have sold the bank to an offshoot of Coutts in London, with Ben Wolfe as a partner. To those who might ask what Mr Fitzroy's part in all this was, you will inform them that he is Coutts's and Wolfe's agent.'

Jess watched while Bowlby, no longer the Banker, scrawled his name on the paper Kite put before him. His aunt was avenged, Caroline Pomfret was saved and would never know how or why. Netherton would keep its bank, which Jess already intended to call Netherton's, having no wish to be known as Banker Fitzroy. Bowlby had muddied that name for him.

He watched Bowlby walk out, with his head bowed.

Kite handed him the paper. Jess took it. Tozzy said, 'A pity you didn't need me. Now may I have that drink?'

'We shall all drink,' Jess told him, 'to Netherton's Bank and to its future.'

To himself he added, And to mine with Mrs Georgie now that this is over.

But not everything in Netherton was quite over…

Chapter Fifteen

Rumour ran rife in Netherton that day and for several days thereafter. No one knew quite what had happened. That Banker Bowlby no longer owned the bank was the only fact which everyone was sure of. What no one was certain of was why he had sold it, who had bought it and when.

Bowlby, it was said, had gone to the bank as usual that last morning, had entered his office to find Mr Jesmond Fitzroy, Mr Kite and a great bully of a man waiting there. Not more than twenty minutes later he had emerged from it, informed his clerks that he had just sold the bank to Mr Fitzroy or Coutts or Wolfe—no-one was sure which—accounts differed—and had immediately returned home.

Later, angry, curious and gossiping servants gleefully reported that there had then been an enormous row with Mr Bowlby shouting and Mrs Bowlby screaming at him that they were ruined and that it was all his fault, although Mr Bowlby later denied this vigorously to a neighbour who called on him, alarmed by the noise. He said that he had decided that he was tired of life in Netherton and wished to try his luck elsewhere. How true that statement was remained a matter of debate.

What *was* true was that, after Mrs Bowlby had rushed to

her room and locked herself in, Mr Bowlby began to arrange for them to leave Netherton immediately and for
good. He had also arranged that the Bowlbys' furniture and
most of their other possessions were later to be packed and
sent after them when they had a permanent address.

The house-curtains were drawn, the servants were summarily dismissed—without their wages being paid—and
before nightfall a carriage containing the Bowlby family
rumbled out of Netherton. What no one knew was that the
Bowlbys were, to all intents and purposes, penniless.

Shortly after Mrs Bowlby had retired from the field,
Bowlby went to his study where he kept a strong box hidden away in a permanently locked cupboard. Inside it was
his secret hoard which Jess had believed might exist: gold
pounds, guineas, specie and a small number of securities
which were there to act as a cushion if final ruin descended
on him.

That moment had now arrived. He silently gloated over
the box's contents before he locked it again—at least Jesmond Fitzroy wouldn't be able to lay his filthy hands on
this! Its destination was the boot of the coach being prepared for his leave-taking. He stole down the backstairs to
the stables, congratulating himself on his foresight the
while.

He had almost reached the coach when he heard a harsh
voice, Tozzy's voice, behind him, saying, 'Like me to have
a look in that box, would you, Bowlby? You sure that it
doesn't contain some of the bank's possessions?'

'No!' exclaimed Bowlby. 'No, it's mine. Family keep-
sakes and bits of jewellery, that's all.'

Tozzy stretched out a beefy hand. 'Then you won't mind
me taking a look in it, will you?'

Bowlby clutched the box to his chest as though it were
a lifeline—which indeed it was.

'Certainly not! You have my word.'

'The word of a swindler? What's that worth, eh? Hand it over and let me look for myself.'

Desperation had Bowlby retreating, which was foolish. The mountainous man approached him, grimly murmuring, 'Now, you know as how Mr Fitzroy doesn't like violence, so don't make me take it from you by force, there's a good fellow.'

It was useless; he might have known it would be. He handed the box over. Tozzy took one look at it, and said, 'The key, too, if you please.'

'I haven't got it with me,' croaked Bowlby.

'What sort of a ninnyhammer do you take me for? Of course, you've got it with you. It's in your pocket. You weren't going to leave without it, were you? Pretty please,' he finished with a grin, the box tucked under his beefy left arm, his right hand extended for the key.

Helplessly Bowlby handed it over and watched Tozzy open the box to reveal its precious contents. Tozzy shook his head at him. 'Tut, tut, game to the last, weren't you? And taking up petty thieving after the real thing. Here's money and other treasure you'd hidden away against a day like this—all of which belong to the bank, not to you.'

'You're the thief,' snarled Bowlby.

'Not I—this goes to my master, who bade me keep an eye on you. He knows the tricks your sort get up to. You're lucky that he's soft-hearted. Were it my shout you'd be gallows-meat, not on your way to cheat other poor fools.'

He walked out of the yard with the box, taking Bowlby's last hopes of some sort of salvation with him.

Netherton knew nothing of this—several of the wiser spirits, hearing the news of the bank changing hands, rushed to Solicitor Crane to ask if he thought that their money was safe under the new ownership, or should they withdraw it in order to bank it elsewhere. After all, they could scarcely hope that Mr Fitzroy would be as honest and straightforward as Bowlby had been.

He had the same message for them all. 'Safe as the Bank of England with Coutts and Ben Wolfe behind it. Mr Fitzroy is their agent merely. I gather that Mr Kite is to manage the bank. You'll find him every bit Bowlby's equal. Leave your money there and you'll not regret it.'

Gradually the news spread out into the country. The next morning, Sir Garth Manning, calling in at the Assembly Rooms to drink the waters—his much abused liver was playing him up—was told by Farmer Unwin of the first excitement in Netherton since his bull had escaped and had run mad down Main Street.

'Fitzroy?' Sir Garth exclaimed, nearly dropping his pewter cup of life-giving liquid on hearing this strange tale. 'Backed by Coutts and Wolfe, the nabob?'

'Aye, very true,' said Unwin. 'Happen he'll treat my loan more kindly—he couldn't be harsher than Bowlby. *He* was threatening to foreclose. Pleasant young man, they say. He and that man of his, Kite, have been working at the bank the whole of yesterday and half the night. Going over the books, they say. They were at it again first thing this morning. They also say they've given that jackanapes of a clerk Bowlby favoured a regular rumgumptious time.'

Dr Shaw, who had strolled up, was listening to this with great interest. If Jesmond Fitzroy was so busy running the bank, then he would scarcely be spending much time with Mrs Georgie Herron. This afternoon might be a good time to visit her and try to persuade her that she owed a duty to her late husband, Dr Charles Herron, and that she could fulfil it by marrying him.

And, if that failed, he knew of other means of persuasion.

* * *

Sir Garth had things on his mind, too—one of which was also Georgie's future. If she refused to marry him, then might it not, after all, be a matter of salvation for him and Caro if she married Jess Fitzroy, seeing that he was rich enough to buy Bowlby's Bank—and possessed powerful and wealthy backers into the bargain. To think that he had spent the last couple of months trying to prevent her from marrying him! It all went to show that betting on the right horse was always a tricky business.

Georgie and Caro, who had heard nothing of Banker Bowlby's sad fate, were eating nuncheon when Sir Garth strolled in, big with news.

'I thought that you had decided to spend the day in Netherton,' fretted Caro. 'Now I shall have to ring for another place to be set.'

'Never mind that. I say, there's been the most enormous turn-up in Netherton, Georgie, you'd never guess what!'

'Wouldn't I, Garth? Has Farmer Unwin's bull broken loose again and charged into the china shop this time?'

'No need to fun, my dear. This is real news—it's probably reached the London papers by now. Your would-be lover, Jesmond Fitzroy, bought Bowlby's Bank yesterday. No one is quite sure whether he actually bought it himself, although it is certain that he has backers of great financial consequence in Coutts Bank, and Ben Wolfe. Crane the solicitor says he is their agent.

'I visited Crane, Caro, to find out whether you ought to keep your account at the bank,' he went on importantly. 'Crane assured me that the Netherton Bank—that is its new name—is even safer than houses with Coutts and Wolfe behind it. I suppose that we ought to congratulate you, Georgie, in netting a man with such powerful friends. I shall be only too happy to dance at your wedding!'

Here was a turn-up, indeed. And not merely the news about Banker Bowlby. Georgie and Caro stared at him.

'Am I to assume,' asked Georgie, 'that my *affaire*—I believe you called it that—with Fitz now has your blessing?'

'If he proposes to make an honest woman of you, yes.'

Georgie burst out laughing. 'And if he doesn't?'

'I should naturally regret that,' said Garth pompously, 'but I am certain that you are sufficiently aware of your own interests to make sure that he does propose.'

Georgie hugged to herself the delightful knowledge that Fitz had already proposed to her and had been accepted. It was as clear as crystal to her that the reason why he wished to delay in making the announcement public was that he did not want it to be overshadowed or muddied by this business with the bank. In doing so, he was showing his usual consideration for her.

Caro said querulously, 'I don't understand you, Garth. Two days ago you were all against Georgie having anything to do with Jesmond Fitzroy and wished to marry her yourself. Now you are urging her to marry him. I did hear you aright?'

'Indeed, you did, and you ought not to need reminding, any more than Georgie does, what a splendid thing it would be for us to be related to such a nabob as he has turned out to be. In my opinion, all this talk about him being an agent is humbug. He's bought it for himself, I'll be bound. That's why he brought that man of his, Kite, to Netherton. He's to do the day-to-day running of the bank, they say.'

They, whoever 'they' were, seemed to be saying a lot of things, but for once, Georgie thought that Garth was showing more sense than usual. While not agreeing that she should marry Fitz solely for his money and his powerful friends, she also thought, remembering the lessons which

Charles had given her, that Garth was correct to assume that Fitz had bought the bank for himself—but that his powerful friends would act as backers on whom to draw if the change-over brought about a run on it.

But by what Garth had said of Solicitor Crane that was not going to happen. People in Netherton would respect his judgement in the matter. She had a sudden longing to see Fitz as soon as possible and share his pleasure—she was sure he would be pleased—at the coup which he had brought off. Moreover, she was also sure that Caro need now have no worries over her mortgage with the bank.

One thing about that interested her—was it Caro's problem which had started Fitz on his campaign to buy the bank? Or was there more to it than that? She would be sure to ask him when next they met. From what Garth had just said, there was little chance that he would be walking in Jesmond House's grounds this afternoon.

She would have to be patient.

Turning her attention back to Garth, she heard him telling Caro of the Bowlby family's departure from Netherton the night before.

Caro said excitedly, 'One of the drawbacks of living out here is that we miss whatever fun is going. Once nuncheon is over, Miss Havisham can take the children fishing and I shall order the carriage to take us to Netherton. Mrs Firth is sure to have all the gossip now that Mrs Bowlby has gone. If she is not in we can take tea in the Assembly Rooms. They are sure to be full this afternoon. Why, Mr Fitzroy might even be there!'

One benefit of Fitz's arrival, Georgie thought, was that Caro was at last beginning to abandon her almost permanent position on the *chaise-longue* and was ready to resume life again. For one brief moment she was ready to join Caro in a trip to Netherton.

Second thoughts, though, told her that she did not wish her next sight of Fitz to be in the middle of an eager, gossiping crowd. If he was foolish enough to go to the Assembly Rooms and brave Netherton's excitement, that was. She rather thought that he wasn't.

'You go,' she said. 'Garth has told us everything of consequence. I would be happy to pass a quiet afternoon on my own. You can tell me everything when you return.'

Caro pouted, but Georgie found an unexpected ally in Garth, who had been so ready to bully her recently, but was now full of consideration. 'By all means, rest, dear Georgie. It might not be tactful for you to bustle around Netherton gossiping about Fitzroy.'

It would also mean that, for a few hours, she would be spared Caro and Garth's company. Marriage to Fitz would take her away from them and not before time. She and Caro had comforted one another in their early widowhood, but there had never been any real friendship between them, and Garth's recent presence had been a constant irritant. More, if Caro was to be no longer in difficulties with money, she would be able to manage without Georgie's subsidies.

For the immediate present she could relax in the drawing room with her canvaswork and her book. Or bring her diary up to date; she had been neglecting it since Fitz had come into her life.

Halfway down the first page she heard someone enter through the glass doors to the garden: looking up in some surprise, she saw that it was Dr Shaw. He was smiling at her, and his smile remained fixed even when she said, her voice severe, 'Pray, sir, who gave you leave to come upon me like this without announcement?'

His smile was vulpine. 'Why, madam, I knew that you would not receive me if I came in proper form. I followed the footpath between your land and Fitzroy's—the one you take to meet him—and then came through the Park. I hoped to find you alone, and so I have.'

Georgie made no effort to rise or even to greet him. She said coldly, 'That makes no odds, sir, I must ask you to leave at once.'

His smile grew. 'Oh, no, my dear, I have much to say to you, and you shall listen.'

He was upon her now and when she raised her hand to pull the bell to summon Forshaw, he gripped her by the wrist and pulled her to him, saying, 'Dear, dear, we can't have that, can we? What I have to say to you is for your ears alone, and when I have finished with you even that by-blow Fitzroy won't want you.'

Georgie, shocked, stared at him and wondered frantically how she was to rescue herself…

'That will do for now, Kite,' said Jess, passing a weary hand over his forehead. 'I think we know how matters stand—in some ways better and in other ways worse than we might have expected. We both deserve a rest.'

Kite nodded and said, 'It's a good thing, though, that Coutts turned up trumps, and that you suborned Crane to support us locally. Without that, saving the bank might have been touch and go—he's been pillaging it for years— and still losing money!'

'True, but that's over now, and between us we'll pull it round. We'll go back to Jesmond House and take it easy until tomorrow. For the time being you might prefer to live above the bank rather than have to travel in to Netherton every day. Take a couple of servants with you and whatever you might need from Jesmond House.'

Kite nodded agreement again. 'I'll arrange that immediately, sir.'

'Good.' Jess stretched and yawned. 'I'll be pleased to be home again and able to get out of my finery.'

He didn't add that when he had done so he would take the path towards Pomfret Hall in the hope of meeting Georgie. He was longing to tell her that things had gone so well that they could announce their engagement immediately. Now that the business of the bank was safely over he could begin to live his own life again.

He was still planning his future when he walked towards Pomfret Hall. His hopes of meeting Georgie on the way— even if she were not alone but had the twins with her— diminished until he came in sight of the Hall itself.

Perhaps she was in the gardens. After all, she would not be expecting him. She was sure to have heard all the gossip about his buying the bank and the Bowlbys' sudden departure. He walked through the wicket gate which opened into Pomfret land, crossed the Park and continued steadily towards the back of the house where he knew that she often sat outside in fine weather.

The glass doors to the drawing room were open.

Jess hesitated for a moment, then walked through them and into the Hall…

If Dr Shaw thought that Georgie was going to be easy prey, he was much mistaken. For one shocking moment she was so overset by his sudden attack that she was unable to think of any way of resisting him.

He had pulled her to him by her right wrist and, brought up sharp against his fat body, she was immediately aware of his arousal and knew the true nature of his cruel intent. She tried to pull away, but his grasp on her wrist was so strong that she was helpless. Her reaction was immediate and instinctive. She bent her head and bit the wrist which held hers with such force that she drew blood—and elicited a cry of pain from him.

Not only that, he dropped her hand and recoiled backwards—giving her the opportunity to make for the door. She didn't quite reach it. Roaring 'you bitch' at her, he caught her skirt with his left hand and tried to drag her back into the room.

Georgie, whom a mixture of fright and anger seemed to have given both strength and initiative, swung round when her skirt tore beneath his detaining hand. Seeing a small bust of Plato, the Greek philosopher, standing on a side table, she seized it, and struck him on the head with it as hard as she could.

Dr Shaw dropped like a stone: so heavily, indeed, that she thought for one dreadful moment that she had killed him. He lay unmoving at her feet, blood slowly trickling from a wound on his temple.

Fright at being raped was rapidly succeeded by fright at the thought of being hanged for killing her assailant!

It was at this moment that Jess stepped into the room.

He did not immediately grasp what had happened. He saw Georgie facing him, her face white, and her eyes wild. She was holding something in her right hand and was staring at the floor as though Hell itself had opened before her.

He could not see that the object of her gaze was the supine body of Dr Maynard Shaw because he had fallen in front of a long sofa.

Georgie opened her mouth when she saw him, but nothing came out. Jess moved rapidly into the room, saying urgently, 'Georgie! What the devil's the matter?'

This seemed to revive her ability to speak. She said stonily, 'I think that I might have killed him, but I'm not sorry—he tried to rape me.'

'Who tried to rape you?' exclaimed Jess, who, fearing

that she was about to faint, so pale was she, had advanced until he was beside her, and was trying to take Plato's bust from her, so that he might comfort her. 'Garth?'

'No, him,' said Georgie, still in a kind of trance, pointing at the floor. Jess, who had been more concerned with Georgie than who had attacked her, looked down to see Dr Maynard Shaw lying before him, blood trickling down his face from a gash on the temple.

'I do hope he's not dead, Fitz. For my sake, not his,' she added. 'I wouldn't like to hang for him.'

Jess, abandoning his attempt to take Plato's bust from the death grip in which Georgie held it, went down on his knees beside Dr Shaw in order to examine him. His first touch elicited a faint groan from the wounded philosopher when he tried to sit up.

Jess was having none of it. 'Lie still, damn you,' he said curtly. He stood up himself, and said to Georgie, 'Unfortunately, you didn't kill him. He's still breathing and ought to be able to walk home. If *I* don't kill him for you, that is.'

'Oh, no, Fitz,' said Georgie. 'He's not worth it. Besides, he didn't even manage to kiss me—let alone assault me—before I hit him with Plato,' and at last she handed the bust to Jess, who began to laugh immoderately.

'Plato! You hit him with a bust of Plato! How extremely rich! You used a genuine philosopher to dispose of a false one! But what were you doing, to receive Dr Shaw at all? I thought that you had forbidden him the house.'

By now he had replaced Plato on his table, and had taken Georgie into his arms.

She said into his chest, 'I didn't receive him, Fitz. He came in through the glass doors—as you did. He thought that he might find me alone. He said some terrible things about us, you and me, I mean, and then he tried…'

She shuddered.

'But he failed,' said Jess.

Georgie nodded. 'He tore my skirt, though, just before I hit him.'

Dr Shaw was now moaning incoherently. Jess made out the words, 'She bit me!'

'Is that true, Georgie? Where did you bite him? Somewhere serious, I hope.'

Georgie, who was fast recovering her normal bright spirits, gave a faint giggle at this. 'I bit his wrist to make him let me go. And then I hit him with Plato. That *was* rather apt, I do admit.'

Dr Shaw gave another faint moan and tried to sit up. Jess, relaxing his loving grip on Georgie a little, kicked him down again.

'You'll stay there until we decide what to do with you,' he informed the prostrate philosopher who couldn't quite make out whether his pride, his wrist or his head hurt the most.

'Nothing, let's do nothing to him, Fitz,' Georgie said into Jess's chest. 'I never gave him the opportunity to do anything to me. In the end it was I who damaged *him*. Let him go. I don't want a scandal.'

'He can't get away scot-free,' said Jess. 'It wouldn't be right.'

He absent-mindedly kicked Shaw down on to the carpet again when he made another attempt to rise. 'Since you fortunately, and through no fault of his, came to no harm, perhaps I simply ought to compel him to leave Netherton at once. Should he be unwise enough to refuse, I'll set Tozzy on him. That ought to do the trick.'

'Tozzy?' queried Georgie.

'I'll tell you about him later,' Jess said. 'Sit down a minute while I dispose of our philosophical friend.'

He pulled the now fully conscious Dr Shaw to his feet and threatened him with the full penalty of the law if he did not leave Netherton forthwith.

Tozzy was not going to be needed, apparently.

'Of course,' babbled the doctor, his handkerchief held to his bleeding head. 'Indeed, I quite misunderstood matters…'

'Oh, damn that for a tale,' said Jess cheerfully. 'Hold your tongue, thank God for our clemency, and be off with you. My man, Tozzy, will come along to help you pack and see you safely out of Netherton. And don't come back,' he added.

Wild horses wouldn't drag Dr Maynard Shaw back to Netherton in the future. His damaged wrist he could hide from his proud sister. Explaining away a gash and heavy bruising on the temple was going to prove a little more difficult.

He left the room with as little dignity as he had entered it, scurrying through the glass doors as though Beelzebub himself was after him, avoiding the eyes of the lovers as he passed them.

'You are really, truly, not harmed?' Jess asked Georgie tenderly when he was out of sight.

'Really, truly,' she sighed at him. 'I'm shaken rather than hurt. I didn't expect that even from him, although I told you that I never liked him.'

'Now you can forget him,' Jess told her. 'He'll not return to Netherton. I know his sort. Puncture his pride and he's finished.'

'And Mr Bowlby? Is he finished, Jess?'

'Yes. He's left Netherton, too, and the bank is saved. Kite will run the day-to-day work for me. Say nothing to Caro, but she and some of the others will be receiving a letter telling them that a mistake has been made, that they are in credit again, and that repaying their mortgages will not prove too difficult. She's in no danger of losing the Hall.'

'Good, now I can sleep easily. You may, if you wish, answer one question for me, and then we'll not talk about that again, either. What made you suspicious of Bowlby?'

'My aunt's financial state when I inherited,' Jess said simply. 'After that, several things were said that made me aware that something odd was going on. Your speaking to me about Caro's situation was the final clincher, though.'

'I never liked him, either,' Georgie told him, 'but I never thought that he was a swindler—just rather distasteful.'

She didn't ask Fitz about the other rumour—that he was enormously wealthy—because she had no interest in that. She loved Fitz and would marry him even if turned out that he hadn't a bean.

And so she told him.

'Well, that's encouraging,' he told her. 'That you aren't marrying me for my money, I mean. I must be truthful and tell you that between us we could undoubtedly finance a small army!'

'Whatever for?' asked Georgie. 'After all, I only needed Plato's bust to dispose of Dr Shaw. But it's nice to know, all the same, that we shan't need to go begging in Netherton to earn a crust.'

Jess gave a roar of laughter. 'That's my Mrs Georgie, and now all we need to do is to get married.'

'All?' queried Georgie. 'Dear Fitz, you have no notion of what a wedding entails. Why, we shall be lucky to arrive at the altar before next Easter.'

'That being so,' he said, with a naughty grin, 'I have nothing against us anticipating the nuptial knot a little, as the parson called the marriage ceremony at Ben Wolfe's wedding. I promise not to go too far, but you can't really expect a red-blooded man to behave like a monk for ten months.'

'Nor a red-blooded woman, either,' riposted Georgie.

'How about now? I gather that all the family's out. I passed Garth and Caro on their way to Netherton, doubtless to join in the gossip about Banker Bowlby and Jesmond Fitzroy.'

'And Miss Havisham is looking after Gus and Annie. I believe that she was taking them to the river to fish.'

'Excellent. Then I will take you in my arms, like so…'

'And I will kiss you, like so…'

Alas and alack, they had scarcely had time to get down to even minor business before the door burst open and Gus and Annie rushed in, followed by their governess exclaiming reproachfully, 'How many times do I have to tell you not to enter a room without knocking?'

Jess and Georgie had sprung part, thanking whatever gods there might be that Gus and Annie had not arrived five minutes later.

'I thought that you had gone fishing,' burst from Georgie, her voice nearly as reproachful as their governess's.

'So we did,' said Gus, 'but Miss Havisham brought us home because the sun gave her a megrim, and when Forshaw told us that you were in the drawing room, we came to see if you would play cricket with us. And,' he roared on, turning to Jess, 'a jolly good thing we did, because Fitz is here and we can play cricket in his paddock now that the workmen have moved on.'

'Augustus,' said Miss Havisham faintly, 'you are not to address Mr Fitzroy in that rude fashion, nor are you to bully him into playing cricket with you. He may have other plans.'

Jess grinned ruefully. He *had* had other plans, but must now abandon them.

Nevertheless, 'No harm done,' he told her cheerfully. 'You go and lie down, Miss Havisham. Mrs Herron and I will be happy to play cricket with Gus and Annie, won't we?'

'Oh, yes, indeed,' replied Georgie, lying in her teeth, trying not to mind too much that she and Fitz must delay celebrating their love, but after all, they had all the afternoons—and nights—of their future life together to enjoy themselves.

'That's that, then,' said Gus briskly. 'I'll go and get the cricket bat and stumps, Annie can put the fishing tackle away, and Miss can lie down.'

'And you mustn't call me Miss, either,' moaned the governess as she led them out of the room, Gus still busily chattering.

His last audible sentences set the thwarted pair he left behind laughing. 'I say, Miss Havisham, wouldn't it be a splendid thing if Fitz and Georgie got married? We could play cricket with them every day—when it's fine, that is,' he added as an afterthought.

'So much for our future life together,' said Jess, grinning, 'arranged to satisfy young master—meaning Gus—not old master—meaning me. I hope you didn't mind too much that I agreed to play cricket with Gus.'

Georgie shook her head at him. 'No, Fitz, we've all our future life together, and somehow it's a fitting end to our story, isn't it? I was playing cricket with them when we first met, and on the day that we are going to announce our engagement and settle down we shall be playing cricket with them again—so we know of at least two people who will approve of our marriage!'

'So we do,' said Jess, kissing her again, 'and one day, God willing, we shall have our own little terrors to play cricket with in the paddock.'

Arm in arm they strolled out into the afternoon sun, not only to wait for Gus and Annie, but for their new and happy life together to begin.

*   *   *   *   *

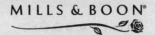

MILLS & BOON®

*Makes
any time
special*

**Enjoy a romantic novel from
Mills & Boon®**

Presents™ *Enchanted*™ *Temptation*®

Historical Romance™ *Medical Romance*™

2 FREE

books and a surprise gift!

We would like to take this opportunity to thank you for reading this Mills & Boon® book by offering you the chance to take TWO more specially selected titles from the Historical Romance™ series absolutely FREE! We're also making this offer to introduce you to the benefits of the Reader Service™—

- ★ FREE home delivery
- ★ FREE gifts and competitions
- ★ FREE monthly Newsletter
- ★ Exclusive Reader Service discounts
- ★ Books available before they're in the shops

Accepting these FREE books and gift places you under no obligation to buy, you may cancel at any time, even after receiving your free shipment. Simply complete your details below and return the entire page to the address below. *You don't even need a stamp!*

YES! Please send me 2 free Historical Romance books and a surprise gift. I understand that unless you hear from me, I will receive 4 superb new titles every month for just £2.99 each, postage and packing free. I am under no obligation to purchase any books and may cancel my subscription at any time. The free books and gift will be mine to keep in any case.

H9EA

Ms/Mrs/Miss/Mr ....Initials...................................
BLOCK CAPITALS PLEASE

Surname ....

Address ....

....

....Postcode ....

Send this whole page to:
THE READER SERVICE, FREEPOST CN81, CROYDON, CR9 3WZ
(Eire readers please send coupon to: P.O. BOX 4546, DUBLIN 24.)

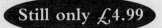